"Robert Burl   ...d keen eye for
detail – emot   ...ectly Broken a
wonderful ride. Fantastic, sharp dialogue and vivid charac-
ters, all in a distinctive, captivating voice. A stunning debut
novel."
– Rosanne Cash, multi-Grammy winner, author of *New
York Times* bestseller *Composed*

"Whether writing about music, parenthood, or life in the
sticks, every page crackles with been-there-done-that veri-
similitude. At turns funny and suspenseful, heartwarming
and heartbreaking, *Perfectly Broken* hits all the right notes,
covering fame and fortune, love and death, success and failure, and fatherhood and marriage. A triumphant debut."
– Greg Olear, author of *Los Angeles Times* bestseller
Fathermucker

"Parenthood, adultery, love, lust, ambition, loss, friendships
gone to seed, a marriage at the turn of this century in full
tilt midlife madness, with rock and roll in the bones and on
the soundtrack. Warren creates a sensory world so sharply
observed, the experience of reading becomes visceral. It
pulled me in and I didn't want to let go."
– Beverly Donofrio, author, *New York Times* bestseller
Riding in Cars with Boys

"Robert Burke Warren's *Perfectly Broken* is an exceptional debut novel that points to greater things in its
author's future. Through its precise prose, the alchem-
ical composition of its story, and the honest emotion
that pervades its pages this book is a study in how to
make realistic minimalism work, one that never puts
the appearance of truth above the reality of it. One that
never forgets fiction at its best is a little like magic."
– The Nervous Breakdown

perfectly broken

robert burke warren

The Story Plant

Studio Digital CT, LLC
P.O. Box 4331
Stamford, CT 06907

Copyright © 2015 by Robert Burke Warren
Jacket design by Mark Lerner

Story Plant Hardcover ISBN-13: 978-1-61188-218-6
Story Plant Paperback ISBN-13: 978-1-61188-240-7
Fiction Studio Books E-book ISBN-13: 978-1-943486-80-9

Visit our website at www.TheStoryPlant.com

First Story Plant hardcover printing: March 2016
First Story Plant paperback printing: March 2017
Printed in the United States of America

0 9 8 7 6 5 4 3 2 1

For Holly and Jack

Perfectly broken
Nothing is too much to bear
Perfectly broken
Nothing to repair

part one

january 2003

chicken bomb

The ache in my thighs reminds me of jumping off speaker cabinets during a show by my former band, Stereoblind. A similar burn troubled my leg muscles back then, in the late eighties and early nineties, when I'd wake up in a strange bed, post-gig, stiff from exertion, ears ringing, the occasional sleeping stranger at my side. All pre-marriage, pre-fatherhood.

This pain is from walking up and down, up and down five flights of stairs all day, removing my family's possessions from our tenement apartment. I straighten up from the final duct-taped box marked "MIXTAPES—'97," and step back from the U-Haul trailer to assess our material goods: TV/VCR combo, vintage (and faux vintage) clothes, furniture salvaged from these very East Village street corners, a dozen or so saved LPs (unplayed for years), my wife Beth's chapbooks and dog-eared spiral-bounds, and my 1962 Ampeg Portaflex B-15 bass amp.

In planning this dreaded day, I'd insisted we forgo professional movers, opting instead to spend hours cramming everything into our '95 Camry and the trailer. Save a few bucks, assert some male brio, compensate for four years of decidedly non-macho stay-at-home dadhood.

Beth did her part, boxing and bagging up our life, working up a dusty sweat. She's in better shape than me. In a threadbare, sleeveless Pyramid Club T-shirt, her anterior deltoids ripple, remnants of a corporate gym membership now months lapsed.

Retired rock star Paul, gone for cigarettes and beer, has kept watch over our four-year-old son, Evan, while

Beth and I work. He is Evan's godfather, although they both prefer the term *padrino*—Spanish for "little dad." On his credit cards, Paul's surname is Fernandez. On liner notes, it's Fairchild.

Of all our friends and neighbors, only Paul came through for us on Moving Day, in part because he has no job. But, as ever, Padrino entertained Evan, shielding him like a jester protecting a boy king from court anxieties. Around noon, he squatted down to inspect Evan's Sharpie art on the moving boxes.

"Hey little man," he said. "What're you drawing? A flying poop? Fuckin' A! That's totally a flying poop, like super poop or something."

After squeals of laughter, Evan said, "Padrino! It's a bee!"

Beth and I watched from the doorway. She sob-laughed quietly into my shoulder, pressing tear stains into the faded black of my T-shirt.

~

A new home awaits us, a furnished rental property courtesy of our old running buddies Trip and Christa Lamont. Their rental, a 1900 farmhouse they call Shulz House, is on a dead-end road three hours north, in rural Mt. Marie, New York.

After 9/11, Trip and Christa headed for the hills, buying a couple pieces of land in the Catskill Mountains, far away from the ashes of the World Trade Center and, they hoped, the memories of eight unsuccessful IVF attempts. They've since adopted a two-and-a-half-year-old Chinese girl named Katie, and all are nesting in a Victorian down the street from Shulz House. In recent emails, Trip refers to our upcoming tenancy in the Lamont "fiefdom." This does not strike deeply indebted me as particularly funny. But Beth and I are desperate and, sight unseen, we've accepted our friends' kind offer of a home.

We've not laid eyes on Trip and Christa in just over a year. Their recent glossy Christmas card showed only tiny Katie, standing in a snow trench before a garlanded porch, her wide, expressionless face framed by a pink snowsuit hood. *Season's Greetings from the Lamonts! Trip, Christa & Katie!* The forced gaiety struck Beth and me as eerie.

I'll be digging snow trenches soon, ugh. I'm hoping global warming will keep this task at bay, as I am pear-shaped where I once was Bowie-thin, and easily winded.

~

I close the U-Haul doors and slide the shackle into the greasy padlock, hands trembling from waning adrenaline, vision sharpened from pain. The cold *ka-thunk* is satisfying. I dread reopening this door to assess our stuff, all of it now connected to loss. For a moment, I fantasize a wave rising from the nearby East River, engulfing the U-Haul, and carrying away our material possessions to the Atlantic forever.

But the only thing I'm actually farewelling is our soon-to-be former home: a red brick 1880 tenement looming in the crisp twilight, vined with cables, Christmas tree lights blinking erratic rhythms on the fire escape.

I drop into the Camry beside Beth and breathe in my family. A groan escapes my lips.

"Papa?" Evan sniffles in his car seat.

"I'm OK, Evan, just a little sore."

Click. The glove compartment light spills over Beth's face. She blinks, the rims of her dark, cried-out eyes glistening. "There's Advil in here if you want," she says.

I wave away the pill. Beth shuts the door and gazes forward.

"Where *is* he?" she asks, meaning Paul. "Why does it always take him three times as long to get anything? We need to go, like *now*, or traffic'll be a nightmare. He *knows* this."

She stares forward. When Paul had asked if anyone wanted a beer for the road, she'd said yes without hesitation, but I do not remind her of this. Nor do I reiterate how waiting for Paul has always been part of having him in our lives. The guy has always made everyone *wait*, friends and fans alike.

Paul's erstwhile band Six Ray Star, for instance: they routinely hit the stage at least two hours past whatever time they were scheduled. It was part of the show, this tardiness, part of the performer-audience contract. Their fans loved talking about it, loved to hate it, loved the heightened anticipation. But it always rankled me, like his blasé attitude rankles me now.

I follow Beth's sightline, as if my attention will make Paul arrive faster, as if Paul is the F train.

The evening waxes on beyond the grimy windshield. NYU students wolf down slices in the pizzeria, lusty-eyed twosomes ascend stoops, breath commingling in clouds. A couple embraces on the curb next to the Camry's passenger-side headlight. The boy lifts the girl, tries to spin her, loses his balance. Beth, Evan, and I gasp in unison as they tumble against our front fender in a tangle of arms and scarves. They right themselves, turn wide-eyed to us, wave laughing apologies, and flee like the children they are.

"Are they OK?" Evan asks, tears rising in his voice.

"Yeah, they're OK," Beth says. "Just . . . careless. It's OK, Evan, it's OK."

Ghostly residue of the young couple lingers in my mind's eye. *Not us,* I think. *That's not us anymore.*

Something crumbles in my chest. Evan's not the one who's going to cry. I am.

Due in part, I think, to Zoloft, Evan has never seen me cry. But our financial troubles have forced me to halve my meds, and here, now, I feel my pharmaceutical buffer diminished. I start the car, crank the heat, and try to summon whatever traces of the drug remain in my chemistry. The Camry fills with distraction, familiar chuffs and rumbles, air warming in the vents, headlights igniting on Paul, crossing in the glow. Perfect timing, as always.

He whacks a pack of Marlboro Lights against his right palm, striding as he did across stages back in the nineties, when Six Ray Star rode Nirvana's raggedy flannel shirttails to indie stardom while I, who'd quit my own band in a huff, watched from the wings. To his godson's delight, Paul has festooned his battered biker jacket with Mardi Gras beads dangling from the left epaulet. A plastic bag at his wrist swings like a purse, bursting with the promised beer.

My lips tighten. Paul's slouchy, hip-first gait suggests a lack of concern for my family's plight. I am refreshingly annoyed, and dry-eyed.

Beth glares as she lowers the passenger-side window. Before she can speak, Paul produces a Rolling Rock from his bag. He grins, Cheshire-cat-like, baring his missing eyetooth gap as he opens the beer with his keyring and hands it to my wife. One fluid motion. No words pass between them. They scan for cops, nod, and Beth drinks deep.

Paul leans in, greasy blue-black hair falling over his forehead. He taps a rhythm on the window frame and laughs.

"You guys look like the Beverly Hillbillies . . . in reverse." His hoarse voice floats on a yeasty cloud. He fits a Marlboro Light in the corner of his plum lips. "You know what I mean? In reverse. Instead of moving to the big city from the country, you're . . ."

"We get it," I say.

Such an asshole.

"Beer for you, Jed Clampett?" he says.

I jerk my head to the waiting road. "Uhm . . . driving?"

"Whatever," he says, put-upon. "You're welcome, *handsome.*"

I glance in the rearview and check my look to see if he's being sarcastic or not. The verdict: sarcastic. Thinning dishwater hair plastered to my forehead with drying sweat, grime-smeared face. Lovely. I look every hour of my thirty-nine years, and then some. I glance at Evan's reflection. My son barely fits in his foul car seat. He shudders with another aftershock sob from a recent crying jag and grips a fistful of his *Toy Story* pajamas. Like all of us, he's upset about moving. These filthy sidewalks where he took his first steps are the only world he knows, and his love for the neighborhood is strong. If this had gone down two years ago, he wouldn't have known the difference, but halfway into his fourth year, he doesn't miss a trick.

My battered black instrument cases flank him, each stenciled with STEREOBLIND. These instruments—my bass, Blackie, and my acoustic guitar, Luther—are as close as Evan is likely to get to siblings.

He is a mini-me of his mother, my son. Except for gender and Beth's distinctive gap in her front teeth, Evan is my wife's clone. He inherited Beth's Black Irish coloring—dark eyes, almost-olive skin, generous lips (now chapped), all set in a heart-shaped face with a pointy, elfin chin dappled with tiny dark freckles. Although Beth's been graying of late, they share the same sable brown, dread-inclined hair. With his modified bowl-cut (courtesy of me) he looks like a little Beatle, circa 1963, a puffy-eyed, upset Beatle.

"You OK, Evan?" I ask.

He nods, looks across the street to the apartment building, raises his hand, and waves.

"Bye, home."

All eyes turn to 244 East Seventh and travel up to the fifth floor.

Paul stiffens. "Hey Grant," he points up with his still-unlit cigarette. "You left the lights on."

"Like we care!" Beth says and sips her beer.

Paul is back in the window. "No, I mean you gotta *take the light bulbs.* Can't leave that scumbag anything. Dude knows you're having hard times, raises your rent! Mother*fucker.* Gotta take the light bulbs. They're yours. Gotta do it."

My wife flashes a bitter smile, and closes her eyes. Hard times indeed. Her employer, *Electra* magazine—"the voice of the hip career woman"—is recently dissolved, her breadwinner editorship no more. A couple months collecting unemployment, and the new lease arrived, our rent increase too much to bear. Due in part to my lack of an income, we are priced out of our long-time neighborhood.

"You didn't do the chicken bomb, Grant." Paul leans further into the car, his face aglow in the panel lights. "So you gotta at least take the light bulbs."

There's a rustling in the backseat. "Papa . . . what's a chicken bomb?"

"Nice going," Beth says, slapping Paul's hand.

"It's nothing, little man," Paul's shoulders are in the car now. He cranes his head toward Evan, forcing Beth to duck. She throws me a glance, a familiar: *Can you believe this guy?* But for a moment, she shines.

"Alrighty!" Beth says, sinking back into her mood. "Thanks so much for the help, Paul, and the bevvies. We should go, Grant."

Paul opens his palm next to Beth's face. "Gimmie the keys, boss lady," he says, grubby digits wiggling in fingerless gloves. "*I'll* get the light bulbs."

A tug at the corner of my wife's mouth may or may not be a smile.

"Wait," I say. "I'll do it."

Beth hands over the keys and focuses on me for the first time today, everything dilating, lips parting.

We're kissing goodbye? Like fourteen years ago, when five minutes was forever?

I'm tumbling toward contact, looking forward to the taste and texture of beer on my wife's lips, when a renegade hair dances across her face. She flinches and jerks back. Her eyes flick to Evan, our unwitting chaperone, then back to me.

"Go," she says, retrieving a case of mixtapes from the floorboards and buzzing up the window on Paul's goofy smile.

~

Paul and I cross the street in the frigid East River wind. He huddles behind me, the plastic bag crinkling. A shadow moves.

"Hey."

We look to the vacant storefront next door to our stoop. Leaning against the pulled-down gate is Beth's junkie little brother Billy, crumpled into a dingy hoodie, shaking with drug hunger chills, eyes popping.

"You guys still need a hand?" he says, his voice raw, faux-casual. He sniffs and rubs his nose, smiling, all overlong teeth and graying gums. "What's up, Paul."

"Hey fly guy, good to see ya," Paul says.

"Thought you were coming at noon," I say, disappointed to see my brother-in-law, yet also validated. I knew he'd been lying about being clean. I look back to the car, hoping Beth and Evan don't see this hepatitis C-decimated wraith.

I'd been relieved he'd stood us up. Against my better judgement, I'd suspended my moratorium on contact between Billy and Evan. Part of our current crisis is due to Billy's recent failed rehab stint, which cost us about twenty-five grand. He'd checked out early, but they refunded us not a penny. That was the final straw for me. But Beth, ever forgiving of her little brother, insisted Billy should be able to see us all off, especially as he claimed to be one month clean, *all on his own*, and we certainly wouldn't be seeing much of him in our new digs.

I'd caved. He'd pitch in, she said. He'd been lifting weights, couldn't wait to show us how healthy he'd gotten. But, as ever: all lies. Part of me wants to drag him to the car to prove I was right, a rising little genie of spite in my gut, ever more familiar these days.

"I got hung up," Billy says. "You wouldn't believe what went down at this place I'm staying at over on Rivington . . . this guy's potbellied pig ate some rotted meat and . . ."

"No time for this, Billy," I say.

"*What?*" Billy says as if I am out of my mind, his usual MO. "What's *your* problem?"

"Potbellied pig?" Paul laughs. "That is rich. Imaginative."

"No bullshit, man! None!"

"OK," Paul says. "OK. I totally believe you."

"That pig is at the Animal Medical Center *right now*," Billy says. "Call and see. Call. She's fucked up, that pig. My friend can't pay. They're gonna put the pig down!"

Paul digs in his pocket. "What do you need, Billy boy?" He produces a crumpled twenty.

"*I* don't need shit," Billy says. "My friend . . ."

"No, Paul," I say, pressing the twenty back. "It's just going up his arm."

"*What?*" Billy says. "I'm a *month* clean, Grant, you fucker. No thanks to you. I just got hung up today. I got hung up. I *know* you don't give a shit . . ."

Billy snatches the twenty and glances over at the Camry, then back at us.

"No skin off your nose, right Pablo?"

Paul shrugs.

"She OK?" Billy says. "My sister?"

"She's great," Paul says. "Evan, too. They're fine. You can catch up with 'em later, right?"

Billy is moving away, energized by the money in his hand. "Yeah, yeah, you know it. I'll be in touch. Tell her I had to bolt, it was an emergency. Tell her I love her, bon voyage, you know."

"We'll do that," Paul says.

Billy races off.

Before I can open my mouth, Paul says, "If she'd seen him like that, she'd have lost her shit, right? I just stopped him from needing to steal something to sell. Admit it: you're relieved, right?"

I have to admit I am.

~

In the stairwell, Paul shifts into raconteur mode, talking half to me, half to an unseen audience, marking time, as always, by what Six Ray Star was doing in bygone days. I'm too tired to remind him I've heard this tale, but that wouldn't stop him anyway.

"The chicken bomb at my Second Street digs was the best," he says. "We were on Matador, before we got on Warner Brothers, and I got evicted for some bull-shit, and Billy was still working at Leshko's and freak-azoid Billy says, 'Chicken bomb! Chicken bomb! Let's do a chicken bomb!' Which we did, the best ever. Billy gets this big gallon pickle jar from the Leshko's kitchen and puts a chicken carcass in it, stuffs anchovies and some other shit in there, pours in some milk, screws it shut, duct-tapes it, and on the day I move my shit out, he hides it in a hole in the wall behind the radiator. It's getting on toward winter, and the radiators come on, like, super hot, and that chicken starts to putrefy and the jar fills with gas and 'round about Christmas—right when we get back from a tour with White Zombie—the fucker explodes! The shithole *reeked* for months! Ho, ho, muthafuckin' ho!"

I turn the Medeco and push open the apartment door as Paul laughs. The thought of chicken bomb revenge is tantalizing. But Beth and I agreed it would be hard on the neighbors. So when Paul offered to facilitate the prank, we'd declined.

Paul never thinks like that. Although forty-one and approaching jowliness where he once was chiseled, he still functions like a kid, with no thoughts of consequences. This "childlike" quality of selfishness, however, combined with a somewhat secret, shrewd business sense, has made him a millionaire in torn jeans and rundown boots.

Six Ray Star did well, mostly from touring, but Paul didn't really score until after they disbanded in '98, and music supervisors came calling. He'd held onto the rights to his songs, so now all licensing fees from commercials, soundtracks, and video games go straight to him. And music supervisors cannot get enough of Paul Fairchild. His most notable coup is a deathless international Nike commercial. If he and his wife had offspring, which they don't (and won't, they say), those kids would never need to work. If anyone's the Jed Clampett of rock and roll, it's Paul.

~

The four railroad-style rooms of my former home lay bare before us, radiators hissing, echoes of the last fourteen years decaying in the shadows.

"What a dump," I say.

Paul lights his cigarette on the stove, drops his plastic bag by the refrigerator, and comes to the twelve-by-twelve space that had been our living room.

"Damn right it's a fuckin' dump," he says, pulling his gray sweater cuff over his fingertips and unscrewing the bulb above my head. Flab pokes out from his sweater hem—beer consumption finally catching up with him.

"Nice gut, Beetle Bailey," I say.

"You're one to talk, Mr. L.L.Bean. The cut of that foxy parka does not disguise your own little spread there, Hoss. And can we discuss the chinos—*chinos!*"

"This stuff was a steal at Goodwill."

"*Huh*," he says, pulling the bulb down. A shadow envelops us. "Listen, I'm jealous. Mt. Marie sounds *great*. What with Manhattan becoming Rich Man's Island, it's practically a bedroom community for the city. You got a *yard*, right?"

"Yeah. So they tell me."

"*Fuck* yeah. Evan'd never get that here. Just dog shit sidewalks and syringes in the playgrounds and shit to worry about. Tell you one thing: I'm looking forward to visiting. I'll bring him something from FAO muthafuckin' *Schwarz.*"

How nice. If I had a fraction of Paul's money, we'd just send *fuck you* checks to the landlord. And we wouldn't have forty grand in credit card debt, with a usurious interest rate. But all I've got is time, patience, and, perhaps thanks to my pharmaceutical crutch, a knack for the parenthood gig. This is a relief and a surprise, as I do not have great role models in the father or mother department. But when I'm charitable, I'll say: *maybe if they'd had meds like I do, things would've been different.* Zoloft, rather than booze and pills, might have done my depressed old man good, might've quelled some of my mom's rage and anxiety. Perhaps he'd still be alive, perhaps she wouldn't have compulsively gambled away my meager inheritance.

~

I stand in what once was Evan's room, where he spent little time. Prior to Evan, this had been my home studio, where I recorded demos for my unrealized oeuvre of imagined solo albums. After wholesale rejection from record companies, music publishers, and fellow musicians, I resorted to proofreading to help pay the bills, stacking manuscripts on my pillowcase-covered recording equipment.

Then, four years ago, my gig changed to primary caregiver-ship for Evan.

This endeavor, unexpectedly, has been a return to the rock and roll lifestyle. In fact, the similarities between hands-on dadhood and my past musical endeavors are striking.

Parenting is not unlike living with a drunken, howling, megalomaniac midget lead singer, a situation with which, having backed up a few of those, I am uniquely familiar (except maybe the midget part). And indeed, Evan and I are up all hours, we eat whenever, and we make a lot of noise. We have crazy hair—especially Evan—and we stink. Plus, if I let him out of my sight: calamity. So all that time in rock and roll bands, during which I often needed to babysit drunken musicians, provided excellent prerequisites for parenting a child.

But none of this, of course, brings in money. "Sweat equity," yes; cash, no. Once we settle into the mountains, I may audition for a wedding combo or a bar band. It'd be nice to make money as a musician again. The last time was when Stereoblind toured the world in '91, buoyed by our Red Hot Chili Peppers-esque hit (that I did not write) "What the Funk Is Up?"

From that to this in eleven years.

~

"Look alive country boy, get those bulbs."

Paul slumps in the doorway of Evan's former room, stuffing the living room bulb into his breast pocket, the space behind him sunk in shadow, the kitchen beyond still aglow. He looks a little more like the indie rock star of yore, standing on a backlit stage.

"Your godson's room," I say. "Lotta good times in here, huh Padrino?"

Paul contracts a little, sucks deep on his cigarette. "Your wifey did a number on me with that godfather trip, you know," he says.

Beth had suggested childless Paul be our son's god-father. She was pregnant; he was forlorn following his band's demise and his wife Melora's refusal to start a family. Back then, before I was a parent and before he was crazy rich, he didn't annoy me so. I'd assented with-out giving it too much thought. I didn't foresee him tak-ing it so seriously, and I had no idea parenting would kill my patience for dealing with adults who behave like kids.

"You're doing a fine job," I say. "Evan loves you."

It's true. As much as Paul gets on my nerves, my son adores him. And Paul is really getting on my nerves now, the rich rock star fishing for compliments.

"Yeah, well," he says, "he doesn't know any better."

"He does. You know that. He sings your damn songs all the time. Drives me nuts."

"I just don't know if I can . . . measure up to . . . I don't know . . . what he deserves, you know?"

As I touch the bulb in the ceiling socket, pain flares in my fingertips. I honor a cruel impulse.

"You know if we die you don't have to worry about bringing him up, right?" I say as the light snuffs out. I head for the bedroom, my fingers burning. Paul stands in the dark, suddenly quite still.

"Yeah, I know," he says, with forced nonchalance. "Trip and Christa, right?"

"They're the ones." I reach for the last bulb, shirt sleeve over my fingertips this time. I recall sitting with Beth in a lawyer's office, assigning Trip and trust-funded Christa stewardship of Evan in case of tragedy. Christa, a devout atheist, balked at the "godparent" concept, and Trip had followed her lead.

Paul clomps over to me, into the halo of light, his icy eyes on my hand. "Looks like your bass playin' callouses wore off, Hoss."

I pull out the bulb, plunging us into silhouette.

"Yeah, I don't get much time to play," I say as I stuff the bulb in my parka, "what with chasing a kid around."

"Beth says you sure could play back in the day." Paul gathers shape behind an orangey cigarette tip. "Says that's what made her fall for you, you know."

"Well, she'd rather I'm here for the kid, I think, even if it's not so sexy."

"You hit the jackpot with Little E, I'm telling you," Paul says.

"He's a handful, you know, that kid."

"You're *lucky*."

Paul's Marlboro Light falls to the floor. He crushes it. "That little dude's a rock star. And you get to give him what you never had. That rocks."

I bristle. This is what I get for frequently proposing the narrative of "giving Evan what I never had." It's a big part of a story I've taken pains to promulgate, often unbidden.

The Camry honks.

"Shit," I say. "This is it. So long, New York. Unbelievable."

"You can come visit us anytime, you know."

The pressure of Paul's hand on my shoulder is oddly welcome, dad-like. He and I have never been so physically close. Time suspends in the dreamlike dark, and for a few moments, as the heat from his hand seeps into my sore shoulder, he's not irritating me.

"I know Boss Lady'll be down looking for work, and you'll need a break from Little E. I can take him to the movies or something, you can get a massage, watch porn, whatever. God knows we've got room. Door's always open."

Beth honks the horn again.

"Time to go," Paul says and heads back to the still-lit kitchen. "But first I gotta show you something."

I stand alone for a few moments, listening to the East Seventh sounds, familiar as my own breath, amplified in the gloom.

"Yo!" Paul calls from the kitchen, a grin in his voice.

I head back through the apartment, my hot fingertips tracing the cool walls. In the kitchen, Paul reaches into his plastic bag for what I assume is a beer. Instead, he pulls out a big restaurant-sized glass pickle jar, the lid encircled with duct tape. Within the glass, a small, grayish chicken carcass sits in a puddle of oily, milky ooze.

"No fucking way," I say.

The chicken bomb is both repulsive and fascinating. I shake my head and peer closer. Paul jiggles the jar. The carcass dances.

He walks to the old stove and pulls it away from the wall. "I can stash this back here," he says, grinning, his eyes wide, "and when they turn on the oven, it'll pop!"

"Beth would freak."

Paul smirks. "Like I don't know that."

"I mean, thanks and all, but . . . we did tell you no."

Paul looks down his nose at me. "C'mon. Our little secret. I can keep a secret."

"What about the neighbors?"

"This one is small, man. It's a damn Cornish game hen. Classy. Explosion'll be localized. I know what I'm doing. It's a surgical strike."

I bite my lip as calculations whir in my mind.

"Don't be a pussy," he says.

As if on their own accord, two words shoot from my mouth: "Do it."

chapter 2

peppercorn

The lights of Spuyten Duyvil, the Bronx, shine across the Hudson as we head up the Palisades Parkway. Since we pulled away from East Seventh—Paul saluting us in the glare of the Pita Palace—no one has said much. I'm trying not to think about the chicken bomb, alternating between schoolboy shenanigans glee and anxiety. My thoughts turn to Trip and Christa.

Trip and Christa Lamont have been together almost as long as Beth and me—about thirteen years. They've always complemented each other—Trip the quiet dreamer, Christa the mercurial doer. Despite his unmet goals as a novelist and their fertility problems, they have a good life. Her trust fund helps. But still, I can't help wondering how they'll be as a family, a trio instead of a duo.

They'd only just settled in Mt. Marie when the call came from China that their baby girl was ready, and off they flew into the adoption labyrinth. After that, radio silence. We were so busy with our own trials—Billy, money woes, depression—that we fell out of touch. Rare emails brought us up to speed: Trip's teaching fifth grade English at the local elementary school; Christa's thrown herself into opening a café in an abandoned diner in Mt. Marie. Then that Diane Arbus-looking Christmas card. Better than nothing, but the epic letters of Trip's and my early friendship, all pre-email, seem very far away indeed.

Nevertheless, those letters clearly helped build a sturdy friendship, because regardless of everything—distance, disappointment—the Lamonts enthusiastically offered us the just-vacated Shulz House. Trip said, "That's what friends are for." He said the vacancy happening just when we needed a refuge was kismet. It'll be like old times, like when we were roommates on Avenue C in the late eighties and early nineties. Except I'll be the only one paying rent.

Once I turn onto the New York State Thruway, the mixtape *Beth's '90s Hits* is in full swing, sidetracking my thoughts. The songs fill the overcast car with memory wormholes. Beth shuts her eyes, wedding ring tapping her empty Rolling Rock bottle. I hit cruise control, wondering where the music is taking her.

Is she reliving our early years, when, after I quit Stereoblind, we went out to see bands almost every night? When, after a few Absolut-cranberries, I routinely piggybacked her up the five flights to our place, where the next morning she would rise at 9:00, drown her hangover in coffee, and be at her job by 10:00? Or is she somewhere else? Is she just worrying about her little brother? I haven't mentioned him showing up on the stoop. We don't talk about Billy in front of Evan because I always rage, and Beth always breaks down. Maybe I'll mention it later. Maybe not. Probably not.

Beth's '90s Hits unspools. Six Ray Star's song "Kiss My Ring" is coming; first will be Nirvana's "Come as You Are," then the Breeders' "Cannonball." This mix gets so much play, when I hear one of these tunes somewhere else, I expect it to be followed by its *Beth's '90s Hits* track list companion.

Soon, the familiar distorted chords crackle in the speaker cones, and Paul Fairchild's nasally talking croon, dripping with irony, meanders over a thumping bass drum. Evan, as usual, joins in from his car seat, mangling only a few words, his reedy voice following his godfather's.

> I am the pauper who became the king
> You want what I got, well you gotta sing
> It's not really much, it's everything
> So kiss my ring, kiss my ring.

Prescient indeed. This is from 1993's *Peppercorn* album. Beth was Six Ray Star's publicist at Matador, before well-financed *Electra* magazine wooed her away in the nineties gravy train years. On *Peppercorn*'s release, Beth had scored Six Ray Star a splashy feature in *Spin*. Nirvana was on the cover, so massive sales of the issue would ensue. We'd attended a celebratory happy hour get-together at Christa's Digital Café on Avenue A.

Digital Café was one of Christa's short-lived East Village business ventures. Before Evan, I'd often nurse a double espresso there, Christa's energy encircling me and everything else in a crackling aura. Hers was quite a routine: batting her green eyes at the deliverymen, corkscrew blond curls falling over her proud Bette Midler nose as she sang at the top of her lungs to a Madonna CD. I still smile at the image of her, sleek in Prada, sweeping the sidewalks, caterwauling "Like a Prayer" while the Ecuadorian kitchen staff watched in numb amazement.

Trip and I had struggled happily alongside each other in the late eighties, sharing a creaky, cluttered tenement on Avenue C and Thirteenth Street. I was fresh off a Greyhound from North Carolina, bussing tables, walking dogs, and playing in fledgling Stereoblind. Trip was a corn-fed Indiana kid-cum-teacher's assistant at Hunter College, MFA-bound, and working on the first of several post-apocalyptic novels that would go unpublished. Around the time Beth and I got together and moved into East Seventh, Trip told us about "a crazy, pretty, rich girl with a sexy schnozz" he'd met backstage at a Soul Asylum show at Irving Plaza. This girl Christa, recent Brown grad, was opening a café with gourmet coffee and computers on the same block as a notoriously mildewy deli where the drug-addled homeless congregated. The prospect sounded insane, but cool.

Digital Café featured a full bar, plus banks of coffee-stained IBM desktops where you could check email or work from a floppy disc. As with her other ventures—a gallery, a clothing line—Christa got a start-up loan from her dad, jumped in with intense enthusiasm, but bailed as soon as the books went in the red. Turned out East Village gentrification had not yet reached the point where a high-end café could turn a profit, and Christa stocked her joint with only expensive coffees, pricey vintages, and top-shelf liquor. This was a decade before folks would nonchalantly hand over three bucks for a latte or eight bucks for a cocktail. And while the checking-personal-email feature was novel, email was only just catching on in the early '90s. Although it began with a bang, the ahead-of-its-time Digital Café was doomed. But it was a fun hang for a while.

During Digital Café's brief heyday, Trip moved into Christa's Gramercy Park co-op. The two of them were comically lust struck and inseparable; Christa's megawatt attentions effectively distracted Trip from his mounting failures as a novelist. Although she offered to float him indefinitely, he returned to school at Hunter, acquired his teaching certificate, and assumed the mantle of Cool English Teacher, which he maintains to this day.

~

As "Kiss My Ring" fades, I'm recalling that day Beth, Christa, Trip, and I met Paul and Melora at Digital Café, ten years ago:

"Can you see the zit on my forehead?" Beth asked, pulling at her hair.

"Nope," I said. "You look great. Your ass looks amazing in that skirt."

She lowered her head, shaking it slightly.

"Really," I leaned, whispering, my teeth grazing her earlobe. "It should be bronzed, your ass. Put in the Smithsonian."

"You and your ass fixation," she said, annoyed and pleased.

"You and your compliment aversion."

Trip was weaving through a sea of leather jackets, sticking out in J.Crew pleats and a fresh haircut. He held aloft a pint of Guinness for me and an Absolut-cranberry for Beth.

He handed her the cocktail and smiled at her infrequently displayed, little-black-dress-encased curves and SoHo-purchased heels.

"I can't believe he lets you out dressed like that," Trip said, looking at me sheepishly. He relaxed at my laugh and pecked Beth on the cheek. "Congrats on all this," he said. "The *Spin* piece looks sweet."

"Thanks," Beth half-yelled over a crescendo in the music, then smiled her gap-toothed smile. She was in her element, glowing in the crush, the racket. The celebratory vibe was all her doing. She wouldn't cop to it unless tipsy, but she was reveling in *success*; squared shoulders, high chin, lips wet with cocktail. From dismally attended readings at Nuyorican Poets Café, where, before meeting me, she tried to be a post-modern update on early '70s Patti Smith, to *this*. If she didn't drink too much, the evening would end well. My fingers itched in anticipation of her hair, the scalloped waistband of the peach-colored panties I'd watched her pull on that morning.

From behind the bar, Christa, in North Beach leather jacket, biker half-boots, and Indian Motorcycle tee, was pouring Moët and pushing hors d'oeuvres, her cheeks scarlet as she bobbed her springy curls in time to a Ciccone Youth tape. She wasn't charging anyone for anything.

"Hey, Handsome!" Christa called to Trip. "Mama needs help!"

Trip gave Beth and me a faux-chagrined shrug.

"I am summoned," he said.

As he hustled away, Beth and I shared a smirk. It was no secret Trip loved to be summoned by his wife. In moments, he was behind the bar, where Christa grabbed his ass, pulled him to her pelvis, and kissed him sloppy and long as onlookers hooted and laughed.

"You are disgusting!" Beth yelled, breaking the spell. "Whores!" Pronounced w*ho-errs*, like an old Irish woman, an imitation of her own Dublin-born mother.

Christa pushed Trip away and gave Beth a friendly middle finger, shook her head as if coming out of a pool, and refocused on the crowd. Trip, meanwhile, stood dazed until Christa tossed him a tattered brown rag and waved her hand over the bar. He bussed glasses, wiped champagne puddles, and removed gnawed-on toothpicks while Christa kibitzed beside him. She leaned over the bar, grabbed people's faces, and pulled them into awkward hugs.

I was about to ask Trip if he needed any help, when the energy in the room shifted.

Beth elbowed me. "There's the band," she said.

Four guys were ambling in, all contrived dishevelment, radiating a gang vibe. Three members of Six Ray Star headed for a booth while the fourth approached us. He was lanky and tallish, with a greasy blue-black pompadour-gone-to-seed, jeans ripped at the knees, engineer boots, and a snug Michael Jackson *Thriller*-style red leather jacket. As he homed in, nodding to admirers, accepting back slaps and air kisses, the lines around his eyes deepened. I realized *he's older than me*, which was kind of a relief. Although I'd not yet seen them live, I knew Six Ray Star had been on the rough indie road for a few years, sleeping on floors and playing dives, and it had taken a toll. He extended a hand to Beth and his abraded lips parted in a nicotine-stained smile with a missing eyetooth.

"So you're the one that nabbed us the press in *Spin*, they tell me." Voice dry and textured as an autumn leaf, husky-blue eyes expressing admiration for my wife with a peripheral intensity.

Beth nodded. "You're Paul, right?"

She knew this was Paul.

"Yeah, and you're . . . Brenda?"

"Beth."

"Bess?" He bent down, offering his thrice-pierced ear.

"Beth!" she shouted into the slicked side of his head. He nodded, pulled back to his full height, and reached into his breast pocket for a cherry-red pack of Marlboros. He held out the pack to Beth. She hadn't smoked in years, but she reached for one. As he lit it, she dragged deep and long.

I offered my hand.

"I'm Grant."

Paul's head jerked back in surprise, as if I'd suddenly materialized. He gave me a limp shake, his hand small and fine. Beth seemed to wake from a daze, encircling my waist with her arm. She shook me, frowning.

"Oh, I'm sorry." She laughed. "This is my husband, Grant."

"Ah. Your husband." Paul proffered his smokes, raised his eyebrows at me.

"No thanks," I said. Although I wanted one. I didn't want to be excluded from the naughtiness.

"So you're married," Paul's eyes tracked from me to Beth and back again. "How long?"

"Almost three years," Beth said. Then, for some reason: "No longer newlyweds. Can't get on *The Newlywed Game* now."

"Yeah," I said. "Cutoff for *The Newlywed Game* is two years, you know."

Paul nodded and pursed his lips, playing along with the "sad passing" of that milestone.

"Well, I've got you beat by one," he said. "That one over there is my Melora, wifey and masseuse. Four years coming up." Paul pointed to a corner of the bar, where a slender-faced, kohl-eyed, dark pageboy-ed woman was in deep conversation with Christa. A study in contrasts: round, large-nosed Nordic fertility goddess and spectral shadow waif. "Wifey is talking that rich bitch into a massage as we speak."

"That's Christa," I said.

"She's our friend." Beth good-naturedly slapped Paul's shoulder.

"Oh, sorry," he said—not at all sorry—from a nimbus of smoke.

"She could use a massage, actually," Beth said. "So your *wifey* is a masseuse?"

"Just got certified, yep."

Paul was not interested in talking to us anymore. His eyes searched the room and widened as he caught someone else's gaze.

"*Peppercorn*'s great!" Beth said, standing on her toes.

"Yeah," I said. "'Kiss My Ring.' Love that tune. It's been in heavy rotation at the apartment."

Heavy rotation, I groaned inwardly. *MTV lingo. Somebody stop me.*

"All right," Paul said, pulling away. "Cocktail time."

"Grant's a musician," Beth yelled, grabbing Paul's sleeve. He let her pull him back into our space.

"Who you play with?" he asked, nodding to someone behind me.

"I used to play bass with Stereoblind, but I'm getting my own thing going."

"Stereoblind!" Paul's eyebrows arched. His genuine focus gave a dark heat. "I love those guys. My band thinks they're lame, kinda white-boy funk-metal schlock, but I'm all about that. My dark secret. *'What the funk is up? What the funk is up?'* Stellar tune. You're like Aerosmith-huge in Holland, right?"

"Well . . . *they* are."

Beth jostled me. "Yeah, I went along once before Grant quit," she said. "It was amazing. *Amsterdam.*"

"We're going over there next month." Paul squinted at me. "Back to the grind, you know."

"I miss that grind," I said.

"So why'd you quit Stereoblind? Didn't fancy a mullet anymore?"

"They wouldn't record this song I wrote . . ."

"Yeah," Beth said, "it's called 'Words Fail Me.' It's fucking great. I'll send you a tape."

"And I did not have a mullet, either . . ." I say, although this is a lie.

"Oh, I'm just joshin . . ." Paul said. "But yeah: gotta get your own songs out there. Gotta do it."

"Grant's got some great songs," Beth said. "Some labels are interested."

She was lying. No one was interested in my songs. I'd emptied my meager savings from touring in a one-hit wonder eighties band and was actually more proofreader now than songwriter.

"So," Paul's forehead creased, "how's . . . that going?"

"It's going great!" Beth said, a little too loud. Her drink now consisted of pinkish ice cubes. "You guys'll be sharing stages before you know it!"

It was actually going disastrously. I'd placed ads and rented rehearsal space for band auditions at which I was stood up.

Paul seemed to sense these melancholy realities in the expressions passing between Beth and me. "Glad to hear it," he said. He fake-coughed, a throaty bark that propelled him away from us, putting a period on the conversation. "Thanks again, Betty," he called from the fray.

"Beth!"

But he was gone, dropping his smoke to the tiles. He sidled up to Melora at the far end of the bar and plopped on a stool beside her, disrupting her powwow with Christa. They made quite a pair, Paul and Melora, starved to flawed perfection, hipster bookends, basking in Christa's unfashionable radiance.

Trip kept the champagne flowing as Christa reared back in wide-eyed appreciation of Paul. Melora jokingly made a grand introductory gesture, all fluid grace, like a silent film actress. Paul took Christa's hand, held it to his lips, and kissed her knuckles.

It was quite a dance of gestures. The beauty of everyone in their prime so captivated me, I missed the chance to be mad at my wife for forgetting I was there for a few seconds.

shulz house

W e're in Shulz House, specifically in The Kitchen That Time Forgot—all crusty chrome fixtures, pea-green Formica, canary yellow wallpaper going brown over the electric stove, the air a potpourri of carcinogenic cleansers and dry rot. Due to roadwork and rush hour traffic, we've arrived about two hours later than expected, and our nerves are threadbare. It's eleven p.m. or so, and the farmhouse is meat-locker brisk. Evan snores into my chest, keeping me warm. Beth, huddled in her coat, reads aloud a note from Trip, her breath rising in thin clouds.

Dear G & B (& E!)

Welcome to Shulz House!

If you're reading this, you found the key under the Creepy Garden Gnome. Sorry we couldn't be here to welcome you. Long story. If you have any emergencies, call and I'll head on over. (Or scream out the window, we'll probably hear. Our house is approximately one-eighth of a mile away.) Essential numbers taped inside cabinet. Use the land line. Cells don't work up here. Also, no TV reception and no cable hookup for you yet. Time Warner won't travel to the sticks. But soon!

You can also call Ricky Shulz, your next-door neighbor (grew up in Shulz House, in fact, before his family parceled up and sold off the land) or you can head over to his doublewide. The one with the green pickup, i.e. the only other Evidence of Life on Shulz Way, ha ha.

Ricky's cool. Wife Jen is library director, daughter Brianna (16, I think) is a sweet kid, also our/your housekeeper. Home-schooled. Good people, the Shulzes, shitty politics. Libertarian. Gun enthu-siasts, 2nd Amendment strong, etc. DO NOT TALK POLITICS.

Fireplace, sadly, is kaput, under code, will smoke the house out (and burn it down) if you build a fire. Furnace is temperamental but should be working OK, if a tad smelly. Thermostat next to basement steps in living/dining room. Howls like a beast when it comes on, so prepare spawn, who must be driving by now (ha ha . . . can't wait to see him. Been too long!).

Hope you like the furniture, some of C's favorite antiques. Sorry about dorky fix-tures n' stuff. We plan to remodel. Some-day. Meantime, pretend its 1981 and all will be well.

Trash pickup is Tuesdays. They come around 8 AM. DO NOT put anything out before that, as Critters will get in and spread it everywhere, even in winter. This is their turf, they make the rules.

IMPORTANT STUFF:
Almost all the doors—extinct American
chestnut—stick. Jiggle the knob and pull
to the left, then push. It's easy, really.
Washer/dryer in mudroom.

Greta's General Store on Main Street,
about a ten-minute walk. Trailways
stops there, buses to NYC, Woodstock,
New Paltz, Kingston, etc. Greta is from
Heidelberg, complains all the time about
everything (esp. Muslims) but sweet
(unless yer Muslim). Hardware-type stuff
in the back, plus NY Times, local paper
(The Huntsman), magazines, etc. Also
overpriced fleece shit, sunglasses, camp-
ing supplies, fishing poles, duct tape.

Mt. Marie Produce & Grocery, aka The
Mildew Mart, catty-corner from Greta's.
Good for basic groceries, beer, diapers,
etc., but DO NOT get fruit, veg, or meat.
Proprietor is Scotty Shulz, Ricky's
cousin. Good guy. Never washes his
hands and apparently can't smell mold.

Good produce, etc., in Woodstock at
health food store Sunflower, bit of a hike
(35-minute drive). Next door is Wood-
stock Pharm, where you can get scrips
filled, etc. DO NOT take scrips to Mt.
Marie Pharmacy and Video, as codger
filling orders will tell everyone about
your Valtrex or whatever. You can, how-
ever, rent vids there. Decent selection.

*C says R-rated vids are stained n' sticky,
but she's making that up.*

*Abandoned cafe is C's new obsession.
She's remodeling it. ETA for Katie's
Kitchen—spring 2003.*

*Come on over for a big Welcome to the
Neighborhood feast tomorrow night,
after I get home (seven-ish . . . I stay after
with special ed kids) and after C gets
done with her various errands (she takes
K everywhere). Will call during the day
with more details.*

*Fresh sheets/quilts on beds, Rolling
Rock in fridge, good coffee in the freezer.*

Welcome to the sticks! More soon.

*Rgds,
Trip & Co.*

"Diapers?" Beth frowns at the note, purple half-moons under her eyes. "Why would we need diapers?"

I shift Evan's weight to one hand and crank the thermostat. The floorboards shake as the furnace rumbles to life, metal fans groaning, ducts rattling. Evan, accustomed to NYC decibel levels, stirs but sleeps on. A thin line of his drool runs down my neck.

"He hasn't seen Evan for over a year, hon," I whisper, flicking light switches on in the living/dining room. Worn antique furniture is scattered among the scuffed, chocolate-brown floorboards and faded Afghan rugs. I head up the stairs, bound for what I hope will be a decent mattress.

"Evan hasn't been in diapers for, like, almost *two years*, right? Fuck's sake," Beth grumbles behind me. She is laden with stuff. The crooked steps squeak, punctuating her words.

Heat rises to the second floor on an oil-scented cloud, where two bedrooms and a bathroom await us. Sure enough, the smallish doors stick in the frames. The first one eventually opens to a crib, which Beth harrumphs at. After a fair amount of jiggling the knob on the other door, the latch gives. Beth reaches in from behind me and flicks the light switch.

"Ah," she says, "Anne Frank chic!"

It's actually a sweet little scene: two dormer windows reflecting light onto a duvet-and-quilt-covered queen-size bed nestled below a ceiling I can touch, plus a rolltop desk on the coiled braids of a rag rug. A single red rose pokes out of a small ceramic vase on a bedside table doily.

"A rose for the poor tenants!" Beth collapses on the bed and brings the bloom to her nose. "A silken rose, at that."

She waves it in my face as I insert Evan into the covers beside her.

"Sweet," I say, taking the flower. As my wife shimmies out of her clothes, I sniff the scentless silk petals and press my finger against the plastic stem, where a thorn would be if the rose were real.

~

"I'm sorry, Grant," Trip says from the teacher's lounge at Mt. Marie Elementary. He sounds marathon-tired, almost stoned, a stark contrast to the tone of last night's note. "We really wanted to be there when you drove up. But we were so fried. We've just been swamped. You got in OK, right?"

"Key under the Creepy Garden Gnome, yeah," I say from the breakfast nook in The Kitchen That Time Forgot, staring through wavy window glass at the waning day, shadows lengthening over Ricky Shulz's double-wide trailer.

Opened boxes surround me: crockery, cutlery, books. I'm twitchy from a couple unsuccessful, teeth-grinding hours attempting to access the Internet via the phone line. My umpteenth coffee warms my guts as the sun edges the mountaintops.

Beth and Evan are returning the emptied U-Haul and shopping in Woodstock. My wife and I spent the day wearing his-n-hers respirators, trying to improve on Brianna Shulz's slack cleaning job. While Evan watched videos on the TV/VCR combo, we tended to the dust felting the windowsills and the mouse shit camouflaged by grime. Although we've scoured every trace of mold we can find, a fungus-y funk lingers still.

"You get my note?" Trip asks.

"The note's a masterpiece. Reminded me of Ye Olden Tymes. Those letters from when you were in France at that workshop?"

"And you were making that record at Electric Lady. Stereoblind days. I've still got those you wrote me from Scenic Avenue C."

"Cool. We should get 'em all out and read through them. You read mine to you; I'll read yours to me."

"That," Trip says, "is an idea."

"Can't thank you enough for putting us up, Trip."

"Of course, of course. You'd do the same for me if . . . you know."

If I'd become a rich rock star? I think. *Like we planned? Or if I married a rich girl like you?*

"I'm predicting you'll go native," Trip says, "with full-on flannel and a cap with earflaps by next fall. Chris isn't so sure."

A school bell rings in the background, shrill and long.

"I gotta go." Trip sounds wasted again. "My kids wait for no man . . ."

"No problem. Where's Christa anyway? No cars in your driveway all day. We were worried, left a couple messages. We thought maybe something with Katie."

"Ha. No, the kid's fine."

Ha?

Trip whispers: "We may need to be institutionalized soon, though, Christa and me."

"What? Why?"

Trip takes a deep breath.

"Well . . . Katie's . . . labor intensive. And Christa's hot to open the cafe, and she insists on schlepping the kid everywhere, to Town Hall meetings, to the Home Depot in Kingston. Will not get a babysitter. And Brianna's offered. And yesterday Christa and Katie spent hours in the café, in piles of rubble—probably toxic—waiting for contractors. They came home filthy. So far, all the local guys've stood her up."

"You'd think they'd be eager to get paid."

"The currency of tribal exclusivity is of premium value, my friend. We are interlopers."

"Thank you, Mr. Lamont. You are my favorite teacher, dude. So, where's your little family today?"

"Excellent question. My wife's probably driving around the mountains, hoping the kid'll conk out."

"Ah. Welcome to parenthood."

A microwave bings in the background.

"Mm," Trip says. "So, you guys coming over at seven . . . ?"

"Oh yeah. We are so there."

"Great. I'll give you more Shulz House info later. It's got a lotta soul, that place. Gotta fly."

I hang up and look around me. Here's what I already know from Trip's emails about Shulz House: Our new home is one of the oldest in Mt. Marie, built by a dairy farmer named Shulz. The Shulzes sold off most of their land in lots in the eighties. Except for Ricky's place next door, Trip and Christa Lamont now own all former Shulz property. Shulz House is on a three-acre plot thick with maple, silver birch, and gnarled, uncultivated apple trees. On the other side of Shulz Way, running parallel to the distressed blacktop, is the famed trout stream, Stony Clove Creek.

Behind the house rises Mt. Marie herself, a three thousand foot, timber-covered peak connecting to the Catskill Mountains. On the far side of the acreage, wreathed in fir, sits another former Shulz residence: the white-and-teal Victorian the Lamonts call home. I can just see it from the porch of the farmhouse. All houses—the Victorian, the farmhouse, and the trailer—form a line, seen from above, I imagine, like bulbs on a string of Christmas tree lights, with Shulz Way being the connecting cord. We all look out our front windows on Stony Clove Creek, sparkling now in the late-afternoon.

Ricky Shulz's doublewide is quite close to us, just over a dry stone wall. The steady white plume ascending from the trailer's smokestack indicates life, and the green pickup with the rusted yellow plow blade seems ready to burst into action, but the only Shulz we've actually seen today is the tireless Lab, tethered to a clothesline strung between the trailer and a sunbaked barn. The dog paces, buries then digs up tennis balls in the muddy snow, and barks incessantly.

After a day spent walking the wide Shulz House floorboards, I know where to expect creaks, and these offer small satisfactions of predictability. All of us are adjusting to the sound of each other's voices in these spaces, still jumpy when someone calls from another room, like hearing a new version of a song you've known for years—familiar, but it takes getting used to.

With the exception of the kitchen, wintry air seeps in everywhere, hovering in pockets, like cold spots in a pond. When one of these breezes touches his feet, Evan says, "Ghosts!" Even after we explain it away as poor insulation, he keeps up the poltergeist drama. I've set up my laptop, boom box, and mixtapes in the breakfast nook, where the gusts do not molest me, ensconced below a window, an arm's length from Mr. Coffee. My perch.

I'm about to give the Internet another shot when my wife and son pull in and get out of the Camry, each bundled in winter wear. Beth directs Evan's gaze to the mauve-peach sunset bleeding across the sky. The panorama against the grayscale mountains is foreign to his city-dweller self. Evan is accustomed to sunlight broken by concrete and red brick. He nods soberly, like he's possessed by the spirit of his future self, like he's seen it all.

chapter 4

ratatouille

Around seven, we bundle up for the short walk down Shulz Way to the Lamonts', crunching through the dark on a thin layer of snow. Evan walks between Beth and me, offering each of us a mittened hand. The air is subtly alive with the trickle of half-frozen Stony Clove Creek and the faraway rumble of the occasional semi on Route 28. When we hit the pavement, Beth gasps and points up.

"Look, Evan! Look at that!"

We stop and gaze at a moonless sky strewn with stars and bisected by the smudge of the Milky Way, which seems creamier than I'd remembered, tinged with purple at the edges.

"There's something you don't see in Manhattan," I say. "Wow."

A drop of light ambles steadily along the soft Catskill peaks.

"Aliens!" Evan says. "Aliens coming!"

"That's a plane, I think, big guy," I say, although I secretly want to pretend it's a spaceship, as I did with my dad when I was very little. My old man had been an original Trekkie. But Evan tends toward the *War of the Worlds*/malign aliens scenario as opposed to *Close Encounters*/benign aliens.

"Yeah, that's a plane," Beth says with extra certainty.

"Yeah? Really?" Evan pretends to doubt us. "Really for true?"

"Yes, Evan." Beth's voice is laced with a smile. "For true."

I let go of Evan's hand and walk to the middle of the street, noting the Big Dipper, Orion's Belt, and Cassiopeia—the only constellations I know. All gain definition as I take them in. The notion of the heavens acknowledging me makes me giddy.

"I could get used to this," I say.

"You're gonna have to," Beth says, leading our son toward the blazing bay windows of the Lamonts' house.

Trip opens the door, a stiff, mirthless smile pulled tight across his face. In twelve months, he's aged five years: sandy hair thinner, deeper crow's feet, a couple more forehead creases. He also seems shorter, stooped, his powder blue button-down hanging loosely on him.

"Hey neighbors!" he says, a little too loud. "Let me take those coats!"

"Big daddy! My sweet landlord!" Beth throws her arms around him. "Been too long!"

Trip pats Beth's shoulder blades and ducks away, overeager to handle our hats and layers.

"Smells good in here!" Beth says.

"Ah," I breathe in a familiar scent. "Trip's famous ratatouille? Yes?"

Trip nods, claps me on the back—a little too hard—and kneels before Evan.

"Wow," he says. "Look at you. You're huge. What do they feed you?"

Evan wraps his arms around my legs.

"Well I hope you like mac n' cheese," Trip says, "'cause I made some for ya. That's all my little one eats, too."

Evan crams his face against my leg, slighting my good friend yet again. My gut twists a little. I was hoping Evan's inexplicable distaste for Trip had waned.

"C'mon Evan," I say, "don't be rude."

"It's OK." Trip straightens up, groaning as his knees crack. He's long since stopped trying to win my son's affection.

"We're still a little shell-shocked, I guess," Beth says.

"Everything OK over there?" Trip asks. "I'm sorry we haven't been able to see you before now . . . things're just . . . I don't know. Crazy."

Beth and I assure him it's OK, although it's really not. It's odd.

"Where's the little bundle?" Beth blinks in the foyer light, her hair standing up with static, recalling punkier days.

"Yeah," I say, "where's Evan's new playmate? Dying to meet her."

"Christa's getting her dressed, or trying." Trip nods to the staircase behind him. "Our little bundle has been in the same pajamas for four days. Pretty rank."

As if on cue, the ceiling shakes with a series of thumps. A piercing shriek rings out above. I lift Evan to my chest, and he buries his face in my shirt.

Beth and I both tense, but before we can speak, Trip answers our unasked questions by holding up his hands.

"Chill, chill," he says with an exasperated laugh. "This is par for the course with Katie." He says *Katie* with loathing, which gives me a start. I've been an exasperated parent, and spoken my kid's name harshly, but Trip's disgust surprises me. Where's his usual sunniness, the same buoyant attitude that got him through all that rejection from literary agents? Apparently, I'd been depending on it.

Trip gives another counterfeit smile.

"Time for a tour," he says. More percussion above: two small feet fleeing two larger ones.

Trip walks us through the handsome house, his Docksiders squeaking on the refinished floors and plush rugs. He opens and closes his right hand nervously as we take in the high-ceilinged dining and living rooms, freshly painted in tasteful, vintage colors. Trip laughs dryly at the names for each color: coral dust, whipple blue, peach cloud. He notes the American chestnut trim on everything. It's a gorgeous place, warm and well lit, kind of hip Norman Rockwell. Until Katie screams again. And again.

Every couple of minutes another outburst erupts on the floors above us, followed by unintelligible vocal sounds from Christa. Trip's face twitches, but he says nothing—at least not with words. Evan claws my shoulders as we stand in the (pale straw) kitchen making small talk. With trembling hands, Trip uncorks the Syrah Beth brought.

Trip is stirring the ratatouille when Christa bursts through the kitchen door. Evan, still in my arms, turns toward the commotion.

The first thing I notice is Christa's red cheeks and the deep black tendrils of hair falling across her ruddy neck. The hair obscures the face of Katie, whimpering and clinging to Christa like a barnacle.

Christa's usually round features have planed out and, for the first time since I've known her, her face bears a hungry hollowness. Her wine-red nose is either a little bigger or her caved-in cheeks make it seem so. The kitchen shrinks around us.

"Hey everybody!" she says, breathlessly. "Heeeere's Katie!"

She pries the squirming child from her chest—I see scratches on Christa's neck—and turns Katie's flailing, fireplug body so we can see her front side. Evan's fascination burns as he tightens his hold on me. He's never seen anything like this. Katie's jet-colored hair, as much a mass as her little torso, lends her a Dr. Seuss quality.

Katie remains in her pajamas—a filthy, spit-stained-and-food-encrusted Lion King set. The shirt and pants fit tight on her round belly—where a diaper pokes out—but hang loose and wet at the neck, ankles, and wrists. Christa walks toward Evan and me, presenting her daughter like a sack of grain.

Katie stops wriggling and swats away her hair, revealing deep black irises. Her gaze widens as she and Evan make eye contact.

Christa laughs, pitching her voice high. "One of your own kind, Katie!"

When Katie is a few inches from Evan, she reaches to touch him.

He recoils and shouts, "Home! Home! I wanna go hooooome! Not the house! Not the house . . . New York Cityyyyy!"

Katie resumes screaming. Beth comes over and protectively encircles our son with her arm, fastening her fingers to my shirtsleeve.

"Ah, shit!" Christa shifts gears from forced gaiety to annoyance. Is that a flash of hatred in her eyes, directed at my son? No. Can't be.

The sound of banging metal draws my attention to the stove.

"Trip, what the fuck?" Christa yells.

Trip is ladling steaming ratatouille into a big Tupperware bowl.

"They can take this back to the house," he says. "This is crazy. She's not gonna let you have dinner, and now she's freaked out Evan! I told you, I *told* you!"

"Wait, wait," Beth says. But I know my wife wants to get the hell out.

I meet Christa's eyes and nod. She inhales deep, her shoulders collapsing in a kind of relieved surrender.

"OK, OK," Christa says. "I'm so sorry you guys. She only gets like this at night. It's a fucking mystery. Plus I dragged her all over creation today, and she didn't nap at all, so she's just toast. She always naps, early afternoon, but not today for some fucking reason. She'll be better tomorrow. We'll come by tomorrow, like three or so. How's that?"

My wife takes the bowl and a baguette from Trip, nodding. "I have a meeting in the city tomorrow," she says, "but I'm sure the boys would like some company."

"Meeting . . . ?" Trip's voice is back to its old tenor. He's smiling, for real.

He is so happy we're leaving, I think.

"Potential publicist gig," Beth says. "This Sasha girl, popstar on the rise . . ."

"Home," Evan cries. "Hooooome!"

We make a hasty exit into the night, carrying Tupperware containers of ratatouille and mac n' cheese through the starlight back to Shulz House. As we walk, Evan sniffles. I glance up again at the celestial realm but keep quiet.

chapter 5

this old man

Once again I wake in the early morning dark, hyper-alert, heart pounding from another dream of my father. When meds were strong in my blood, these dreams were infrequent, usually seasonal. But now, as I'm tapering off, two nights in a row—our first night in Shulz house, and now our second.

I throw back the covers and sit at the mattress edge, bed warmth eking from my skin. A bittersweet ache I define as my father's presence shimmers inside me.

The dream is always the same. The old man is smiling, whisper-close, shape-shifting, yet definitely my father. He fluctuates from cipher to an elder version of himself, an alternate-universe dad, one who sobered up and survived, living on in another reality; wispy white hair swept back from his broad, lined forehead, gunmetal-gray eyes gazing from deep sockets, cheeks russet with health, thin upper lip, fat lower, square jaw, hands crosshatched with pulsing veins, and big feet in beaten Weejuns. No socks.

In the border between dream and wakefulness, I am flush with the wildest of implausibilities: the old man's death has been a misunderstanding, an elaborate joke. Joy bubbles up, accompanied by a summery forgiveness, a weightlessness, freedom from the ballast of past events. This fragile state never lasts long; with each breath, my personal timeline clicks in, my mind recalibrating to consciousness, drawing me back, sandbagging me with memory.

A heavy, long sigh escapes my parched lips. I inhale the cool, mold-stung air like a man surfacing from a great depth, and I am back.

I opt not to wake Beth, curled now like a mama squirrel around our son. Over the years, my wife and I have expended a lot of energy hashing over how my dad's suicide shaped and damaged me, especially as I was the one who found him; we rake over notions of my problems springing from that dark event, as if it is the root of some clinging vine I'll always need to manage but never be free of. A great story, that. But I'd just as soon not hasten the return of my vindictiveness, encroaching now from the horizons of my thoughts like rot at the edges of a leaf.

I pull on my sweatpants and robe and head downstairs, where I turn up the furnace, ignite all the eyes on the stove for additional warmth, and busy myself with coffee, trying to hold onto the decaying echoes of my father's presence. I shun the light switches, trying to remain in his shadow.

The sky is paling, mountains distinguishing themselves against the blue as the oncoming morning pushes against the window. Coffee scent rises. Warmth from my steaming mug courses from the ceramic into my palms and up my forearms. Finally, I surrender, sitting at the nook as recollections unspool like a movie into my forebrain.

~

It's July 2, 1973, the summer of my ninth year. My folks, who separated several times, have reconciled again. But my journalist dad cannot quite get his shit together. After numerous missed deadlines, the Charlotte *Observer* has fired him. My mom is transitioning from edgy flower child to Mary Tyler Moore hip, working in administration at Mercy Hospital. Daddy's home, typing away with manic focus on his electric Smith Corona, cigarette burn on the SHIFT key. He's writing letters, making carbons, swigging PBR from a can, sort of keeping an eye on me, but not really.

I'm leaving for the neighborhood pool. Daddy is distant, but my observation that his typing sounds like tap dancing elves reels him in. He laughs from the corner of his mouth and advises me to stay out of the deep end. It is my last memory of him alive. The laugh, and the advice. Stay out of the deep end.

A few hours later, I'm walking home. Due to my flaxen hippie hair, the black kids on neighboring porches call me Cream Head. I like this, even more today than yesterday. I am unreasonably amused by their good-natured jeers. Prodigal dad is awaiting me and I'm happy. I'm looking forward to a syndicated *Star Trek* rerun, maybe some ice cream.

The screaming fights between my folks are over. All is forgiven. Daddy's been playing "Take Me Home, Country Roads," "If I Had a Hammer," and "The Lion Sleeps Tonight" on a 1970 Gibson Hummingbird acoustic guitar that will soon become mine.

As I walk, the ebb-and-flow rhythm of the cicadas in the bushes reminds me of the sounds of my parents fucking in the night. Since my father's return, I've heard them—my parents fucking, that is—more than usual, often right after I've been tucked in. Surely they must know I can hear them, but their hunger is undeniable. I am OK with that.

The whack-whack-whack of the headboard, the rhythm of the bedsprings, the muffled coos and humming of my mother, the grunts and sighs of my dad, the stunned laughter of both of them—all of it comforts me. I have no words to explain this feeling, not yet, but I know the same carnal heat from which I sprang is a big part of what keeps us together as a family; it defies the darkness, the stale beer breath, my father, red-faced from screaming, prying open an ochre prescription bottle and dry-swallowing pills.

Medicine cabinet snooping has revealed VALIUM. Right next to my mom's flying-saucer-looking birth control pill dispenser. VALIUM. Like a *Star Trek* villain.

Over the years I will add acquired knowledge to jig-sawed memories, and I'll see my father as a mood-swing-prone alcoholic pill head, likely bipolar; I will get to know my mother's rage, which, after my father's death, will intensify. My questions to my mother regarding the old man will be met with terse silence and will eventually cease.

It's that summer afternoon again, 1973. I'm almost to the house. My shadow is taller, ahead of me now, leading the way. I'm proud to go barefoot the whole distance from the pool without needing to jump into the grass. I've got Indian feet.

I enter the house expecting tap-dancing elves but find only thick, buzzy quiet. In the ensuing decades, I will tell myself I knew right then, but I'm not sure this is true.

"Daddy!"

As ever, the house seems really dark. My eyes are still in outside-sunny-pool mode, plus Daddy keeps the blinds down all the time. So I stand at the door, eyes adjusting, blinking wetness back into them. I smell shit. Did I step in dog doo on my way back from the pool? Again? No. My toes are clean. Relief.

Daddy's bare foot is the first thing I see, sticking out over the arm of the sofa. The TV flickers blues and browns, but the sound is down. *The Hollywood Squares* is on. I know because of the colors. Paul Lynde's face is orange and grainy. Daddy is very still and he stinks. The shit smell is him. Now that I'm close, I smell other things, too—beer, pee, something sharp I can't name. He's different. Foam like from root beer is crusted at the edge of his lips. On his forearm he's written "I'M SORRY" in blue ink. Beer cans are everywhere, plus a pill bottle on the coffee table, upended, empty.

"Did you scream?" people will ask.

No screams. The calm spreading through my limbs will be identified by experts as shock. It serves me well in the short term, enabling me to call my mother and to sit quietly watching a pantomime of *The Hollywood Squares* while paramedics burst in, brusquely assess my father, and carry him out on a gurney as my mother skids to a stop outside. Her powerful slam of the Super Beetle's door wakes me from numbness. She crumples on the porch, saying, "Mother*fucker*, mother*fucker*, oh you motherfucker," and my body commences trembling. At that point, the recollections grow mercifully indistinct.

chapter 6

black stars

By the time Evan and Beth awake, I have reassembled and restocked our VHS shelves, set mousetraps under the sink, unpacked our crockery and cutlery, plugged several holes in the sheetrock walls with steel wool, and sucked down an entire pot of Maxwell House. I've peeled duct tape from a box marked "Beth—Misc Work, '89-'90" and affixed a haiku of hers to the refrigerator with a magnet. She'd scrawled it on a Post-it and left it on the bedside table sometime in our first year together. I was still in Stereoblind, and she was working ten to six at APCO Worldwide, making her way up the PR food chain, yet to go indie, and still performing occasionally at Nuyorican Poets Café poetry slams. I awoke with her scent on me and these words by my head:

> *After the small death*
> *A bittersweet breath of us*
> *In the ceiling fan.*

It's been four hours since I caught sight of our next-door neighbors' sixteen-year-old, Brianna Shulz. Around eight a.m., a glossy Subaru packed with a couple other teenagers and a ponytailed dad driver pulled up. Fellow homeschoolers, I guessed, going to someone's house to "study" who knows what. Ponytail honked and Brianna emerged with the handsome yellow Lab. *So that's Brianna*, I thought. Average height, apple-cheeked, magenta-red hair poking from under a black toque. Backpack on her shoulder, she strode on stick-thin bluejeaned legs, hunched in a pea-green parka with a faux fur collar. She led the Lab to the clothesline, hooked him up, nuzzled his neck, and trotted to the Subaru. The dog barked after her, which was sweet. At first.

Four hours later: incessant barking, echoing off the bare mountains. Not at all sweet.

Perhaps he's not a mindless barking machine, sent to further test me and my family. Perhaps he senses something I do not. *Or maybe,* I think, desperate to entertain myself, *maybe he is singing,* because for a few moments, his barking rhythm sounds like "Jingle Bells." I am grinning on the lip of my coffee mug when Beth clomps down the stairs in clunky heels.

"That damn dog," she says. "It's insane. Christa and Trip did not mention *that,* did they?"

"Mommy! Bad word!" Evan says from a nest of empty boxes in the living room. With most of our stuff unpacked, he's fashioned a cardboard fort surrounding the TV/VCR combo. I'd thought he was engrossed in Disney's animated *Tarzan* for the hundredth time, but a quick look from the kitchen table reveals him doodling furiously on his fort with a Sharpie, paying no attention to the cartoon or the Phil Collins soundtrack songs I now know by heart.

"Cut mommy some slack, Evan," I say. For some reason, he is bothered only by his mother's cursing, no one else's.

"*Damn* is a bad word," he says, face on his work.

Beth grunts at his protest. Evan catches this, processes it like it's an actual sentence in their private mother-child nonverbal lexicon, and grunts back.

Beth is in business mode: hairspray-and-cosmetics scent, gray pegged trousers and matching tapered jacket from her favorite NYC boutique, plus laptop and a large shoulder bag. The interview with old Manhattan cronies is afoot, a potential freelance gig publicizing well-financed, rising young R&B singer Sasha, whose music, unfortunately, is not our cup of tea: heavily processed, mostly synthetic pop that will, in all likelihood, sell gazillions for Universal, one of the only major labels still kicking. The Manhattan-bound Trailways leaves from Greta's General Store in a half hour.

"What's this?" Beth asks, looking at the haiku.

"You remember that," I say. "That's a fave."

She nods, slowly, then strides to the mirror by the kitchen door and frowns in it.

"You look great," I say, taking her in as blood flows below. I stand behind her and, sadly, catch my own reflection: unshaven face, greasy hair, sleep-starved eyes, stained sweatpants, distressed wool socks, and tattered flannel robe open to a fleshy gut. Did I brush my teeth today? I did not.

"You think so?" Beth purses her lips in the mirror.

"I know so. You'll knock 'em dead. You foxy."

She rolls her eyes, but I do not look away. The East Seventh tenement was opium-den dark, so I am unaccustomed to seeing her in natural winter light filtered through blown glass. The glint of the sun on her thick, dark hair, dusky skin, child-broadened hips—all good. I note once again how Evan's birth altered her proportions, making her curvier, more anchored to the ground, to me.

Then I recall her recent disinterest in sex. My lust— enhanced, I'm sure, by my lower dose of Zoloft—morphs into irritation.

"You're welcome," I say.

She adds milk to her coffee and slugs it down. "Thanks," she mutters, walking to Evan's fort, her heels clop-clopping on the floorboards.

"I'm off, baby boy," she says, pulling back a cardboard flap to find our son scribbling.

Evan drops his Sharpie and holds up his arms. "Huggy time," he says. His hands are filthy with ink.

"Evan, your hands!" Beth says. She turns to me. "You know about this?"

"Yeah. It'll come off. It's happened before."

"When?"

"I don't know. Two months ago. In the city. You were out."

"Huggy time," Evan says, a little louder.

"It'll be OK, honey," I tell my wife as a draft brushes my ankles. "Really. It comes off pretty easy."

This is a lie.

"Huggy time!"

Beth takes a deep breath and kneels before the boxes. "No huggy time today, baby boy. But kissy, yes."

Evan stands, looks in his mother's eyes, and nods, awaiting instructions.

"No dirty hands on my outfit, 'K?" Beth says.

"'K, Mommy."

Beth places Evan's hands in her hair as he plants dewy kisses on her neck. He sees something and draws back, squinting.

"Mommy."

"Yes, my love."

"Your silver strands are gone away."

Beth casts me a quick glance, then faces Evan. "Yes, sweetie, I put a little rinse in my hair."

"When?" I lean down to Beth's head. Although her mussed hair hides her eyes, I can feel irritation troubling the space between us. Her hair is, in fact, a shade darker. The recently visible few threads of gray are gone.

"Yesterday," she says. "After we cleaned up."

"I miss the silver strands," Evan says, sticking out his lower lip. "I miss them. Bring them back!"

"Oh they'll be back, don't worry" Beth says, her forehead against Evan's. "They'll definitely be back."

I suddenly feel about fifteen pounds heavier. "I . . . I didn't notice. Sorry."

"I noticed you didn't notice," she says and meets our boy's eyes. "Only Evan did."

Evan grins.

She looks up at me, sighs, and squeezes my calf, sending electricity upward. "It's OK, you got a lot on your plate, I know." She turns back to our son and points to a tiny circlet of reddish-brown moles on her forehead. "I still got my angel kisses."

Evan pokes her moles gently. "Angel kiss, angel kiss, angel kiss . . ."

"I love your fort," Beth says, nodding toward the stacked, graffittied boxes. "You're artistic like Uncle Billy. Are you and Katie gonna play in it?"

"If she wants to," Evan says warily. Then, assuming Beth's voice, he parrots something he'd heard her say last night: "She was Looney Tunes."

"She's just shy." Beth smiles and strokes his hair. "She needs a friend. It'll be better today, right Papa?"

"Yeah," I say, happy for this distraction. "I think Katie was just tired last night. We all were." *I still am.*

Beth pulls our son into a tight hug. He makes a show of keeping his inky hands at his sides, like a tin soldier. "I'm gonna miss my boys," Beth says, voice muffled in Evan's hair. She kisses him full on the lips. "Later, tater."

"Soon, raccoon," he says and disappears into his fort.

Beth heads to the mirror in the kitchen, where she finger combs her hair and whispers to me, "I hope it goes OK today . . ."

Evan and I are expecting Christa and Katie in a few hours. Christa had called earlier to assure me her daughter is not, in fact, feral but is just "moody" and will do much better after a nap. I only half-believe this. Turns out, in the nine months they've had Katie, they've not yet attempted to socialize her. Evan is the first non-Chinese child Katie's seen up close.

Beth's in the kitchen by the back door, spending an inordinate amount of time on the buttons of her coat. "I'm not sure how long it'll take, you know, this meeting," she says.

"Might need to stay over at Paul and Melora's. Might try and track down Billy, too."

I bristle at the thought of her seeking out junkie brother Billy but know better than to try to dissuade that.

"Well, Paul and Melora do have the room," I say, as jealous bile rises in me. "Only East Villagers I know with a guest room." Then I let it come: "Bet you're psyched to miss that poor freaky kid. Looney Tunes."

"What?"

"Oh, come on. You can't wait to get out of here so you don't have to deal with Katie. But that's OK. Leave it to me. It's what I do. It's all I fucking do."

Beth squints at me. I know I'm picking a fight, and at the worst possible time. But I can't stop. Or I won't, rather.

"I need to do this interview," she says in a forced whisper. "I'm not looking forward to being away."

"Yeah. Right. Why deal with putting a house together and kid-wrangling when you can spend the night in the Christadora House, drinking expensive wine with your favorite old rock star? And his wifey."

"What's wrong with you? Why are you making this harder than it has to be?"

"It's hard? You can't wait to get on that bus. Be honest."

"Yeah." Beth grabs her scarf from a hook by the back door. "And if I'm lucky I'll get the shit-smell section, next to the crusty grandpa who'll pass out on my shoulder."

"Mommy!" Evan calls from the living room. "Bad word! *Shit* is a bad word!"

Beth's dark eyes burn into me. "Nice. Look what you did."

"Oh, now I'm the potty mouth."

"Everything was fine until you . . ."

"Oh yes, it's my fault. Of course."

She looks at her watch. "I would love to stand here and soak up more love and support from you," she says, "but I have to get this bus and go sell my forty-two-year-old self so maybe, if we're lucky, I'll get to help pimp this anorexic little stripper puppet so we don't end up on fucking welfare. Unless you've got some work lined up."

"Mommy!"

"Look around you," I say. "Look in that room over there. That little guy. That's my work. OK? Making sure Looney Tunes doesn't go for his jugular—that's my work. No small thing. OK? You have no idea. Really. No idea."

"I really have to go earn some money," Beth says, "so we can get you back on your meds. You're impossible."

"I feel great, actually," I say. This is true. In these pissy moments of righteous anger, I feel like I'm tapped into high octane fuel, like some kind of truthing avenger. Blood rushes back to my groin. If Evan wasn't in the next room, I'd make a pass at Beth. A quick look into her eyes shoots that fantasy down.

I decide it's imperative I drive her.

"Let me drive you."

"You're kidding, right?"

"I'll get Evan into his snowsuit, strap him in, and I'll drive you. It'll take, like, a minute. I'm skilled."

Beth looks me up and down, focusing for a millisecond on my gut.

"I don't think so," she says, pulling on a black wool hat with a suddenly ridiculous pompon on the crown. "I can get there faster by walking. You make me need to rush because you were browbeating me, you feel like a shit, that's your problem."

"Mommy!"

"I love you, sweetie!"

"Love you, too!" Evan's voice is disturbingly undisturbed.

My wife gives me a *fuck you* frown, turns, and pulls on the back door handle. This door in particular is a problem, and it sticks as if glued shut. She jiggles the knob, pulls, and kicks the base, rattling the old glass panes.

"SHIT! This fucking door. What the fuck am I doing here?"

"*Mommy!*"

I reach for the knob, my fingers closing on her hand. She jerks away and stands steaming by the hat rack. I pull, twist, say a prayer, and the door gives. Frigid air flows in as Beth adjusts her various burdens and heads out.

The Lab is barking even louder now, straining against his leash, pacing in the muddy snow.

"I'll call you later to check in, let you know what I'm doing," she says, choking back a sob as she blinks in the sun. She winces at each bark.

"I can drive you."

"No." She pulls out her Ray Bans and boom, I am shut out. "Go take care of our kid. Make sure he doesn't think I'm a bitch."

"Come on. I'm the bitch."

She nods and heads off, making pretty good time considering her unsensible shoes, bags bouncing against her wool-enshrouded body. "I'll call later," she says over her shoulder, "let you know what's up."

"The color looks great," I say. "Your hair! Looks great!"

She slows down a little, as if she's going to stop and turn around. But she just raises her hand vaguely before picking up speed again. I want to yell after her to be careful if she goes to check on her brother, but I don't.

The dog is going crazy. Ricky Shulz, broad at the shoulder, narrow at the hip, zipped into mustard Carhartt coveralls, opens his door and steps onto the front deck. He sort-of waves, his salt-and-pepper bearded face crumpling in a micro-expression of both irritation and apology as he attends to his Lab.

"King! No!" Deep voice. Baritone.

I am shivering on the flagstone stoop, wondering if my new neighbor caught any of Beth's and my argument. I wrap my robe tighter around me. My teeth chatter as my nostril hairs stiffen. The previous epiphany at my sorry appearance recurs, and I want to bolt back inside, but I feel like some words should pass between my new neighbor and me.

Ricky unhooks the now quiet King and leads him up the deck steps. He glances back.

"He'll calm down once he gets to know you," he says.

"Totally OK. Just doing his job, right?"

Ricky sort-of nods as he leads his dog into the trailer.

There's a tug at my robe. I turn to see Evan reaching across the threshold, pulling me back inside.

"Papa," he says. "You have to come and see my pictures." With his jaw set tight, he is distracting both of us from fight fallout. I admire this and wish I'd done it when my parents fought. I was passive, though, always hiding, waiting for it all to blow over. Evan's more like his mom in this regard. Willful. A doer.

I allow him to pull me back in. He helps push the door closed. Now that Beth's gone and my head is clearing, regret bears down on me like an instant hangover.

"Was that Ricky?" Evan asks as he leads me into the living room.

He must have overheard Beth and me talking about our new neighbors.

"Yeah, Evan, that's him. Ricky Shulz."

"Is he nice?"

"He seems OK."

"Is his dog nice? Mommy doesn't like his dog."

"King's OK. He's barking so much 'cause he doesn't know us yet."

"He won't bark if he knows us? If we're friends?"

"I hope so. We'll see."

Evan points his finger at an imaginary presence, as if laying down a law, and says, "Friends don't bark at their friends."

We're back in the living room. Evan has arranged the boxes so his pictures are on display. The Sharpie drawings are large heads sprouting stick legs and arms, with prickly blobs for hands and feet. The faces are all swirly eyes and wavy, smiling mouths, the heads crowned with wild clumps of hair. This is business as usual with Evan's art. There are several groups of three, smiling. Above the trios are random globs.

"Wow, Evan, cool," I say. "That's me, you, and Mommy, right?"

"Yes. Me, you, and Mommy."

I point to the globs above the figures. "What are these?"

"Stars. Black stars."

"Black stars?"

"Yeah. Sometimes stars are black."

One simple circle floats among the black stars.

"What's that?"

"Spaceship. Aliens coming."

He'd never, to my knowledge, drawn a spaceship before. "Cool," I say. "Friendly or not?"

Evan pauses, cocks his head, and says, "I don't know yet."

chapter 7

playdate

Around three, Christa shows up to Shulz House with Katie. She raps at the back door, then lets herself in. Evan and I enter the kitchen like it's a minefield. Beneath a huge down coat draped over both of them, Katie is still in her *Lion King* pajamas, clinging to her mother's waist, face buried in breast.

"Sorry my breath smells like ass," Christa says, kissing my cheek. "Ladies and gentlemen," she says, reaching into her Coach tote, "kiddie crack!"

She pulls out a bag of Robert's American Gourmet Pirate's Booty. Katie grunts, tightens her stout legs around Christa's clingy sweater, and claws at the crinkling bag. Christa reaches into a kitchen cabinet for a bowl.

"Look at this, Grant!" Christa pours the puffs into the bowl as her daughter flails. Neither mother nor daughter is using hands to hold on. "These women at the orphanage said they'd never seen a kid with such strong legs. She's like a spider monkey."

"Wow," I say, dimly wondering if Katie's unusual lower body strength bespeaks some medieval orphanage conditions. Evan is frowning.

"What's kiddie crack?" he asks.

It occurs to me that Christa, who hasn't been around my son in over a year, doesn't realize Evan now understands almost everything adults say.

"Watch it, Christa," I say. "Evan's pretty sharp these days."

"What's kiddie crack?" Evan says again, louder.

"I meant kiddie *snack*," Christa shoots me an apology with her eyes.

"That's not what you said." Evan, as usual, knows he's being lied to.

"People make mistakes, Evan," I say. "Ease up."

"Hey, Evan," Christa says, pitching her voice high, "you still into Thomas the Tank Engine?"

Evan nods, eyes wide.

"Well, I brought . . . *Thomas and the Magic Railroad!*" Christa pulls a VHS from her bag. Katie gasps.

"Oh man, hallelujah," I say. "Evan loves him some Thomas. And we don't have that one yet."

"Great! It's Katie's favorite, too!"

Katie releases a throaty wail. She snatches the videocassette, squawking as she waves it in the air like the spoils of war. The hair stands up on the back of my neck.

"She's got a future in rock," I say.

Christa grins and buries her lips in Katie's hair, kissing furiously. For the first time I see Katie smile.

"My leetle rock star!" Christa punctuates her baby talk with raspberries on Katie's plump cheeks. "The next Joan Jett! See how sweeeeet Baby Rock Star is when she's had her nappy nap?"

"Let's watch! Let's watch!" Evan says as he runs into the living room. He ejects Tarzan and motions for Katie to bring him the tape. Katie unhooks her legs and plops, wild-eyed, to the linoleum. She runs to my son, wide feet thumping with more force than I would have thought. In seconds, Evan inserts *Thomas and the Magic Railroad*, and the two kids are side-by-side, fidgeting, waiting for the previews.

Christa deposits two grape juice boxes and the snack bowl before the TV. Katie and Evan shovel fistfuls of Pirate's Booty into their mouths, never taking their eyes off the screen. I foresee excavating wet, half-chewed mush from the crevices in the antique rug. But in the scheme of things, it's OK; scraping masticated food, like wiping clay-textured crap from the toilet seat and pee from various surfaces, has become "the small stuff" I do not sweat. Another violent tantrum from Katie, however, will go a long way toward ruining my day.

Christa scoots back to the kitchen.

"Thomas the Tank Engine, the great equalizer," I say, shaking my head. "Who knew?"

"Right? And it's the worst piece-of-shit movie. I mean it's awful, right? Or is it me?"

"No, we saw it in the theater and were stunned by its badness. But Evan loves anything Thomas. Thanks for bringing it, Christa. Good call."

"Mom of the year," she crows, going for the never-empty Mr. Coffee. She stops short over the sink. "Grant, what the hell?"

For a second I wonder if it's yet more mouse shit, but I see the Woolite bottle and remember.

"Just doing a delicate wash," I say. "An old shirt I haven't worn in a while. Cotton-silk blend."

"Dude, there's *underwear* in here. Sexy stuff."

"Those aren't mine." I don't tell Christa adding the lingerie helped assuage my guilt over being a dick to Beth. "Laundry's part of my gig, you know."

Christa dips a wooden spoon into the suds and lifts out my favorite old rock star shirt, a black star-spangled thing I wore a lot in Stereoblind.

"I remember this," she says. "You wore this at Lollapalooza '91, right?"

"Unbelievable."

"Long-term memory still intact," she says. "Short-term, however, is fucked." She gives me a quick glance, focuses back on the shirt, and says, "You looked wicked hot in this thing."

"Thanks. I came across it when I was unpacking some clothes. Road manager for Jane's Addiction offered me two hundred bucks for it."

"You can't put a price on sexy. You made the right choice."

"I could use that money now, though. God knows."

"Will I see you in this at the next playdate? Not that the robe-and-sweatpants look isn't a feast for the eyes."

"No ma'am," I say, blushing. "It reeked with BO going back to '91, so I just thought I should clean it up. Threw in some of Beth's unmentionables to keep it company."

"Ah." Christa nods. She drops the waterlogged shirt back into the sink with the camisoles and French-cut underwear. I see her black tights are slack at the seat, riding low, the waistband of a thong poking out. The droopy look is a first for her. She's always been proudly "hippy but happy," opting for snug pants. Country life seems to have whittled her down. She spins and catches me.

"Your neck . . ." I say, focusing on the scratches.

"Oh," her cheeks bloom. "Katie. Little hellion. Gotta trim her nails."

"You think?"

She points to the sink. "If you wear that shirt tonight, I bet you get lucky."

I laugh. "Not likely. First off, Beth's probably staying over at Paul and Melora's . . ." My gaze goes to the big toe protruding from my sock.

"Ah. And secondly . . . ?"

Secondly, I think, *we haven't fucked in a month.*

"Well . . ." I say, glancing in the direction of the kids.

"I get it," Christa nods. "Katie hasn't been the biggest aphrodisiac either."

The image of my friend Trip pops into my head, with piercing clarity.

"How's Trip, anyway?" I ask. "He recover from last night?"

"Oh, my Trip." Christa's face falls, and she stares into space. "Katie's kinda kicked him to the curb. Me too, a little. He doesn't like to talk about it. He was so nervous about you guys coming over, and it all went just as horribly as he knew it would."

"Sorry."

"No, it's OK. She needs to get *socialized*, all the books say. And we love Katie so much, it's just we had no idea." She slaps her hand on the counter and smiles. "Why didn't you tell us?"

"Tell you . . . ? That's it's, uh, work?"

"I knew it'd be that, but you're so lucky . . . your kid's . . ."

Normal.

Her face clouds.

"Would it have changed your mind if I warned you?" I ask.

"No," she snaps, recovering. "I wanted a baby. Damn my plumbing. We wanted a baby."

"OK, then."

A surge of saccharine music wafts in from the living room and Christa rolls her eyes. She goes to the stack of mixtapes by my laptop.

"Mixtapes! Love your mixtapes. Our Pathfinder doesn't have a damn cassette player, you know. You gotta start with the mix CDs already."

"One thing at a time," I say as I drain the water from the sink.

"*Beth's '90s Hits*," she says. "Oh, this is sweet stuff. Nine Inch Nails, Butthole Surfers, Oasis, Nirvana, Pavement, and of course," she groans, ". . . Six Ray Star." She inserts the tape in the boom box and presses *play*. The chugging, folky opening of "Wonderwall" fills the room. Liam Gallagher's Lennon-y vocal drowns out *Thomas and the Magic Railroad*.

"So you don't like Six Ray Star anymore?" I'm wringing my wash. "'Kiss My Ring' is kind of a nineties totem, right?"

"Yeah. Very alternative. And perfect for a Nike commercial."

"Please don't start with that." I drape the under-things on the open cabinet doors and the shirt over a kitchen chair.

"So Beth's staying with them, you think?"

"I would if I was her. We had a spat. I was not at my best."

"Oh?"

"I'm . . . coming off my meds. If I keep breaking the pills in half, I'll have about three month's supply left, then I'm done."

"Ah. Interesting. You do seem a little more . . . edgy."

"It's a mixed blessing."

"Why the change? You been on meds for, what . . . ?"

"Couple years, since that time when Evan was a baby . . . in the park."

"Right. I remember . . ."

I shudder: The Junkie Incident, late summer, 2001, Tompkins Square Park. In the future review of Grant Kelly's Life, I predict The Junkie Incident will be one of the top five defining moments.

chapter 8

the junkie incident

It was a normal stay-at-home dad day for me. I was chatting with a nanny; tall, thirtysomething Dominique, broad-shouldered in a sundress, big hands like fluttering pigeons. She was paying her daughter's college tuition by watching a pair of three-year-old twin boys whose parents sold antiques in the West Village. Dominique held the attention of me and a couple of moms—Juliet, a single bartender, and Sage, an erstwhile graphic designer whose husband renovated brownstones. They had a toddler each. As usual, I was the only dad in the park. But caregiver-ship trumped gender. I was, essentially, one of the gals.

The "caregiver" brand of gossip was especially salty, a potent antidote to the tedium of hyper responsibility we'd all taken on. We rarely talked about the pressures of parenthood or nanny-hood; we just alleviated those pressures via curses, righteous airing of grievances, and loose talk.

Dominique's Jamaican accent lulled us. She was bubbling over about her employers' marital problems, and it was juicy stuff. She'd walked in on the husband *in flagrante delicto* with another woman. She omitted nothing, her alto voice caressing each detail—*him look like a plucked chicken, dis guy, and him cock is like a acorn.*

None of us were watching our kids. Had I not allowed myself to be seduced by Dominique's tale, I might've taken more notice of the junkie.

I'd seen the junkie on my way into the park—maybe twenty-five, maybe forty, splayed on a park bench near the playground gate, raw-faced, skinny, Harpo Marx hair, greasy, stonewashed jeans, grimy blue flannel. I even recall her shoes: sewage-colored high tops, unlaced, flapping around festering sores on her ankles. Dominique, Juliet, and Sage had seen her too, but junkies were not uncommon in our neighborhood; less prevalent than in the Dinkins years but not unheard of. No big deal.

No one actually saw the moment of abduction. Evan was about twenty feet away from me, toddling alone around the gate, fascinated by a squirrel. He did not cry out when the junkie pounced. When she bolted from the playground and into the park with my son in her arms, Sage, miraculously, looked up at precisely the right moment.

"Grant! Grant! That junkie's got your kid!"

After that, it's a jump-cut horror film. Like a fairy in a changeling tale, the junkie vanished with Evan. It was the longest three minutes or so of my life. And I only say three minutes because that was the general consensus. Sage said five, but both Juliet and Dominique said, oh no, it was only a couple minutes.

I spent however long it was running through the park, heart pounding in my ears. The voice in my throat, yelling my son's name, rose from my gut, an unfamiliar, primal bleat upsetting pigeons and sparrows.

Sage, Juliet, and Dominique fanned out, running to the sidewalk, to Avenue A, yelling to other moms to watch their charges while they searched. I scanned the paths, the grassy areas, even the lower boughs of the trees, as if the junkie had alighted there with Evan. My head whiplashed as I asked strangers if they'd seen my son: *dark longish hair, this big, red T-shirt, blue shoes.* Some people shook their heads even before I started talking.

I ran behind the dilapidated band shell, and there they were. The junkie had placed Evan on a disused pigeon-shit-crusted bench. She'd stepped back, frowning at him, itching a boil on her neck, nodding as he pointed at pigeons beating their wings overhead. For an instant, it seemed effortlessly intimate, like I was intruding on a tender moment.

I ran and gathered Evan up. The junkie backed away, waved scabby hands and said, in an indignant bark, "I . . . thought he was mine." She was annoyed, either at me, or at her last shred of sanity that had whispered *put the kid down.*

Did Evan really look like a child from her past? Her child, taken from her? Or was this drug-sick delusion? Had she planned to ransom him for dope money? Deliver him to a perv waiting in a boiler room? I will never know.

I sank to the bench and inspected Evan's moist flesh. The junkie's pissy BO emanated from him, stinging my nostrils. My mind reeled with images of needle pricks or bite marks, but I found only a quarter-sized dollop of some kind of effluvium, snot or drool, in his hair. I beat at it with my trembling hand. Then he started wailing.

The junkie did not approve. She yelled, "Hey! Asshole! Hey!"

Sage, Dominique, and Juliet found and encircled us. I called out, "He's OK, he's OK, he's OK," like a general yelling *stand down!* to his troops. The junkie, caught up in conversation with herself, didn't care. She sauntered through them, saying, "I thought he was *mine.* Looks just like . . . You did not. You're a *liar* . . . I did too, you . . . *scag.*"

By the time the cops arrived, she had vanished again. The Ninth Precinct guys studied my posse and me with a kind of hostile weariness and silent, leaden judgement. They asked if I wanted to fill out some paperwork. I said *no, thanks* and they thanked me with tired eyes and rumbled off.

I never saw the junkie again.

I considered not telling Beth, but when Sage called to check up on me, she said the news was all over the neighborhood. The blabbermouth woman at the dry cleaners, where Beth took her work clothes, couldn't stop talking about it, which meant it would get back to my wife. She would have known something was up anyway, because I lost my mind.

Desperate to cleanse Evan of the junkie's presence, I cut his hair extremely short, in a jagged punk-rock-meets-trailer-trash 'do. Then I bathed him in the sink, scrubbing every inch with undue force. The first bath he endured with little complaint. When I ran the water a third time and once again went to work with the anti-bacterial soap, he began whimpering. That's when Beth walked in from work and stood in the litter of Evan's dark locks on the dingy white tile.

"What are you doing?" she asked. Then, with horror: "*What happened to his hair?*"

I told her a version of The Junkie Incident in which everything happened much quicker, and he was never actually out of my sight. I did mention the junkie's BO getting on him and said it was time for a haircut anyway because, well, his hair was really dreading up and such a nuisance. I didn't mention the snot or whatever that was.

"Oh my God," she said and rushed to him, pulling him out of the sink and drenching her blouse. "You should have called me."

"Mommy!" Evan said, happy to be freed from my insane clutches.

"He's fine," I said, my voice shrill. "See? He's fine. He's OK."

Beth looked at me over his sudsy shoulder, her breath quick. She closed her eyes and inhaled. My heart leapt as I waited. *She's going to lose it . . . here it comes . . .* Evan cooed some nonsense and pawed her hair, freeing it from a clip. Her shoulders dropped, and she softened all over. When she opened her eyes, they were wet.

"And you?" she asked. "You OK? That must have been . . . a nightmare. Such a nightmare. My God."

She reached for me so that all three of us embraced in a puddle of suds and toddler hair, the windows open to the hot, noisy summer night, the oscillating fan breeze wafting over us.

"Go put him to bed," I whispered. She nodded, dried him off, and headed back to the bedroom. I stood there, drinking beer until she returned. Without a word, she embraced me. That's when I began to cry, offering the first of many apologies as my wife stroked my hair and assured me it was OK, it was all OK.

It was not OK.

Beth's forgiveness was not enough. I thought the adrenaline would sink back into my bloodstream, but it didn't. My mind fixated on a single channel of 24/7 horror films, projected non-stop on an overstretched canvas just behind my eyes. In them, the junkie snatched Evan again and again, and/or Evan was brutally injured on my watch, falling from the slide, pulped by a speeding taxi on Avenue A. My father's suicide was intercut with the waking nightmares, his cooling body, glassy eyes, agape mouth leaking ooze, leaking life. A voiceover—my voice—intoned: "If only you hadn't gone to the pool. If only you hadn't turned your head to listen to that story . . .

"The Junkie Incident wasn't an aberration," I'd hear, "just a pulling-back-of-the-curtain on Reality, *Wizard of Oz*-style. You are powerless, you are fucked! Like your own dad, you are *not* cut out for fatherhood. What were you *thinking*?"

At night, the movies and voices intensified, drowning out the polyrhythms of Evan and Beth sleeping. Their interlaced breath, mixed with the street sounds from below, had often lulled me to sleep. But now, two or three hours of rest a night was the best I could hope for.

Where I'd once been energized by play, by singing Evan songs from *Yellow Submarine* and *A Hard Day's Night*, the very sight of Luther, the heirloom Gibson Hummingbird, exhausted me. I thought to smash it, because I did not deserve it. I almost did smash it, more than once.

The slightest need from Evan rankled me, and I relied ever more on television to keep him occupied, which exacerbated my guilt. I stayed away from the park, no matter how beautiful or hot the day. Evan and I roasted in the oven-hot TV glow in the apartment. Calls from my park posse went unanswered. I never picked up the phone unless I heard Beth's voice on the machine, sometimes not even then.

My son seemed clueless, but I told myself he'd suffer from my inattention, his brain would turn to mush because I was not up for this. I was ashamed to put my fears into words. Speaking them, I reasoned, would make them even more powerful. I didn't identify the cause-and-effect then, but I recognize now my only moments of relief came when I hassled Beth, which I did, a lot.

Because it was somewhat aberrant, she put up with my bullshit for a couple weeks. She knew I was reeling from The Junkie Incident, and she wanted to help, but any mention of it triggered put-downs from me. She implored me to *get over it*. But Teflon-resilience was her style, her gift. Not mine. Not at all. Yet she insisted I could use my "creative soul" to *get past it*. She knew I could do it. As when I'd tried to be a songwriter, she believed in me. But increasingly, as I became ever more sullen, doubt shaded her words.

One night, she was really late getting home from *Electra*. They'd been closing the September issue. As Evan slept in our bed, exhausted from a full day of the Cartoon Network and videos, I laid into her, lambasting her lateness, questioning her devotion to us. It was the only time I felt good that day.

She insisted we enroll Evan in the Little Missionary Day Nursery on St. Mark's Place. This sent me into a rage. I took it to mean she was proclaiming her husband an unfit parent, not unlike his own dad. I hadn't broken the cycle after all. As in so many other pursuits, I was a failure. That's the code I deciphered.

But all I actually *said* was, "Fuck no, he stays with me."

"I just figured you could use some relief from the pressure. What the fuck is *wrong* with you?"

"Oh I don't know, maybe watching a kid for twelve hours on no sleep has me a little, I don't know, *stressed*, maybe? But you wouldn't know about that."

"And you wouldn't know about closing a fucking *national* magazine when the publisher's breathing down your neck, and your writers have missed deadlines, and you have to rewrite their fucking articles, and . . ."

"Yeah, because no one would dare, would fucking *dare*, to entrust a *loser* fuckup like *me* with that kind of responsibility, right? Because that is what you're saying. Right? Admit it. Just admit it, for once."

"What? I'm not . . . I'm calling the fucking daycare in the morning. I'm doing it."

"No. That place is like a TB ward. I've looked through the windows, which, I'm sure you didn't notice, have bars on them like a fucking prison . . ."

"All New York schools have that, genius. It's the law."

"Kids get hit, get bit in there, get . . . sick, get lice, get *meningitis*! Do you not give a shit about *that*? Unbelievable."

A Little Missionary Day School attendee had, in fact, contracted meningitis and died in 1997. It was neighborhood lore and likely had nothing to do with the school. All the other stuff I made up.

"Of course I . . . Grant, this has got to stop. You've got to forgive yourself for what happened. All's well that ends well. It could've happened to anybody."

"No. It could only happen to *me*. And we are not talking about this, remember? Unless you want to get off on trying to make me feel bad. Again."

"We'll send him to another daycare. You need a break."

Part of me said, *she's right*. But all that came out of me was, "Fuck. No. He stays with me."

Beth closed her eyes like she could not bear to look at me. When she opened them, they'd shifted from flinty anger to dull, teary disappointment.

"He stays with me," I said, more pleading than declaring, which was not my intention. Even though I knew I was in over my head, I wouldn't admit defeat, and I knew I had the ace card, which I was unfairly playing. She couldn't force me to do anything. Even if it was the right thing.

Beth sighed and stomped back through the apartment to our sleeping son, no doubt for refuge; if anything remained sacrosanct in our lives, even when all else was fraying, it was Evan's sleep.

After a few minutes, I peeked into the bedroom. She'd fallen into deep, seemingly untroubled slumber. This further enraged me. It was all I could do not to wake her and reignite our argument. Instead, I carried on in my head as if she were still awake, stewing into the early morning, rehearsing and refining my rejoinders as I polished off a six-pack. I obsessed on the unencumbered lives carrying on in the apartments above and below, on the sidewalks five floors down, where bar crawlers hooted to the skies.

When I awoke after a fitful, alcohol-sodden drowse on the futon couch, Beth was striding past me, indignant, freshly showered, bent to her day with exceptional fierceness, yet also, I thought, displaying what I risked losing if I did not get my shit together. Her towel was barely adequate. Our usual morning banter hovered ghostlike in the rooms. As I moped, she dressed in our bedroom, and, to my surprise, carried the woozy Evan to me, plopped him in my lap, kissed us both, and strode out the door, trailing the perfume I'd half-jokingly asked her never to wear to work, and sporting a pair of trousers I'd often cited as particularly ass-flattering.

Later that day, I called Trip. He dropped by after he got off work at PS 188. As Evan zoned out to the *Teletubbies*, I let all my fears loose. It was the only time my old friend had seen me cry, and it was heavy, snot-laden bawling. It felt good. Trip reminded me of how his pharmacist dad spoke glowingly of the antidepressant revolution. He suggested I get a regular checkup with my GP—I hadn't done so since we'd gotten insured through *Electra*—and broach my dilemma there.

I did, and it was a much shorter visit than I'd anticipated. Before I could go into detail, my doctor diagnosed PTSD and generalized anxiety disorder, prescribing 150 milligrams of Zoloft. As he scribbled my script with a Zoloft pen, I noticed the Zoloft clock, the Zoloft Post-its, and his desk littered with sample boxes of Prozac, Paxil, and several other drugs with frequent *Z*'s and *X*'s in their names.

Only after he handed me the prescription did the doctor ask, offhandedly, about my past. When he got an earful of my suicidal, druggie dad and feckless, rageaholic mom, he said he was surprised I hadn't sought meds before.

"Parenthood brings a lot to the fore," he said.

While dampening my sex drive, putting fifteen pounds on me, and increasing my cholesterol level, Zoloft certainly made me easier to live with. It softened my guilt and diluted my anger. I slept again, for eight hours at a stretch, dreamless, restorative slumber. I laughed, and let things go. The drug seemed to help me concentrate on being present for Evan as I had been before The

Junkie Incident. His world reopened to me, albeit with muted colors. I found my voice and sang to him again, even put a fresh set of strings on the Hummingbird.

I was able to check my compulsion to make my wife feel bad. And she forgave me for being an asshole and stopped insisting on daycare. This felt like a vote of confidence for me, a vote that I could, indeed, "give Evan what I never had."

When 9/11 happened a few weeks later, I knew the drug was rooted in my blood. We watched from Paul and Melora's rooftop at the Christadora—the highest in the neighborhood. Christa wild-eyed and panicky in stoic Trip's arms, Melora quiet and remote, Paul inappropriately cavalier, Beth smoldering angry as she and I tag-teamed, each distracting Evan in the condo while the other went to the rooftop to stare, look away, stare, look away.

The Towers fell, the city reeled, the world changed in a day, but I was numb.

It was the first time I was conscious of an emotional tidal wave broken by the wall that is Zoloft. An odd sensation, to feel a vague sense of trauma, yet your surface self remains affectless. I recall thinking, *If I wasn't on meds, I'd be crying*. At the time it seemed a blessing. I had a kid to raise. I didn't need that shit.

And, of course, Zoloft probably saved my marriage. No. It definitely saved my marriage, and my nuclear family from shattering. At the time, this was worth anything to me, any Devil's bargain, *to give my son what I never had*.

I remained curious, though. Zoloft did not blunt that. I researched the broadening menu of antidepressants, eager to find *why* they do what they do. No one—not even the manufacturers—seemed to know, but I was undeterred. No one was certain about long-term side effects. So what? I didn't want to be a divorced single parent; I wanted to keep laughing, and I wanted access to Evan's imagination while it was still wild and wooly. I rolled the dice, took my pills, and did my part to help create a multibillion-dollar pharmaceutical industry.

chapter 9

scratch and sniff

Christa pokes me.

"So," she says, "why go off your meds now?"

"Mostly money, but also . . . I don't think I need to fret about, you know, scary junkies. Not many of those in Mt. Marie, right?"

I also want to know I can parent my kid without drugs. Break the cycle on my own.

"Well you know what?" Christa slaps my shoulder. "I'm *on* meds now. Effexor."

"Whaddaya know."

"Better living through chemistry."

"It is that, in some ways, I guess . . . And?"

"I can get out of bed now and take care of the kid. Once we got her home from China I went into some kind of tailspin. Bad. But it's better now."

"Jesus. I had no idea. You should've called."

"No. You guys've had your own hellish year. And damn, you sat through all my moaning about my IVF nightmares, all that shit before we moved. And Trip . . . he didn't want to . . . burden you."

"OK. I guess. So how're your side effects?"

"Couldn't sleep at first. But I've got another scrip for that. Ambien. Trip's got one, too. Plus he's on Paxil. We're like fucking Sid and Nancy. But we sleep like the dead. Trip does sleepwalk sometimes . . ."

The tape spools around to "Kiss My Ring." Christa turns and focuses on the music, the naked guitar chugging over ramshackle drums, fret-buzz bass, all intentionally shambolic. She sings along in a whiny voice, making fun of Paul. My mind fixates on my wife and Paul and Melora, sitting around drinking Bordeaux. I sense an opportunity to bitch about it.

"You've seen Paul and Melora's place on Avenue B, right?"

Christa rolls her eyes. "God, yeah, it's so tacky. Having a Lichtenstein so close to the toilet is . . . don't let's start. We haven't hung out with them much, you know, Grant, the last couple years or so. Paul's not one of the things we miss about the city. Since Trip became a teacher, his patience for Paul's bullshit has worn pretty thin. Plus, I don't really trust that Melora. Never have. She gives my man the hairy eyeball."

"She gives everyone the hairy eyeball."

"So you noticed, too. God forbid we say something."

I remember Melora's overlong hugs, especially after a few cocktails, her unusually big masseuse hands pressing at the small of my back, her small breasts against my ribs. Not an unpleasant memory. After we made Paul Evan's god-father, Melora got still more touchy-feely, even with Beth. I got the feeling we'd relieved some tension from Melora and Paul's marriage by allowing him to act out some of his paternal instincts on our kid.

Like me, Beth had never expressed offense at the over-long hugs. We never spoke of these things. So busy, so many distractions.

Christa, despite herself, is moving in time to "Kiss My Ring."

I pour myself another coffee and top hers off, drain-ing the carafe. She leans in the living room doorway, softly bangs her head on the jamb in time to the song, and watches the catatonic kids for a minute or so, her face uncharacteristically slack, her Cleopatra profile softening before my eyes.

After a hissing segue, a hypnotic, programmed beat pulses in the boom box. Christa stiffens. The throbbing sub-bass and blasting snare ricochet off her tightening body. She turns, open-mouthed, as the compressed sneer of Nine Inch Nails' Trent Reznor pours forth.

It's "Head Like a Hole," rocking the breakfast nook, all synthy noise and defiant guitar snarl. I smile in the rising racket.

"God, this one takes me back," Christa says, hips bucking slightly.

"Papa!" Evan calls, still riveted to Thomas. "Too loud!"

I move to turn down the volume. Christa is behind me.

"Trip and I used to fuck to this," she says, low and husky.

I stiffen. This is a first.

"He was so skinny," she whispers, "his fucking pelvic bones bruised my hips." Her breath is brackish with coffee, her hair sweet with sweat.

"I guess you need a copy of this tape, then." My voice is thin. All energy gathering below my waistline.

"I guess," she takes a deep breath and heads back to watch Evan and Katie. I exhale and rearrange myself, tying my terrycloth sash tighter, hands in my pockets to disguise my now-deflating predicament.

A question rises in my mind: Effexor? She's always been flirty, but this is different. When I researched Zoloft, I looked into the potential side effect profiles of other drugs, too. Effexor's were particularly daunting: "insomnia," "engaging in dangerous activities," "loss of one's sense of identity," "mania."

Yet, meds or no, I am a combination of flattered and uncomfortable. I hope she and Katie will leave soon, while at the same time I'm whetted for more open-petal intimacy the likes of which I have not felt in ages.

"Evan still got that boy-crush on Paul?" she says, eyes on the kids, jaw tight. "Still calling him Padrino?"

Paul. Let's rag on Paul. Good.

"I don't think I'll ever be rid of that asshole," I say.

"Why not?"

"Evan just loves him. He's like punk rock Barney. Whenever Paul came over to the apartment, Evan was just so psyched. Part of me wishes he'd have fucked up when he was babysitting. But he never even cracked a beer when Beth and I went out."

"Well, now you've got us," Christa says. "Babysitters right down the street. Anytime. See how good they are together?"

My left eye twitches—my caffeine critical mass gauge—as I recall Katie's tantrum, the scratches on Christa's neck. But my son and his playdate companion seem content, in their expanding, thickening crumb circle.

As if in response to my thought, I hear the distinctive burble of a juice box sucked clean. Katie flings her empty at Evan's fort.

"Hey," Evan says. "That's my fort!"

Christa runs to the juice box. "It's OK, it's OK," she says. "I got it."

Katie snatches Evan's juice and lobs the box at the fort, narrowly missing Christa. Dark purple spills out, staining Evan's stick figure art. The girl has quite an arm for a tot.

"Hey!" I say, running to Evan.

"No!" Evan bolts up and stamps his foot. "No, Katie! No! No! No! My pictures! My pictures!"

Christa flees to the kitchen with the juice boxes. Katie launches herself at Evan, swatting like a cat. I hear a rip.

"Jesus, Katie!" I yell, kneeling between the kids just as Evan's mouth gapes open in a silent, and then a very loud, scream. I take him in my arms and he crushes himself into my chest, grabbing fistfuls of my robe. I meet Katie's blank eyes as a knot tightens in my forehead.

Whatever my face is doing sends her to the kitchen wailing. Christa scoops her up.

"What happened? What happened?" Christa asks.

A quick look at my son's exposed skin reveals two fresh scratches on his left hand.

"She scratched him," I say. "She fucking scratched my kid, Christa."

"Are you sure?"

"Yes, I'm fucking sure!"

"Katie," Christa says. "Did you scratch him?"

"What the fuck, Christa? Trim her fucking nails, OK?"

I carry my son to the tiny half-bathroom beneath the stairs and slam the door behind us. Evan is trembling. He shudders and snorts back snot.

"It's not so bad, big guy," I say, washing the scratches and spraying them with Bactine, worrying about the funk under that girl's fingernails.

"Papa . . . ?"

"Yes, sweetie?"

"Your breath smells really, really bad. It smells like ass."

"Shhhh," I say as a grin creeps across my face. "Bad word."

He smiles, flush face still wet with tears. I sit on the toilet seat lid and pull him onto my lap. He leans against me and lets out the heaviest sigh I've yet heard from him.

There's a knock and my son tenses. Beyond the door is quiet: no video, no Katie screaming, no mixtape.

"Everything OK?" Christa asks.

After a few seconds, I say, "We're OK. Give us a few."

"I think we're gonna go. Katie's got a full diaper. Should I leave T-H-O-M-A-S?"

"Thomas," Evan whispers.

"Yeah, sure," I say. "Thanks."

"OK . . . I'll call you later. You need anything? Food? Wine? Beer?"

Valium.

"We're good," I say.

"OK. The V-I-D-E-O is in the player. I'll get it tomorrow. Breakfast, maybe?"

No fucking way.

"We'll see. Give a call or something."

"Right. Can I borrow this mixtape?"

No.

"Uh . . . OK."

"Thanks! Say bye, Katie."

Silence.

"OK," Christa says. "Bye-bye!"

After about a minute, Evan sighs again, pushes open the door, and pulls me back into the living room. We watch the rest of *Thomas and the Magic Railroad* together, in silence. It's not as bad as I remembered.

chapter 10

like that's a bad thing

I'm watching Evan in the half-light. He's been out for about twenty minutes, swaddled in quilts from which he will gradually extricate himself like a sleeping Houdini. His face is angelic, smooth. The Muppet Band-Aid on his hand is coming off. I resist the urge to yank it.

It's getting on toward eleven p.m. The apology call I expected from Christa never came, and Evan and I spent the post-*Thomas and the Magic Railroad* evening playing Candyland, then watching *A Bug's Life* while eating ramen noodles. I considered calling Beth's cell, but another disastrous playdate discussion would no doubt end badly. While I am tempted to rain on her parade, just out of controlling malice, my guilt from our fight keeps me in line.

Evan got past everything remarkably fast, as is his wont. I envy his lack of vindictiveness, his ability to move on from crisis, to willfully follow Uncle Walt and Pixar & Co. down a digitally enhanced garden path and get lost in the world on the TV/VCR combo. If any long-term damage results from his hard day or the overall recent uprooting of his former life, I see little evidence of it, especially now, as his chest rises and falls with clockwork precision.

The phone rings. I run to pick up the cordless while Evan rolls over and slumbers on. My feet pound down the stairs as I answer.

"Hello?"

In a wash of noise, I hear my wife's voice.

"Hey, it's me," she hollers. She's in a crowd.

"Hey there." I'm back at my kitchen perch. "How'd the meeting go?"

Distorted noise. Beth talks to someone in the slurry rhythm that tells me she's drinking. She laughs.

"Hello . . . ?" I say.

"Hey, the meeting went great. I think I got this gig. I'll know tomorrow or maybe the next day. But I may need to come down once in a while, at least until the tour starts."

"That's great. How's the money?"

Another pause, intermittent drop-outs as the signal scrambles.

"Hello . . . ?" Beth shouts. "Hello? Hello?"

"Hey, how's the money?"

I hold the phone about a foot from my ear.

"It's OK," she says. "It's . . ." crackle, pause, ". . . afloat . . ." More static, silence, crackles. "Sasha's actually very nice."

"Good. So I guess you're staying over." I open the last Rolling Rock.

"Is that OK? You guys OK?"

"We're great."

"Paul wants to talk to you . . ."

Paul's voice: "Hey there, Hoss! How's it going?"

"It's fine Paul, it's all good."

"How's Little E?"

"He's good. Sleeping away . . . asked me when you're coming to visit."

"Soon, soon." More distortion, drop-outs. Where are they?

"Where the fuck are you guys, Paul?"

"I got us on the guest list to see the Strokes at Bowery Ballroom," he says, then laughs at something. "You oughtta be here. Remember when Six Ray did our last show here? In '98?"

"Sure."

"That was great, right?"

"If I remember correctly, yes." Sold-out show, screaming fans, a drunken girl "ironically" throwing a tattered Bon Jovi T-shirt onstage. I remember.

"You really oughtta be here."

"Wish I could be. Kinda swamped."

"I bet. Heard the Lamont kid's a little wack-a-doo!"

"Is Melora there?"

"Naw. My wife hates the fuckin' Strokes. Says they're a buncha rich kids pretending it's 1981. Like that's a bad thing."

"Right."

"Hey, speaking of rich, I got a proposal for you . . . you feel like doing some rocking?"

"Not following you, Paul."

"I got a call from this guy, this Nike honcho, wants Six Ray to reunite to play his fortieth birthday in Portland in May. They all still love them some Six Ray Star at Nike HQ. That's where the party'll be."

"A birthday party? What's the punch line?"

"The punch line, my brother, is a hundred grand plus expenses."

"Sweet. And? You gonna do it?"

"Need a bass player. Otto's not into it; he's become all Buddhist and shit."

"Wait. Are you asking *me*?"

"I am. There's ten K in it for you. You get a little smaller cut 'cause you're kind of a sideman, but still . . . pretty nice scratch, right?"

I'm stunned. I'm excited, insulted, and irritated that he already assumes I'll say yes. Which will happen. But I hold my tongue.

"Listen," Paul says, "band's coming on soon. You think about it, let me know. I figure a couple rehearsals, you and me getting together up thataway. Something."

"Uh . . . yeah . . . thanks . . . I'll let you know soon. Thanks a lot."

"We'll be in Portland for, like, five days, bein' wined, dined, sixty-nined, you know. Then one ninety-minute set, then home again, home again, jiggety-jig."

In the background I hear Beth ask, "Is he into it?"

93

"Your lady here thinks you should do it," Paul says, a smile in his voice.

"Right. Hey, can I talk to her?"

"Here ya go. Talk to ya . . ."

Beth's voice: "Pretty cool, huh?"

"Yeah. We need to talk about it, though."

"Uh-huh. I'll be on the earliest bus I can get tomorrow, OK?"

"Sounds good."

"New York 1 said there may be a snowstorm, though. Is it snowing up there?"

When did she get a chance to watch New York 1? Paul and Melora's, I guess. Probably went there to decompress after her meeting.

I press my nose to the cool windowpane and sure enough, fat flakes are tumbling in the square of light from the kitchen. "Yeah, looks like the real thing . . ."

She says something, but it's lost in the band's crashing first chord and a subsequent multi-voiced cheer overloading the cell phone's tiny receptors. Then silence.

~

I shower and shave as the house creaks around me, rodent toes scratching in the walls, furnace humming while the temperature falls. Snow whispers down the siding, accumulates on the windowsills. I don the my still slightly damp star-spangled black shirt, smiling at the clash with my sweatpants. In the living room, I lift my precious old bass from its battered case, fire up the stereo and my dusty Ampeg B-15 Portaflex bass amp. The scent of the warming tubes actually arouses me.

I can't recall the last time I held my bass. Black Fender Precision, 1962, bought at Matt Umanov's in Manhattan with part of my share of the Stereoblind advance in 1989. Traveled the world with me. Back dimpled and gouged from the metal buttons of the jeans I once favored, maple veins revealed in the blemishes. This nick from when I tripped over a cable in Belfast. That scratch from the idiot stagehand in Tampa knocking it from its stand. Even though the strings are dead, unchanged for years now, and the neck is a little bowed, and some frets buzz when I press on them, it feels good to play, to feel the contours of the instrument's body slide against my ribs, to smell the mix of oil and sweat-soaked wood and wire.

Remarkably, the old Fender is only a little out of tune. As I turn the pegs, a memory flits across my mind: Beth watching me play. We'd only been together a few weeks. We'd made love in the hot afternoon, rattling the tin ceiling of Trip's and my little Avenue C hovel.

I bite my lower lip, almost hard enough to draw blood.

She'd showered afterward, and I took out this bass and sat naked at the edge of the soaked bed, playing, unplugged, eyes closed, deep into it, endorphins still aswirl under my skin, bass pressed into my thigh like a cool, firm hand.

After a minute or so, I'd realized I was out of tune, so I tilted my head down, stared into space, eyes unfocused, and turned these pegs until the frequencies slid into accord, like two presences melding together.

Just when I hit the harmonic sweet spot, the air shimmered at the corner of my eye. I turned, and she was standing naked in the kitchen doorway, a towel wrapped around her hair, watching me. No one had ever looked at me that hard, of that I was—and still am—sure. I shivered, and we both laughed.

"I love your face when you tune," she said. "Love it."

"I don't look catatonic?"

"Maybe a little. But mostly you look like you're inside it, inside the music. I know it sounds corny, but you're free, you know . . . in the moment. No worries, no regrets. Like your soul is showing. It's sexy."

~

I rip open the box marked "CDs—Q thru U." Between Shonen Knife and Elliott Smith, I'd filed Six Ray Star's decade-old *Peppercorn* CD alongside their other releases, *Pledge, Bodega Perfume* and *Turpentine*. The now-iconic *Peppercorn* cover has been slid in and out of the cracked jewel case many times, especially by Evan in the last couple of years. He frequently studies the insert, folding and unfolding, even smelling the deepened creases, his eyes scanning the annoyingly illegible fonts. The glossy, dog-eared insert features a close-up of a stray peppercorn on a stained calico tablecloth, the edges of the image ragged, as if seen through a hole torn in a cardboard box. On the back cover, a blurred, wide-angle shot reveals Six Ray Star gathered around the same table, which we now see cluttered with old-school crockery, coffee cups, and ketchup-smeared plates scattered with stray fries. It's the old Williamsburg diner, Cosimo's, now lost to urban development; a working-class-men aura hangs over the surrounding booths, and the band is—obnoxiously—trading on that rundown gravitas. Nobody smiles. Paul wears Vegas-era Elvis shades, his engineer-boot clad feet propped on the table. I snort to myself, for perhaps the two hundredth time, and get to work.

The CD glides into the player. The songs are almost nursery-rhyme easy. Musically, Six Ray Star was more about texture and attitude over chops, atmospherics over hooks. Except for "Kiss My Ring," which is an earworm if ever there was one.

Would my glammy, star-spangled rock star shirt pass muster? I think not. In their day, the band, as evidenced on

the CD cover, cultivated an air of studied unprofessional-
ism—of we-just-stumbled-onto-this-stage-after-working-
at-the-Hess-station—which was horseshit, but certainly
nabbed them an ardent following of twentysomethings
(now thirtysomethings) who bristled at notions of "corporate rock." As if Six Ray Star was not itself a corporate
entity, the current soundtrack to the most profitable ath-
letic-wear corporation in history.

Even in the band's earliest days, when they were on
Matador, they were, as with any band that signs a con-
tract, corporate. Wasn't Matador, like SubPop, 4AD, and
KillRockStars, et al, a corporation, filing taxes as such?
Of course. Paul has always known he was corporate, but
back in the day he never dared say as much to his fans.
He played his role well. I'll give him that.

As I commit the tunes to memory via my ears and fin-
gertips, I smile bitterly at my memories of Six Ray Star.
I floundered after quitting Stereoblind in 1993, despite
Beth's constant encouragement: *this is your year.* Six Ray
Star's concurrent ascent brought forth in me ever deepen-
ing shades of green. I pretended to be proud but was not.

They were a mess. Bassist Otto, of the raggedy bowl-
ing shirt, playing out of tune to thunderous applause;
Chas and Roberto, guitar and drums, respectively, in
ill-fitting cords, Keds, and ironic T-shirts, barely negotiat-
ing the songs yet getting laid with astonishing regularity;
Paul, the only member to cop to some rock star style,
patron of Aqua Net, acting as if he was embarrassed
to be onstage yet able to imbue the slightest move with
dark charisma, breaking so many showbiz rules, turning his back on the crowd for half the set, stopping mid-
song because "I don't feel like playing this song after all,"
imploding into himself, risking stillness, often wielding
his chipped black Telecaster as a prop, haphazardly
banging out intentionally soured chords when he bothered to play at all.

Yet, for all the band's alleged anti-show-business shtick, Six Ray Star did put on their version of a performance, one where the mostly white, college-y, affluent audience was as much a part of the event as the group, where indeed, fan and band looked almost exactly alike: dressed down yet orthodontically pristine. (Paul's missing eyetooth the glaring, much-emphasized exception.) With my glammy inclinations, I never felt part of this clique, but I had to admit the foursome did generate a palpable greater-than-the-sum-of-its-parts energy, for which its substantial fan base paid real money for a decade. And now their songs blare from THX movie theater speakers, televisions, and Xboxes, almost all the resulting revenue going into Paul's pocket.

As I nail the songs, the prospect of the Portland birthday party for the Nike exec grows rosier, although the knowledge that I'm getting paid less than the other band members is starting to bug me. I wonder if I can ask for more. But when I spend the ten grand in my mind, my will to negotiate crumbles.

Ten grand: five will go to pay down credit cards, alleviating a little monthly bill stress, and the other five maybe goes toward another car. The notion of adding to the family coffers combines with a vision of me stepping to the lip of a stage, rekindling the earlier horniness coaxed out of me by Christa. Although the *Peppercorn* tunes are no challenge, I begin making mistakes, losing focus. When thinking about money and fucking, I can't navigate the songs. Some things I simply cannot multitask.

~

In the middle of my second run-through of the *Peppercorn* track list, I hear a rumbling engine outside, followed by two door slams and tapping at the back door. The clock says twelve-thirty a.m.

Just outside the kitchen, two figures hover behind a flashlight beam. I flick on the light and there's Trip's face, pressed up against the pane. By the time I reach for the knob, I see Ricky Shulz's beard behind Trip. Just beyond, in the cab of Ricky's idling truck, King is panting in the panel lights, watching us.

In seconds they're standing in the kitchen, each dusted white: Ricky in a shirt jacket, cap and boots, big Maglite; Trip in a long cashmere coat over flannel pajamas, shearling slippers dampened with fresh snow, hair wet with melt. Ricky's cigarette-coffee-soap scent is dominant, with a hint of Trip's slightly sharp, acrid body odor, imprinted on me almost fifteen years ago.

Trip does not look right. His eyes are wide but unfocused. He's not drunk, though. No alcohol smell, red face, or sloppy vibe. I am amazed to recall the time he and I did mushrooms in the eighties, at the Harmonic Convergence in Central Park. We'd only just met, both just out of our teens.

"I think he's sorta sleepwalking," Ricky says, pulling on the bill of his oily cap. "I was coming home from some plowing, almost killed the sumbitch. Just walking in the snow, headed this way. Picked him up. He told me to come here. It's that Ambien shit."

"What?" I lead Trip to the breakfast nook, moving my laptop and cassettes away. "How do you know it's Ambien?"

"It's a common side effect, you know, walking around, doin' stuff while part-a your brain's offline." Ricky's gaze drifts over my rock star shirt/sweatpants ensemble. He clocks it, frowns, and looks away as if I'm naked.

"I read up on it," he continues. "Big Pharma doesn't want you to know the side effects of these meds. It's a fuckin' conspiracy. People do all kinds of crazy shit on Ambien. I'm tellin' you. They drive to the store, buy a buncha crap, get in bed with the wrong folks, gamble online.

No memory the next day, none. Big Pharma doesn't want you to know that. They got billions, *billions*, keepin' it outta the mainstream press. *Billions*. Guess Lamont here's kinda lucky, all things considered."

I think about my side effects from Zoloft, the fine print in my Devil's bargain: passivity, weight gain, spiked cholesterol, anorgasmia. At least I don't unconsciously walk around in the snow in my pajamas.

"Second time this's happened," Ricky says. "Last time I almost shot him. He was in my yard, sitting on a stump, humming some crazy shit. Thought he was my daughter's ex, stalking her. Lamont's wife told me it was the Ambien. She does love to talk. Sure enough, he didn't remember anything the next day, probably won't remember any of this tomorrow."

Trip starts humming what sounds like *The Flint-stones* theme. He scans the kitchen.

"Looking good in here, Grant," he says. "Homey. I like it."

"Should we call your wife, Lamont?" Ricky asks.

"Want me to call Christa?" I say.

"What for?" Trip says, wiping beads of water from his cheeks. "I wanted to come visit. Here I am."

Ricky huffs. "I gotta get my coffee and go back to work," he says. "S'posed to get like two feet tonight. Probably more. Weatherman don't know shit. I gotta go."

"Thanks for picking him up, Ricky." To both men, I say, "I was just practicing for a gig, a, uh, show."

Trip, my one-time number-one fan, does not react, just continues staring dumbly at the walls, nodding, humming. I haven't gigged in years, yet this big news hangs in the air, unseized. I consider saying it again, louder.

Ricky softens. "Lamont's wife said you were kind of a famous musician back in the day."

"I still am. A musician, that is. You know that Nike commercial with Michael Jordan flying over the court?"

"Sure, sure." Ricky is both impatient and, in spite of himself, interested.

"The band that does that song is playing a gig, and they want me to play bass with them. They're called Six Ray Star and . . ."

"Oh, that song . . ." Ricky nods. "My daughter sings that song all the damn time. You know the guys that play it?"

"Guy that wrote it is my son's godfather. My wife Beth's hanging out with him in the city as we speak, in fact." The bitterness coiling up from my stomach meets a fake smile as I rush to cast everything properly for Ricky Shulz. "She went for an interview. She's a publicist, helps promote people, get 'em in magazines, on TV, that kind of thing."

"Hm. Is that so? And you're like Mr. Mom, like in that movie."

"Yeah, like in that movie. Four years now. Nice work if you can get it." How many times am I gonna say that fucking phrase?

"OK, then." Ricky absent-mindedly pulls on his cap bill, processing all the info, swishing spit in his mouth, the corner of his lips twitching into a kind of tight smile as he shakes his head. "Well my daughter can come babysit if you need a break or something, she's good with kids. I'll have to tell her you know that guy . . . she'll be impressed."

Paul will love that. "So you guys homeschool?"

"Sure do. I know Lamont here's part of the system, at that white elephant of a school down the road. God help him. Waste of tax money, that place. If you were a homeowner you'd feel the same. You wouldn't believe what I pay in school taxes. It is criminal. I know it's a drop in the bucket to Lamont here and his wife, but it just about does me in."

Trip registers his name. He looks up, as if waking from a nap.

"Grant, Grant," he says, like he just remembered something. "This man . . . is a saint." He grins at Ricky. "He pulled me out of a ditch last month."

"That was nothing, Lamont," Ricky says. "You gotta take that curve slow when it's icy."

"Thanks anyway. Thanks for plowing, too. Thanks for being you."

"Trip . . ." I lay my hand on my friend's shoulder and shake him a little. "You sure I shouldn't call Christa?"

"No, no, no." Trip pats my hand. "You'll wake up the kid. Bad move. Do not do that. Just don't."

Ricky huffs again and turns to go, raising his hand in a cursory farewell. "I'm outta here. Next time, Lamont, just do a double shot of Maker's Mark and smoke a joint. Works wonders for me. Don't need to feed Big Pharma anymore . . . they're only in it for the dough."

"How's it feel being in the kitchen where you grew up, Ricky?" Trip says. "Lotta memories, huh?"

Ricky spins and focuses on Trip, frowning under his cap. A flick of his gaze to me, and he checks himself, shakes his head, exhales, deflates. The kitchen fills with his heavy breath. He turns, effortlessly opens the door, and strides into a blur of snowflakes.

I go to the window as Ricky passes in front of the idling pickup's headlights and pounds up his steps. In the truck, King tracks him, ears pricked. When Ricky is a few feet from his welcome mat, the storm door swings open and the porch light flicks on, revealing a small fig-ure wreathed in warm lamplight from within the trailer. It's his wife, Jen. She's about a head shorter than Ricky, dishwater hair pulled into a French braid. A fluffy pink robe renders her shapeless, like a little monk. She smiles into Ricky's eyes, her pale face angled up, crinkled with mischief.

Jen furrows her brow as she places her right hand against her husband's chest, denying him entry. I'm guessing it's his boots, which, in fact, left much muddy snow on my kitchen floor. In her left hand Jen brandishes a silver thermos, which Ricky takes. She grabs a scarf from just inside the door and ensnares his neck, pulling him in for a long kiss, during which his cap falls to the snow and his entire back slackens like he's been shot. He places his free hand at the sash of her robe, and she angles herself into his palm, rising on her toes. Then she pushes him away, spins, and shuts the door, leaving the scarf dangling around his neck.

Ricky is still for a few seconds, snow accumulating on his greasy hair and bowed shoulders. He bends to his cap, catches my stare, and stiffens back up, pulling the bill over his brow. I turn away from the now-fogged window, busted, watching peripherally as he hurries, head down, to his truck, which he backs out of the driveway, spewing snow. In the street named for his ancestors, he drops the steel blade to the pavement and scrapes away.

Trip is still humming.

"Let's get you home, Trip," I say.

"Aw. We're not gonna hang? Like in Ye Olden Tymes?"

"Not tonight. Maybe tomorrow. I'm pretty bushed."

Trip sighs. "Promise? I wanna hang. Just us. No. Ladies. Or. Tots."

"You got it."

I check on Evan. He sleeps on, spread-eagled, free from his bedclothes, deeply unconscious. I've never left him alone, haunted as I am by the The Junkie Incident. But waking up Christa will bring too much drama. I'll make it fast. Five minutes, tops.

Cursing these fucking Lamonts as my heart rate quickens, I throw on my parka and boots and escort Trip through the snowfall. Flakes tumble in drifts from surrounding branches, shushing us as we walk. The temperature seems milder than earlier, as if the snow is absorbing some of the cold. Or perhaps it's due to distress; I'm panting with anxiety. Distant plow blades squeal on the surrounding roads. My friend says nothing, just hums the *Flintstones* theme and kicks at the accumulating white. The Lamonts' home, bereft of light, is smaller and slightly sinister. Motion-sensitive floodlights illuminate the frosted yard as we approach.

Inside, I pull off his fine coat and guide him to the stairs, but he plants his feet and shakes his head, pointing to the living room, where the muted TV flickers on the Home Shopping Network. The couch is made up with quilts and big feather pillows.

"My bed," he says.

"Great. Go. Go back to sleep."

He nods slowly, eyelids heavy. He burrows back into his nest of covers as I reach for the remote.

"No," he says. "I need that on. Leave that shit on." He yawns and closes his eyes, the bluish TV tint bathing his sluggish body, his pillow darkening with moisture from his hair. I pat his shoulder and bolt.

I sprint through the snow, hating my friends, hating myself for being unable to prevent my family from landing in this situation. Each step brings visions of junkies emerging from the closet shadows and stealing my son, and/or Evan waking up terrified, and/or the house suddenly erupting in flames from a gas leak. Or something. Before I can decide if these notions indicate a healthy wariness or a Zoloft-depleted mind teeming with paranoia, I am bounding through the front door of Shulz House and taking the stairs three at a time.

chapter 11

mermaid parade

Snow melts from my boot soles onto the rug. Each breath draws the image of Evan, in exactly the same position on the bed, deep into my body. I'm whispering *thank you* again, unreasonably grateful.

I towel myself off in the upstairs bathroom and consider calling Beth. Surely she's awake, hanging out with Paul somewhere post-gig, post-successful interview, enjoying her respite from domestic life, celebrating the increased likelihood of her family's renewed cash flow. Although I contract with jealousy, I also crave her raw voice, the way it gets when she's been cheering a band, drinking beer, sneaking cigarettes. That particular sound is like nicotine to me, or some other vasodilating sister stimulant. I'll complain or worry aloud about something—the Lamonts, money, getting old. Then she'll say it's all going to be OK; Trip and Christa will be OK, we'll be OK, it'll all work out. At this, blood will flow easier in me. My mind doesn't believe any of it is true—none of us is "OK"—but some carnal part of me wants to hear it and will respond.

Evan calls out in his sleep, a short, strange, speaking-in-tongues harangue. I fold him into my arms, luxuriating in his body heat as he nestles against me, his respiration a steady rhythm. A wet hay scent mixes with little waves of mint from his nighttime teeth-brushing. My hand alights on his sternum; beneath the wash-softened flannel, his heartbeat thumps along at a strong, sure clip, a tireless little turbine of life, radiating heat and as-yet-untapped potential, hope personified.

When the midwife turned up the volume on the Doppler stethoscope and we heard his heartbeat during Beth's first sonogram, my wife and I both laughed at the similarities to heavy metal drumming at its fastest, most awe-inspiring, and most ridiculous. Evan's prenatal heartbeat was about one hundred eighty beats per minute. As he's gotten older and bigger, his heart has slowed appropriately, but it's still pretty much at rock and roll tempo, and his temperature hovers at standard packed-club level—around ninety-nine degrees.

I reach for the light and catch sight of some framed photos I'd haphazardly set on the bedside table. There's the shot Billy took of Evan, Beth, and me at the Mermaid Parade, the official start of the Coney Island summer. June 2001. Two-year-old Evan is asleep in his leopard print stroller, a tiny Styrofoam trident atop his chest. I am shirtless, possessed of pre-Zoloft torso—about fifteen pounds lighter, hipbones jutting above the waistband of low-slung cutoffs. I wonder what became of that seashell necklace I'm wearing. Beth has only recently stopped nursing Evan, and her enhanced breasts are snug in a green bikini top decorated with scallop shells. Fake seaweed garlands tumble from her hair. Scantily clad drag queens surround us, and an elderly potbellied man in a metallic blue Speedo is brazenly sizing up my wife's green mini-skirted ass. We'd used this photo for our 2001 holiday card.

~

"Suh-weet!" Billy said, handing the camera back to Beth. "You are a hot little mermaid, sis."

"Thanks, little brother. What do you think of your nephew?"

Billy knelt before the stroller. "This is not the same kid. You traded him in for a bigger model, right? 'Cause this guy's a butterball."

"What a difference a year makes," I said, my hands sweaty on the stroller handles.

In a sleeveless Coney Island tee and clean indigo 501s that actually fit, Billy looked better than ever, which made it easier to suspend my moratorium on engaging with him. He'd put on a little weight and cut his mangy mouse-brown dreads. Sunglasses perched atop his head, his dark eyes—almost identical to Beth's—burned alert, the whites clear around the irises. Cabled forearms sported recently-inked tribal tattoos, a Celtic and Maori mix, some still scabby, swirls and swoops obscuring track marks and abscess keloids. Circling his upper arm was the phrase from the back cover of Patti Smith's debut album *Horses*: "Charms, sweet angels, you have made me no longer afraid of death." This was a copy of his big sister Beth's one tattoo, a ring of text encircling her left ankle.

Accompanying Billy was his Narcotics Anonymous sponsor, Zoe. Beth had gotten wind of Zoe, but before this day we'd not yet met her. Zoe had channeled amps of energy into working out six days a week at a store-front gym, resulting in arms that looked as if they were wrapped in piano wire, an onion butt, pulsing thighs, and gladiator shoulders, all quite visible in black bike shorts and a midriff-baring yellow Lycra top. Ink vined her limbs, danced along her lower back and up the nape of her neck; dragons, Bettie Page, thorny roses, and stars. She claimed to be two years clean and had taken Billy under her wing six months previously. From Billy introducing us until we went our separate ways, her shades stayed put. As did mine.

"I knew we'd see you guys," Zoe said, wiping sweat from her upper lip as we all moved away from the parade to a mustard-smeared boardwalk picnic table. Her tail-light-red tresses, pulled into a bun, stank of floral hair-care product borne aloft on her considerable steam.

"I told Billy," Zoe went on, hoarse like she'd been screaming, "I says, 'I bet Grant and Beth and the baby'll be there!' He was worried, actually, right, babe?"

"No, no, no." Billy laughed dryly, all receding gums, missing bicuspids. Yes, he'd been worried, which made me glad. The fucker. He'd stolen our stereo receiver last year, plus an heirloom pocket watch, and sold them for junk or crack, I couldn't recall. After changing the locks, we'd cut him off. Beth had caved a couple times, met him in Tompkins Square Park, probably gave him cash, but I'd stayed firm, which made me feel righteous.

"It's OK." Zoe pulled one of Billy's belt loops. "Now they can see you're better than ever. Six months clean!"

"That's so amazing." Beth's hand went across the table to her brother's. "So amazing. So good to see you."

"Workin' the steps," Zoe said. "Workin' the steps."

"Couldn't do it without Zoe here." Billy bumped against his sponsor. "She's all about unconditional love."

"Tough love!" Zoe pinched Billy's arm, then glanced down at our sleeping son. "You gotta use tough love on this kid here, too, you know."

"You got kids?" I asked.

"God, no." Zoe laughed.

"She's got me, though," Billy said.

"And he is more than enough to keep me busy." Zoe slapped the table. "But the baby here, what's his name again . . . ?"

"Evan," I said.

"Evan, yeah, I knew that, my brain, fuck! So. You gotta know, he's gonna need more than our Billy here got as a kid. If you wanna break the cycle."

"What do you mean, Zoe?" Beth's voice was edging up.

"Your folks, I hear from my Billy here, they weren't exactly good at their job, is what I hear. Not the most loving parental units."

"That's not what I said, Zoe." Billy's eyes skittered between his sponsor and his sister.

"Let's not speak ill of the dead," I said. "I knew 'em, they were cool."

A couple years after Beth and I married, Billy and Beth's mom had died from bone cancer; within a year, their dad passed from heart disease. Not long after, Billy had gone off the rails, dropping out of the School of Visual Arts and descending into drug hell, rapidly burning through his inheritance.

"What did he tell you, Zoe?" Beth asked. "Did he mention our dad left him fifty grand, and he put it all up his fucking arm?"

"Whoa," I said, my hand on Beth's stiffening shoulder.

"Here we go." Billy's lips tightened, and he nodded. "See, Zoe? See what I mean? No forgiveness."

"You gotta forgive, sister," Zoe said, cool and triumphant.

"You gotta stop telling me what to do," said Beth.

"This is the kind of stress that will infect a kid, you know," Zoe said, standing up and snapping her waistband. Billy rose and cleaved to his sponsor.

I said, "Aren't you supposed to be focusing on your own shortcomings, not others'? Isn't that part of the program?"

Zoe looked at me for a second, back to Billy, back to me. "You're right, Billy," she said, nodding. "So right about this guy. Bitter. No wonder."

"Bitter?" I replied. "About what?"

"I know, I know," Zoe said. "I bet it's hard to give up chasing the spotlight and be a kept man."

Beth laughed mirthlessly at this, which made me glad. A quick glance to her face, however, revealed rising tears, of which only I seemed aware. Her painful history with her brother was a pile of combustibles that needed only a tiny spark to ignite.

"I didn't say he was *kept*." Billy poked Zoe's bicep. "I said he stayed home with the kid while my sister works." He looked at me. "That is what I said, Grant."

"Whatever," Zoe said, pursing her lips. "Looks like *The Life of Riley* to me. How hard can it be?"

Evan, perhaps sensing his cue, began to stir. He pushed his trident out of the stroller and looked around in confusion, bleating and grunting.

"Look who's up." Beth's forced gaiety barely concealed her irritation. "Just in time to see Uncle Billy!"

Beth gave Evan a water bottle. He grunted and sent it rolling on the foul boardwalk, almost tripping up a buff, middle-aged Poseidon. Combined with his mother's upset, to which he always seemed attuned, the lost bottle was a tragedy to our son. His fussiness soon became desperate woe.

"He's probably hungry," I said, fetching a Baggie of Cheerios from the stroller.

"Definitely." Zoe squinted at the rising distress from the stroller. "He really does look like his Uncle Billy when he cries."

Billy nudged Zoe. "Guess I'm still having my terrible twos, huh, babe?"

"We should get moving," Beth said, kicking the brakes loose on the stroller. "Movement will chill him out." Her words were contoured with oncoming tears.

"Right." Zoe nodded as she pulled Billy to her hip. "Nice to meet you guys at last." She sounded sincere, as if no tension had arisen.

"Talk to you soon, little brother." Beth blew her brother a kiss, spun the stroller, and barreled back into the crowd of leathery revelers. My flip flops slapped as I ran to catch up. I glanced back at Zoe and Billy. She held his face in her hand, her forehead creasing as she spoke. Billy was nodding, a vacant look in his eyes.

Beth's fake seaweed hair bounced against her shoulder blades as we threaded through the crowd. Evan wailed, drawing the inevitable judgmental glances from passersby. The drag queens in particular seemed put out. After about a minute, we reached a less crowded section of boardwalk. Seagulls keened above us. Beth braked the stroller, freed our boy, lifted him out into the sunlight, and pressed him tight to her chest, shushing and cooing, kissing his tears, running her fingers through his sweaty hair, rocking him.

As usual, this calmed him. His pudgy hands found her cheeks, wet from silent crying.

"No, Mommy," he said, suddenly calm and clear-eyed. "No sad. No sad."

"Billy looked good, though, didn't he?" I said. "I mean . . . I was surprised. Right?"

Beth nodded, then whispered into Evan's scalp, "I don't want to talk about it, 'K?"

"OK."

She placed her hot palm on my hand. "I'm so glad you're here, Grant. I'm just so glad."

I encircled them with my arms, inhaling the distinctive scent of my little family: tears, sweat, and breath mixing with sunscreen, baby shampoo, and the filthy surf. In my embrace, Beth's shoulders relaxed and Evan fell back against her breasts. He fixated on the scallop shells attached to her bikini. She laughed away a sob. Evan giggled in response and she laughed again, throaty and loud.

My heart swelled. *I'm supposed to be here. I can do this. I can help her through this. I'm supposed to be here. I can protect my son from freaks like Zoe. I can make my wife feel better. I'm supposed to be here.*

Certainty filled me with all-over happiness, blotting out my annoyance toward Billy and Zoe, cancelling the little irritations of our high-maintenance day, our life littered with constant renegotiations and backtracking. It had been a long time since I'd felt pleasant clarity. After the "babymoon" of Beth's maternity leave was over and she headed back to *Electra* magazine, I'd settled into constant insecurity, running on shaky, inefficient faith that I was doing the right thing. Doubt had plagued me, and I'd gotten used to it. The Junkie Incident was yet to come, and it would ferment that doubt into something dangerously, darkly intoxicating indeed.

But on that Coney Island boardwalk, my doubt receded like a scummy wave. For an hour or so, as we huddled on the steamy, fetid F train back to our neighborhood, Evan nodding off again in his mother's lap, I secretly reveled in my certainty. I decided not to try to vocalize it, spoil it by exposing it to air, to speech. Beth remained intent on a copy of *Bazaar.*

My feelings of successful crisis negotiation morphed into lust. Beth's thigh against mine created friction, a growing heat. I wondered if she felt it.

My mouth watered and my tongue twitched with muscle memory at the distinctive shape and feel of her clit against it. I actually tried to distract my erotic thoughts with disgusting images, an activity I'd not engaged in for at least a decade. Repellent images were in ready supply on the F train. I stared at the yellowed tufts poking from the earlobes of the bent old man in front of us. But even that did not work; I became the dreaded man on the train with a hard-on.

I hoped Evan would stay asleep, because I wanted to peel off Beth's sweaty bikini top and hike up that green skirt as soon as we got home. We'd put a latch on the flimsy door leading to our bedroom to ensure against Evan walking in on us as we fucked in the living room, but we'd only actually done it on the futon a handful of times, furtively and quickly.

As our train tunneled below the East River, I reveled in ardor and wonder: Everything has led me to this moment and thus everything is right and I have been blessed among men. *I am where I should be.*

Evan awoke in his stroller as we turned onto our block. After getting a bath in the sink, he ate twice as much dinner as usual—almost an entire takeout bean burrito. Having napped an excessive amount, he was up very late, nestled wide awake between Beth and me as we watched *SNL* in bed, all of us freshly bathed, an oscillating fan whirring by the antique clothes rack that served as our closet. Beth was the first to drop off to sleep, then Evan.

Desire still ran tepid in my veins, and I hoped Evan would sleep late in the morning, and Beth, if she awoke in time, might be game for Sunday morning futon sex, moving together in cycles of fast and slow as the bells of Iglesia de Cristo chimed down the avenue and up the airshaft. I sighed against a parched throat and tongued the inside of my lip until it was very wet.

On the trip back from Coney Island, we'd pointedly not spoken about Zoe and Billy. It had been easier for me not to engage in bitching about my brother-in-law, consumed as I'd been by my Moment of Clarity and subsequent lust. But now, as I stood in my boxers and tank top in the refrigerator light and popped open a beer, I replayed my memories of Billy and Zoe, seeing them through a mind's eye now equipped, I believed, with clearer vision.

I felt a swelling regret that I'd not been as kind to Billy as I should have been. One beer led to another, and I decided to call my brother-in-law, connect with him. Perhaps we could meet somewhere. I needed him to know we were really proud of his latest attempt at getting clean. The desire to be good filled me like a sugar craving.

I was flipping through our address book when I heard Beth's footsteps, the creak of the door to our bedroom, and the latch on the lock. I put the phone down and made my way into the shadowy living room. My wife, in a threadbare white Cramps T-shirt that reached her upper thighs, was lighting a votive candle. Her hair was loosened and wild, obscuring her eyes, but her hungry smile drew me in like prey. All of her energy angled my way, her scent mixing with the dissipating sulfur of the spent match.

"Turn off that light, you," she whispered hoarsely as she switched on the box fan in the airshaft window. It rattled to life and drew the still air into the humid East Village night, not quite full-on summer yet, still dewy with lingering spring.

Beth pulled her shirt over her head and stood in her underpants in the flickering light. She reached for my beer, took a deep sip, placed it on the end table, pulled my T-shirt over my head, and kissed me, sloppy, beery, and hard, her lips salty from sleep sweat. Her shoulders still bore slight indentations from her bikini top; lavender scent rose from her clavicle and neck. She slipped her hand under my waistband and found a cock swelling in her hot, slick palm.

"Come on," she said, reclining on the futon, peeling off and flinging her panties to the floor in one motion.

I dove for her abdomen, tongue making a beeline southward on the thin strip of hair below her navel, but she wanted no foreplay. She grabbed my head and pulled upward, pelvis rocking as she pushed my boxers to my knees, placed me just inside her, then angled her hips up, letting out a little laugh-sigh as I sank in.

We soon hit our "quick-before-Evan-wakes" rhythm. In pre-Evan days, Beth would have uncoiled a gut-deep series of animal moans, and a distant sliver of my awareness would clock the likelihood (very good) that our neighbors heard us; these days, all of that was funneled into a humming song that resonated in her body like sound waves in an overheated vacuum tube amplifier.

I felt as hair-triggered as a sixteen-year-old virgin. I withdrew several times to stave off coming, but Beth wasn't having it. She wrapped her legs around my back and laughed again as I shook my head *no, no, no*. This sent her over the edge, and she tightened up, then shuddered and pounded her fist against my shoulder as she came, groaning alto-low as I let myself go inside her, ripples of electricity coursing from my lower back to the nape of my neck.

The door strained against the lock.

"Mommy?"

We scrambled for our underwear, like teens who've been busted in the barn or the backseat of a car.

"Evan!" Beth called out, a little too loud. "Is that . . . you?" Pant, pant. "What are you doing up?"

"Mommy? Papa?"

Beth flicked on the light, blew out the candle, undid the lock, and opened the door. Evan was accustomed to seeing us either naked or very nearly so, so he didn't flinch at us standing there in our underwear, out of breath and sweaty. Evan himself was nude, a perfect little vision of an innocent, uncircumcised toddler.

"Wa-wa, Mommy."

"You know what?" Beth gave me a quick, sly grin and lifted our son. "That's a great idea. Let's get a drink and go right back to bed."

Evan's nose wrinkled at the lingering, popcorn-y scent of recent sex and candle wax clinging to the air. We all headed to the kitchen, where we squinted in the light, drinking cold New York City tap water, my wife flushed from our romp, her neck bearing my teeth marks, a shiny trickle on her inner thigh. Evan nattered on, gesticulating in her arms, his clear-eyed gaze meeting her complete attention with boundless trust.

I am where I should be, I thought. I smiled in an endorphin-heavy stupor as my eyes drifted over my fleshy little family, all of us free from the difficulties of the day and unconcerned with our blindness to the future.

chapter 12

in good hands

Ring.

Evan frowns at the ringing phone. We're engaged in Lego play. At his request, I'm building a spaceship for a character he's making.

I sigh and put my work aside. He grabs my robe sleeve.

"No," he says. "No."

"I gotta. Could be Mommy."

I consider letting the machine get it. In four rings, our outgoing message—my voice—will engage: *please leave a message for Grant, Beth, or Evan at the sound of the beep, or try Beth on her cell 646-261-4939 . . . thankyouverymuch.* (Elvis flourish at the end.)

It's most likely Beth calling, checking in from Paul and Melora's, letting us know how the Strokes fared, whether she's heard from Sasha's "people" about the publicist gig, etc. It's noon, and I'm sure she slept in and is probably a little (or a lot) hungover. I am preemptively jealous. Yet I'm also enjoying my revived Lego skills. Evan has inherited my fascination with the plastic blocks—as a child, I built whole multicolored cities—and my son deems my creations works of genius. I'm allowing myself to think he's oh-so-perceptive, and this softens my creeping umbrage. A little.

Ring.

I could lie about why I couldn't answer. We were playing outside in the snow. Hmm. And Evan, smart as he is, hasn't yet grasped the deception of "screening calls," so he won't rat me out, I don't think. But maybe he would, even unintentionally (that's happened before). He's in a "quantum state" of development at present; his progress—vocabulary, abstract reasoning, empathy—is difficult to predict.

A glance at the window discourages me. Sleet is needling the house, coating massive white mounds with an icy glaze. Hardly a winter wonderland. We were playing outside in the snow. Bad lie.

Ring.

I realize Beth may be marooned in NYC. Ricky cleared our sidewalks and driveways around ten a.m. but still advised us not to go out all day. Accidents all up and down the Thruway and surface roads, he said.

I shake free of my son's grip and head to the kitchen.

Ring.

"Hello . . . ?"

"Billy's dead!" Beth cries.

I hold the receiver away from my ear and gasp. First thought: some mistake? He's gone missing for weeks at a time in the past, and we'd feared the worst, but he always showed up eventually.

"What?" I say.

Evan looks up from his work, noting something in my voice, something for which he does not yet have words. I meet his eyes for a second, mash the phone back to my ear, and retreat, wobbly-kneed, to the stove, where he can't see me.

"My little brother . . ." she says. "I can't believe it! Fuck. Fuck!"

I sink to the floor. "Shit," I whisper. "Shit. Goddamn it . . ." In that moment of broadened awareness, I notice a tinge of mold at the curling edges of the linoleum.

Beth wails into my ear. My hands shake as I run my fingers through my hair, scratch my scalp.

"Slow down, honey . . . slow down," I say, my hands going numb.

This is it. The Call. Beth and I have talked about getting The Call, the news that Billy, after many scares, has finally shot the wrong stuff, crossed the wrong dealer, fallen on the third rail, collapsed from hepatitis C complications.

"He . . . he . . ." Beth gasps like she's been running. "Oh shit . . ."

Melora commandeers the phone. "Grant?" she says, her thin voice steady.

"What happened?"

"He . . . nodded out with a space heater going in an apartment on Rivington," Melora says. "He was crashing with some Irish musician guys in a one-bedroom . . . the firemen think the space heater shorted out and a fire started in the walls at, like, four this morning. They put it out, the others got out, but the smoke got him. He was on the nod. They think he never woke up."

Beth wails in the background. Paul's voice is low, calming her.

"I'm coming there," I say. "Now."

"Grant, we've got her. She's in good hands. I've got some Xanax. You stay put. The roads are really, really bad, especially where you are in the fucking sticks. Should be better tomorrow. Day after at the latest . . . We all knew this was coming, right?"

"I guess . . . So it's really bad, the roads?"

"City's shut down, practically. It was beautiful before the sleet hit."

Beth wails again.

"Let me talk to my wife."

"Right."

"I can't believe it . . ." Beth's hyperventilating. "My little brother. What do I do, Grant? What do I do? Damn him!"

"Where is he?"

A simple question reels her in. "At the morgue. I just identified him. They called my cell hours ago, but it was off. We were . . . out late. He had my number in his wallet. I didn't want to call until I knew . . ."

"Oh, honey. Honey, I'm so sorry."

"I said . . . goodbye . . . for you . . . and Evan. He just looked like he was asleep. They cleaned him up a little. Smelled like he'd been camping. His hair. Smelled like . . . woodsmoke, y'know. The morgue's right up on First Avenue, near Bellevue, did you know that?"

"I didn't know that."

"Thank god the fire didn't get him, thank god, thank god, thank god, thank god."

"Listen, listen, honey? You need me to call someone?"

"No. Thank you. I guess Trip and Christa, although I know they didn't like him. Assholes."

"OK. Zoe . . . ?"

"She can rot in fucking Bridgeport or wherever the fuck she is."

"OK."

"I'm talking to the morgue later about . . . arrangements. I'm next of kin. I'm . . . seeing about cremating him somewhere. It's what he wanted, he said . . . some time. I don't know when."

"I'll find some way to get down there."

"No!"

I hold the phone away.

"No," she says lower, through her teeth. "The weather channel says do not get on any roads today. I can't deal with thinking about you in an accident. Stay with Evan. That's what you can do. Stay with Evan . . ."

More crying.

Evan wanders in the kitchen with a humanoid-looking Lego creation.

"This is the Alien Man!" He plops the figure at my feet, his eyes widening with curiosity at my sitting on the ragged linoleum. Beth gasps at the sound of his voice.

I give Evan a thumbs-up, try to smile, but my face is frozen. He opens his mouth to ask why I'm on the floor.

"I'm talking to Mommy," I say. "She's at Padrino's house in New York City."

"I want to talk to Padrino." No interest in my sitting on the floor anymore.

"Not right now, big guy. Mommy and I are talking important stuff."

"I'll get Paul," Beth says, sounding eager to bid me goodbye.

"Hey Grant," Paul says. "Fucking hell, right? The asshole got away."

"Yeah." I lean away from my son as he reaches for the phone. "Thanks for . . . everything. Here's your godson."

Evan mashes the phone to his ear and says, "Hey . . . When you coming to visit? I want to show you my pictures. I drew a alien and I made a Lego guy and his name is Alien Man and he's half alien and half person and he's a superhero I made up . . . Yeah you can make one too . . . And then they can fight. But mine will win. Yes, he will . . . Yes, he will . . . Yes, he WILL . . . That's a bad word, you're not supposed to say that."

"OK, give me the phone," I say.

"I have to go . . . Papa says . . . Yeah . . . Soon raccoon."

Evan takes Alien Man back into the living room. Beth's back on the phone.

"What do you want me to tell Evan?" I ask.

"Nothing yet, OK? Nothing yet. It's too horrible."

"Right. I'll keep it secret."

"I'm so glad our parents aren't here for this."

"I hear you."

"Now all I've got is you. And Evan."

After a moment, I say, "Yeah. You do. You've got us."

Within the soft ocean of digital noise, my wife draws a sharp breath. Fear pricks at me.

"I'll call you later, OK?" she says, her voice thinning. "Let you know . . . what's what."

I don't want to let her go. I want to gather her back. My hands begin to tremble again.

"Grant . . . ?" she says.

"I'm here. I hate this."

"I do too. But I'm in good hands."

"I love you."

"Love you, too."

~

The kettle is whistling as Trip, Christa, and Katie arrive at the kitchen door. They're huddled beneath a single, huge Metropolitan Museum of Art umbrella, sleet bouncing up from the taut fabric with percussive pops.

"Keep your voices down," I say as they shake themselves out of their coats. "Evan doesn't know yet."

Christa and Trip nod. They are flush from the cold and seem energized, frowning yet radiating excitement. Whether this is from their bracing walk or something else, I can't tell. I'd told them they didn't need to come over, but Christa had insisted, telling me to put the kettle on, we're all going to have Swiss Miss, a box of which she pulls from her Coach tote. This out-of-left-field idea, ventured in the wake of my relating the news about Billy, blotted out all other thought, and I'd just said OK. As soon as they walk in, I berate myself for shitty judgement, feeling like I've betrayed Evan, still in the living room putting Alien Man through his paces.

Trip rips open packets of Swiss Miss, saying nothing about last night's Ambien walk. I resist the urge to ask. Either he remembers and doesn't want his wife to know, or, as Ricky had said, he's clueless. The now-dreamlike visit of my friend and the sex-and-violence overtones of yesterday's playdate hang in the air like pressurized clouds.

Katie is clinging to her mother, as before. Christa sits in the nook, pries her loose, and unzips the girl's bubblegum-pink hooded fleece snowsuit. Lion King pajamas are intact, giving off a cheesy whiff. Christa plops Katie on the floor and pulls another bag of Pirate's Booty from the tote and waves it under Katie's nose. The girl snatches it and digs in.

"You sit, Grant," Christa says, "and tell me again what the fuck happened."

I whisper the story again, about the space heater, the smoke, Billy being on the nod, unable to escape, impending cremation, Beth handling it all from Paul and Melora's place.

"I knew it," Christa says. "I knew he wouldn't make old bones from that first time I saw him. When was that? Was it '92? Yeah, '92."

Katie, sensing Evan's presence, rises from the floor and turns toward the living room. Christa grabs her and waves the snack bag under her nose again, refocusing Katie's energy.

"Hurry up with that chocolate, pops," Christa says to Trip.

Trip is merrily stirring the cups, swaying as if a song is playing. "Coming up. So . . . Beth's OK? She can't be surprised."

Christa musters a mask of compassion for a few moments and says, "Poor Beth. But I know she's been expecting this."

"She's bad off," I say, irritated, taking a mug. "I'm worried for her."

"Not the best time to be coming off your meds, huh?" Christa says. Trip glances over. He is in the know.

"I guess," I say. "But I reckon I can take this. I should feel this." No more 9/11 numbness. Three more months of halved pills and I'm done.

"How about Paul and Melora?" Christa asks.

"They seem OK. I think they're probably enjoying having something to do."

"That's a shitty thing to say." Christa smiles. "Although totally true. You *are* coming off your meds."

Trip puts an ice cube in a sippy cup filled with hot chocolate and places it before his daughter. I realize he's not made one for Evan.

"Evan!" I call. "You want some Swiss Miss?"

Evan runs in, and I brace for his reaction to Katie. But he's thinking only about the Swiss Miss. He stands in the doorway, eyes wide, mouth a perfect "O," as if he's on a game show winning thousands of dollars. As if the Lamonts are not even there.

"Swiss Miss!" he says, then does a jig. "Swiss Miss dance, Swiss Miss dance!"

Katie rises, crumbs cascading from her pajamas, and does the Swiss Miss dance with Evan.

"Look!" Trip says. "They're buddies!"

"All is forgiven, I guess." Christa hands her hot chocolate to Evan. "Here ya go. Made special, just for you. Don't spill it." She roots in her tote. "I brought some sandwiches for everyone. *Beth's '90s Hits* is in here somewhere, too."

"Cool," I say, surprised she's returning the cassette so promptly. "Thanks. Fork it over and we'll listen to some tunes, get our minds off things, while educating the kids about the music from . . ."

"Ye Olden Tymes," Trip says.

"Where is it?" Christa says as she slaps wax-paper-wrapped sandwiches on the table. "Uh-oh." She sticks her hand through a rip in her bag. "Oh! I've been meaning to get this sewed shut! These things are never supposed to wear out!"

"It probably fell out back at the house?" Trip says.

Oh no. No, no, no, no.

"You've got a dub of it, right Grant?" Christa says.

"No, I don't." I bolt up and run out into the storm in my sweats, T-shirt, and bare feet. A municipal snowplow trundles by.

"You'll get frostbite!" Christa yells through the rattling applause of the sleetfall. "Stop!"

My feet are instantly prickly with pain. Ice nails into my skin as I blow on my hands and scan the wintry mix for the cassette. *Fuck fuck fuck.*

"Papa! You'll get frostbite!" Evan's voice, high and faint.

I run toward the Victorian, frozen shards slipping between my toes. Sleet and snow weigh down the birch and maple branches lining the road; they bend now like a ruined white canopy.

Just how much damage will the wetness and cold do to a five-year-old cassette? Not much, maybe. Bullshit. A lot. Unless, of course, Trip is right and it's back at the house. But somehow I know he's not right.

Trip runs up with the MOMA umbrella. He's carrying my snow boots. He holds the umbrella over my head, allowing me to stop squinting in the downpour. A bit of black juts out from a recently plowed berm. My heart sinks as I run and dig it out, my fingers aching at all contact.

Beth's '90s Hits is destroyed, scooped up and crushed under the plow blade. The case is splintered, and black tape guts spill from within. On the soggy insert, label script runs like watery blood, drawings smeared in an indistinct mass, a Xeroxed photo of Beth's smiling eyes peeling from sodden cardboard. The cassette is a smashed face; the spools are dead eyes, the broken rectangular window a mouth.

"Is it OK?" Trip asks.

"No it's not fucking OK!" My teeth chatter as I slip the ruined mixtape into my pocket.

I made *Beth's '90s Hits* for my wife's thirty-seventh birthday, when she was pregnant with our son. She'd noted with a sigh that it was her last birthday before crossing a threshold she never thought she would cross—parenthood—and she was excited but also a little blue. I'd wanted to enshrine her favorite music from a less careworn time; we both knew we were diving into deeper cares than we'd ever experienced. So I cobbled together songs from our first few years as a couple, our long honeymoon.

I'd stayed up very, very late the night before the big day, a packet of high-bias, pro-quality cassettes and a huge mug of coffee at my side. I used both LPs and CDs, even a few singles, obsessing over the sequencing, tinkering with fade-ins and fade-outs. I even needed to restart a couple times with a new cassette. While she was at work the next day, I labored over the art, cutting and pasting a photo-booth pic of her. I surrounded her beaming face with drawings of flying CDs and LPs.

I'd only made one copy of *Beth's '90s Hits*, for Billy. He'd been at the little birthday party we'd given on East Seventh, and he was on good behavior. He kept convulsing with joy over the songs, and in a moment of sweet weakness, I made him a copy on the double-cassette deck. That dub is no doubt lost. And now he's dead.

What a fucking day.

"We'll make you another, OK?" Trip says. "Give us the tracklisting, we'll make you another. OK? OK?"

My mind goes numb. I can't feel my feet. A strange rising feeling spreads through my chest, like I'm on the first drop of a roller coaster.

"C'mon, Grant, back to the house." Trip is pulling me along Shulz Way. He's still carrying my boots. I don't want to go back. I stand rooted at the snowbank, shivering, listening to the constant *shhhh* of the sleet on the snow, like tinnitus, the ticking of the hard drops against the tree bark.

I jump as something swirls to my left over Stony Clove Creek. Vulture? No. A bald eagle. Circling the water, hunting. Trip sees it, too.

"Holy shit!" he says.

It is massive, the biggest bird I've ever seen outside a zoo, and my first sighting of a species I was told would one day be extinct due to DDT. I may as well be seeing a pterodactyl. It moves as if under water, barely pumping its wings, unfazed by the sleet. It is aware we're watching it, glancing over for a millisecond. Something inside me bends beneath the weight of its yellow gaze.

"Holy SHIT!" Trip repeats.

"Shhh."

The eagle overwhelms all thought and sensation. I may still be trembling, I don't know. In a flash, I understand bird watchers. Each circle over the creek reels us ever further in, until the eagle alights on a birch about twenty feet away, folds its wings, and gazes at us full-on. Trip and I each take a sharp, involuntary breath.

I'm back at that blissful place, where I am free of vindictiveness; I bear no ill will toward Christa for her carelessness, to Billy for being a hopeless, heartbreaking addict, to my father for checking out and knowing full well I'd find him, to Paul for his success, to my wife for her inattention, distance, and success, to anyone for anything.

After a span of unmeasurable time, our new friend unfolds his wings and launches himself skyward, sending glistening bits of ice flying from the recoiling branch. He makes one wide circle over Stony Clove Creek and heads toward Mt. Marie, releasing our attention, disappearing in frozen rain and low-hanging clouds.

"Papa!" Evan yells from the doorway. Has he been yelling for a while? Yes. He's been calling me, and I've not processed his voice. All is clicking back in place. I'm cold. My anger over the mixtape is refreshed. I miss my eagle friend.

"I'm coming, Evan!" It comes out more irritated than reassuring.

"You're gonna get frostbite, Papa!" Evan's voice is pitched high, quavering with worry, bordering on panic.

"I'm coming, I'm coming!"

I'm having trouble walking. Evan may be right about frostbite. Trip is talking.

"That was pretty amazing, right? Did you see that?"

I nod.

"Maybe it was Billy," Trip says to his feet. For a moment, and for the first time, he seems sad.

"M-m-m-maybe."

~

Back in the kitchen, I sit in the nook and wrap my prickling feet in a towel. Christa's made me a fresh cup of Swiss Miss. The kids are engaged in parallel play, silently making Lego creations in the living room, as if yesterday never happened. Trip is in there, half-monitoring them while tinkering on my Mac, working on the dial-up connection.

"I've got all those songs on CD," Christa says as she massages my feet through the terrycloth. "And what I don't have, I'll buy, I swear. It'll be even better quality than the one you made. I just can't believe that happened."

"These things happen," I say, employing one of the more useless modern mantras in an effort to preserve my eroding forgiveness. "Mixtapes aren't meant to last. Just like people."

Her green eyes focus on me as she squeezes my defrosting toes. "Morbid, but true. So let's make it count before we get plowed over or smoked out, eh?"

I nod.

chapter 13

anywhere but here

When Evan and I walk into Greta's General Store, bells tinkle, but no one notices us. The place is as Trip described it: Fly rods against the wall, camping equipment, packaged food, magazines, dry goods, everything hazy with oily heat and evaporating snow melt. All poorly lit with fluorescent ceiling tubes.

Behind the counter, a blonde, zaftig woman perched on a barstool exudes annoyance, flinching at a gaggle of twentysomething skiers clustered around her register. In her lap sits an abandoned crossword and a mug of something thick and brown. Greta. Her customers—florid of face, brimming with health, encased in Lycra and wool skiwear—are unloading fleece hats, energy bars, glossy magazines, and lip balm on the glass top. A rack laden with sunglasses creaks as a girl spins it around to the mirror. She admires the enormous aviators on her face.

"Those rock, Eleanor," her friend says. "Now we'll all have shades from our Madcap Mt. Marie Weekend!"

"They are quite expensive," Greta's German-accented disdain thickens the close air in the cluttered store. Her hostility confuses me. The Storm of '03 has been a godsend for the local winter recreation businesses, yet Greta seems unimpressed by her good fortune. She absently stirs her mug with a pen, curling her thin lip at the kids. They raise their eyebrows but don't put anything away.

Evan pokes around in a bin full of after-Christmas sale items, mostly Santa refrigerator magnets.

"Excuse me," I say. "Are you Greta?"

"What?" she demands, as if we've known and been annoyed by one another for years.

"Sorry . . . I'm . . . just here to meet the Trailways." Why am I apologizing? "It's coming soon, right?"

"It comes when it comes." She shakes her head, shrugs.

"My mommy's on it," Evan says. Greta notices him for the first time. She cranes her neck over the counter.

"Who are you?" she asks, smiling, the blood rushing to her lips and cheeks. Like a magic trick.

"Evan."

"I'm Greta."

"Hello," Evan says, all Tiny-Tim-like. "Is this your store? We moved into the house over that way."

"Shulz House," I say. "I'm Grant."

She nods at me. "The bus will be here in five, Evan," she says. "You want a Santa magnet? Take one."

"Really?" Evan's face lights up.

Greta nods. At my prompt, Evan thanks her, which reignites her irritation. She turns to the kids, monitoring them with a willed scowl.

Evan pockets his trinket, and we stand by the fogged-over glass door and watch for the bus. In the time we wait, the skiers rack up over a hundred dollars' worth of crap. They scuttle past us in a thin cloud of teen sweat and perfume, leaving Greta to sigh and sink back into her puzzle. She makes no move to chitchat with us.

The bus hisses to a stop beside the massive plowed snowbank, sending a diesel plume into the crisp air. Aside from contrails expanding in the winey sunset, the sky is unbroken, purpling like a bruise.

Beth, flush behind Ray-Bans, descends the steps, hand luggage and laptop case dangling like ornaments. She clutches a brown bag to her chest. Billy's clothes and, I assume, his ashes.

"Mommy!" Evan throws his arms around her legs as I unburden her. She looks thinner, as if she's cried away a part of herself over the last four days. So much crying into her cell phone, and, I'm sure, during all the activities following Billy's death: the cremation, the collection of his ashes, papers to sign. Paul and/or Melora had shepherded her through the worst of it. She's exhausted; one question will send her spiraling.

She hands me the bag. It reeks of oily metal and ash. I brace for Evan to ask about it, but he doesn't, which is odd. He's excited to show off his Santa magnet.

"I missed my boys so much!" She kneels before Evan, kissing him several times on both cheeks. I wonder when we'll tell him about Uncle Billy. The official excuse for putting it off is "we're worried he'll be stricken with grief," but that's not really so. I don't think he'll be too upset at the loss of his uncle, whom he barely knows. Although she's not said so, my guess is Beth is afraid of exactly that: the prospect of Evan facing Billy's death impassively. As with most four-year-olds, he has not yet learned to lie, so whatever his response, it'll be pure. Either way, it's something we can't govern, and we'd just as soon not add one more uncontrollable aspect to the mix of our fraught life.

"Mommy, look at all the snow!"

"I see, I see."

She straightens up and kisses me quick, her lips like grosgrain ribbon. She pats my shoulder, making brief, bleary eye contact over her sunglasses. I feel a heavy woe in her gaze but also a kind of fear, which I attribute to her being so recently close to physical death.

After my father's suicide, death shadowed everything. It was like I possessed second sight; summer leaves browned in my mind, people aged until I blinked them back to youth. My mother withered in my imagination, leaving me alone, standing over an imaginary, bottomless abyss. I spent countless afterschool hours watching the driveway, praying for her safe deliverance from her job. Yet, as soon as the Super Beetle pulled in—and it always did—I'd run to the TV, hiding my relief with fake boredom.

"I got the gig," Beth says, forcing a smile.

"With the stripper puppet?" Evan asks.

My wife and I laugh a little. "Don't say that, Evan!" Beth says.

"But you said it."

"It was a mistake, baby boy. A mistake. A big mistake. Her name's Sasha."

"OK," he says. "Sasha." He lets the "A" ring out. It is a fun word to say.

"Yeah," Beth says. "Sashaaaaaah."

"Congrats!" I hug her sideways.

"With that and the Six Ray gig, we should be able to get our heads above water before too long." She ducks into the Camry.

"What's a Six Ray gig?" Evan asks as I strap him into his seat. I haven't agreed to anything regarding the Portland party. It's been all about Billy these last few days.

"Daddy's gonna play music with Padrino this summer. With Padrino's band Six Ray Star. They're doing a concert. Getting back together for a party."

"Oh! Oh!" Evan squirms under my hands. "Will you be playing 'Kiss My Ring'?"

I glance at the front seat. Beth's applying lip balm in the rearview.

"Looks that way," I say. "Looks that way."

~

Back at Shulz House, Rolling Rock in hand, Beth vegetates in front of a VHS of *Annie Hall* borrowed from the Lamonts. She's not really watching, just gazing at the mid-distance between herself and the screen, where perhaps another movie plays. Evan is at her feet, doodling on my instrument cases with a silver Sharpie and yawning. He was up late last night and woke early this morning anticipating her return.

I stash the Billy Bag in the cabinet under the sink and haul her stuff upstairs, emptying her clothes on the bed, where I will sort them, then do a wash. As ever, she's crammed the dirty stuff in a plastic bag. A button-down shirt, a bra, and a couple pairs of socks and underwear, sexy panties, gifts from me on either Valentine's Days or birthdays past. One black Victoria's Secret skimpy lace thing, mostly sheer, one pair of burgundy red, faux-vintage boy shorts from a little boutique in the East Village.

But why take the sexy stuff? Why not the utilitarian "Bridget Jones" briefs? The three-for-twenty-dollars variety, of which she owns at least a dozen. Clean. I should know.

From the Victoria's Secret pair, something drops onto the quilt. A light blue scrap, a torn piece of something, the size of a fingernail. My heart leaps to my throat, and a low thrumming begins in my ears. My knees buckle. I drop to the quilt, gaze at the scrap, blood rushing from my hands and feet, leaving them cold and clammy.

The light blue scrap seems to pulse with life, like it'll run if I reach for it. Its metallic sheen clashes with the soft peach of the quilt. I pick it up: the corner of the light blue foil wrapping of a Trojan lubricated condom. Having bought and used Trojan "blues" in the past, I'd recognize it anywhere. But I'd rather not recognize it here. Anywhere but here.

Footsteps on the stairs. Slow, grief-heavy. Sock-clad. Beth. I grab the scrap and pitch it behind the headboard. Something to do. Good. Ask now? No. She's broken. Not now. And really: What do you know about it? Nothing. You only surmise. You know nothing.

I wince as the condom wrapper scrapes along the drywall and settles to the floor like a snowflake. If only. If only it would melt. But it won't. I will need to deal with that later. All of it. That's my choice. Later. Definitely. Definite. Something definite.

I clear my throat, as if letting someone know I'm in the bathroom, in a compromising position in which they'll not want to see me. A courtesy.

A deep stratum of my voice rises inside me, quelled by a strange paralyzing guilt at knowing something I'm not supposed to know.

"Grant?"

I snap into action, pantomiming surprise and industry for . . . whom? My reflection in the darkening window? Yes, apparently. That guy.

"Yeah?"

Not bad, perhaps tuned a little high, a little pitchy. Breathe in. Good. Brain chems stabilizing, serotonin flowing, time speeding back up. Maybe I shouldn't come off the Z after all, with money coming in, maybe I could stay on it, insurance be damned.

A few moments of magical thinking: maybe that Trojan wrapper is one that Paul used with Melora, left on the floor where Beth threw her clothes down, and it somehow got caught in the fabric.

This thought is like sugar in my blood. I breathe easier, busying myself with the underthings. I ball them into a silky wad, a beached sea creature, tentacles dangling. The door creaks. Beth's presence heats up the back of my neck as I cast around for something else to do that will not involve facing her. Facing her will break the spell of the denial. Amazing human trait, that: denial. Knowing yet forcing ignorance. Yes, it's from Paul fucking Melora, that's what it is. Of course. It makes sense.

No.

The bedroom door closes. Her arms encircle my waist, fingers under my sweater and T-shirt, up my ribs. She is already shirtless, her breasts against my back, hardened nipples scudding along my spine.

"Evan's asleep," she whispers, beer breath on my shoulder blade, teeth grazing my skin. "Downstairs, on the sofa."

She's coming on to me? She's coming on to me. First time in months. I drop the underthings to the bed. The fact that Evan is so close and could very well awaken and burst in does not deter her, which is unusual. Once upon a time, she was brazen, but the last couple years, she's grown wary. The surprise novelty of her renewed courage flicks a switch; time, distance, action-and-reaction, logical consequences, reality in general, all fly out the window as an erection strains against my pants.

I spin and pull her jeans from her hips as she scrabbles at my waistband. She has lost weight; her pelvic bones jut for the first time since before she got pregnant.

Christa's voice rings in my head: "He was so skinny, he used to bruise my fucking pelvic bones."

I'm not skinny, but I will bruise your fucking pelvic bones, Beth.

Her ass bobs in the window reflection. I reach for the light switch.

"No," she says, more begging than demanding. "On. Leave it on."

Also new. Her nails dig into my thighs, she's kneeling and I am in her mouth, gasping. This hasn't happened in many moons, and never with such conviction. Ever. Not in fourteen years. Like she's starving, not doing me a favor. My eyes widen as the event horizon of an orgasm approaches all too quickly. I push her away, lift her by her armpits onto the soiled clothes, rip her jeans from her ankles, and duck between her legs, partly because of hunger, partly because I don't want this long-awaited sex to end abruptly from too-soon-coming on my part.

She bucks against my mouth in a steadier, more dogged rhythm than usual. But for her distinctive taste and texture, the mole at the crease of her left thigh and torso, appendectomy scar, palimpsest of stretch marks around her shallow navel, Patti Smith tattoo on her ankle, she could almost be another woman. My hands cup her ass, feel this new rhythm. Within a minute, her hips arch and she's thrashing as clothes fall to the floor. She grabs a fistful of quilt and moans deep and low into the old cloth, like Nina Simone letting loose a long, slow note. That sound alone almost coaxes cum from me. I back away and stand, jeans at my ankles, cock free of contact from anything that might set me off, grateful for the cool of the room.

Beth moves as if I'm already inside her, eyes glazed, pelvis rocking, grinding into the darkening quilt, angling up, slightly stubbly legs open wide. We have not met on this terrain in a long time.

I close my eyes and wait, breathing deep as if preparing to dive to the drain at the deep end of the pool, willing the blood away from my abdomen, wishing for the control of my twenties. At last the heat recedes, my heart slows slightly, and I touch the tip of my cock to her clit. She pushes me inside, and we gasp together.

The still-pulsing coal of suspicion flares into anger. I grab her wrists from my lower back and hold them over her head, something I've never done. Instead of protesting, she rasps as her lips peel away from her teeth. The mattress creaks beneath us, an annoyance that seems lost on her—also new—even as I release a wrist to keep the headboard from banging the wall, something she would have done once, amid annoyed sighs. Her free hand nestles at the crack of my ass, also new. We settle into a polyrhythm of gasps, thrusts, and creaks. I withhold for a minute or two, grateful, for a change, for that Zoloft-induced anorgasmia.

"Come . . . inside . . . me," she says. "I . . . want you to. Come . . . with me." As she wraps her free arm around my rib cage and shudders, I do, rising over her, pounding.

Involuntary grunts escape my throat. Hot chemicals spill into my veins. She contracts around my torso, coiling up and banging her forehead into my collarbone. Then she releases me, and I collapse beside her.

A minute passes. Just beyond the glow of the house, a snow-weighted branch cracks and plummets from its parent trunk, *ka-thump*-ing in the mounting drifts.

My wife and I have neither kissed nor made direct eye contact, and it seems oddly inappropriate to do so now. Questions hover at the far edges of my thoughts. My forearm rises and falls on Beth's chest. We are shiny with sweat, mouth-breathing out of time with each other. Conscious awareness of her scent dawns on me; she's been bathing with other soaps, high-end bars, likely from Barney's, whispers of soft floral perfumes, Chanel or something, and traces of what I guess are Melora's massage oils, lavender, bergamot, I don't know. Also Paul's Marlboro Lights in her hair. All thickened in sex haze.

As if hearing my thoughts, Beth tenses, then tries to make it seem as if she meant to do so because she's going to check on Evan. She wipes a tear and says it's sweat. She's looking for something to put on. Can't make a decision. I pull the faux-vintage boyshorts from under my ass and toss them to her. She snatches them from the air and steps into the lace as the furnace yawns to life in the bowels of the house.

The lamplight shadows dance across her curves; her physique twists with defiant animal grace, unapologetic, elemental like a flame, engorged with blood, moving independent of her drawn, guarded face.

She grabs what she calls her Granny Robe from the hook behind our door (she'd not taken that to NYC, no she did not) and hustles down the steps, leaving me with ebbing endorphins and a clatter of voices all making different demands. Face it. Leave it. It's not what you think. Just ask. Not now. Later. Never. Now.

I bargain. Refrain for now, but take one peek at the scrap of condom wrapper on the floor while reflecting: I will never forget what just happened. I will be deep into my dotage, unaware of my own name, balls at my knees, on my deathbed, and I'll remember this. I am old enough to realize how few life episodes retain clarity. This will be one.

A murmuring of voices below. Beth is talking, the cadence of her voice rising in a series of questions. Evan's awake? Did we wake him up with our fucking? I throw on my pants and head down.

Evan is sitting in front of the TV/VCR combo, a mess of bedhead, the bag of ashes in front of him. He holds his silver Sharpie and looks at Beth with wide eyes, dark bangs on his brow, head cocked like a puppy's. Beth is breathing heavy, hand in her tousled, glossy hair, shoulders tense around her ears. Evan has doodled on the bag, a stick figure surrounded by stars.

"Hi Daddy," Evan says evenly, turning his gaze my way. "I'm drawing on Uncle Billy's bag."

Beth turns to me, shaking her head, eyes unfocused. She mouths words before finally saying, "He . . . he got the bag from . . . the kitchen . . ."

"Did you . . . ?"

She shakes her head more forcefully.

"Uncle Billy's . . . died," Evan says. It's the first time I've heard the word *died* from his lips. "I'm making his bag all pretty."

"How did you know?" I ask Evan as Beth collapses in my arms. Her forehead scrunches against my chest. Did he hear us talking? Did he catch any of my phone conversations? I thought I'd been so careful. Why had he not said anything if he knew?

Evan doesn't answer me. He seems not to know how he knows. He comes over and wraps our legs in a hug. His arms are surprisingly strong. "It's OK, Mommy," he says. "Uncle B is flying now. He's OK. Just like in my picture."

Evan's words, Beth's tears, the sight of the doodled-on bag, and decades-old memories merge with the opiates in my blood; together, they are the notches on a combination lock clicking open, revealing a heretofore unknown space inside me, a vista expanding at hyper speed, like the universe emerging from the size of a dime after the Big Bang. The far corners are dark indeed. I assign my knowledge of the condom scrap and its implications to that vista. Evan squeezes us tighter, and the door to that space slams shut. For now.

part two

april 2003

chapter 14

meltdown

Spring has arrived overnight, courtesy of a record-breaking heat wave. Three months' worth of snow is melting fast, casting a gauzy glow over Mt. Marie. I'm taking advantage of the weather and my family's absence, scrubbing persistent black mold from the pukey kitchen linoleum with Evan's ratty old *Toy Story* pajama bottoms. The doors and windows are open to ventilate the place, which reeks of barely diluted Clorox.

Beth, Evan, Trip, and Katie are at the Kingston Mall, taking in *Piglet's Big Movie*, while Christa preps Katie's Café for tomorrow's grand opening. Ricky Shulz is there, detailing, seeing to plumbing concerns. Christa offered him twice his usual rate, which, apparently, was the only way to make him show up punctually and whip the place into shabby-chic shape.

Rather than join the mall excursion, or subject myself to the chaos at Katie's Cafe, I remain here, on my knees with a toxic rag. And yes, this is where I'd rather be. I'll clean the kitchen floor first, where the greasy fungus creeps under the cabinets and refrigerator, then overhead, where a colony of dark speckles blooms on the ceiling.

I will not miss the snow. It's melting beautifully, working an eerie spell on Shulz Way. Mist shrouds Ricky Shulz's snowbound trailer, blurring the well-rutted, muddy pathways. A corner of the previously hidden "Michael Badnarik: Libertarian for President" yard sign pokes like a little shark fin from a slushy swell. King, usually pacing on the clothesline in a dingy snow trench, pants beneath a dripping maple. He is jittery, rimed with mud, shivering despite the rising temps. He has not barked once today.

Ice cracks on the swollen, tea-colored Stony Clove Creek. Teenagers speed alongside it, racing down Shulz Way, windows rolled down, hip-hop blasting, salty grit spewing. Icicles drop from gutters as birds clamor in the weird weather, either joyously or in confused terror, I can't tell.

The heat wave rolled in early this morning. The tail end of it will bring torrential rain, due tonight. Meanwhile, another storm is traveling up the East Coast. Weathermen on the local NPR station say the two systems will collide above the Catskills. As I suited up in my respirator and rubber gloves, the news turned back to the recent US invasion of Iraq, for fuck's sake. I switched it off and found myself pining for my erstwhile laid-back, medicated self. But no, I said. No. No more numbness. Anger and despair are appropriate here. People will die for horseshit, yet again. A stream of curses has flown freely from my mouth all morning, and that feels good. Turns out there are advantages to being left alone and unmedicated in a little poison cloud.

Since the last mold scouring, my respirator has sprung a leak, but I ignore the tinge of bleach in my nostrils. As I work up a noxious lather, I huff Darth Vader-style into the black plastic. I could use Beth's respirator, but I'm not. A little Clorox won't hurt me. All those over-chlorinated pools of my childhood did me no harm.

I focus on Beth's scent lingering on my lips and the stubble just below my nose. We'd engaged in quiet, intense sex last night, and I did not shave or wash upon waking, wanting to lengthen the memory of her grinding into my face. Sex is a regular activity these days, nighttime and occasional afternoon romps. Since ambushing me when she came back from Paul and Melora's, Beth's desire hangs in the air like a presence, an entity from the substrata that frequently rises and overtakes her, like when we were first a couple, lo, those fourteen years ago. My respirator fogs.

Another reason to clean up is the imminent arrival of Paul and Melora, tooling up the Thruway tonight in a brand new Saab. The Portland Six Ray Star gig looms, along with my promised ten K fee. My relationship to this assured windfall has, of course, changed; pocketing a princely sum as a one-time hired gun in Six Ray Star is bittersweet. Like the Lamonts satisfying our need for shelter, I welcome it and hate it at the same time. While I get a chance to play again, I'm anticipating awkwardness; to my knowledge, I've never shared a stage with a friend who, in all likelihood, has cuckolded me. (I keep telling myself this must've been what it was like to be in Fleetwood Mac in the '70s.) But since I've not reneged on the gig, we've set aside this weekend for me to run through Paul's songs and for us all to "catch up."

The Lamonts are having everyone over for dinner. She'd never admit it, but Christa, being old money, is obsessed with showing up nouveau riche Paul, rubbing his nose in "the right way" to be rich.

Paul and Melora are just back from wintering in St. Croix. According to their postcards, they hung out with Sting and Harvey Weinstein, talking truffles, wine, and potential soundtrack placements for Paul's songs.

Scrub, scrub, spray, spray, spray, scrub, scrub.

The bitterness at the back of my tongue reminds me of the taste of that final half-Zoloft, washed down with coffee ten days ago. The recollection of a teenager-y hard-on waking me up these last few mornings, however, cheers me a little. Plus, my waistbands are looser, hipbones emerging from antidepressant-and-beer flab, and my gray, circa 1990 bespoke rock star pants, courtesy of a Studio City seamstress, almost fit.

Still not sleeping well, though. Still entertaining dreamtime visits from dad, and tempted ever more to bum an Ambien from Trip, possible sleepwalking be damned. But I am loath to ask for yet one more thing from our friends-cum-landlords.

Thankfully, due to nerves or spring or a need to overdo "pulling my own weight," I am doing stuff constantly. Locomotion keeps the demons on the run, or at least the trot. And there is much to do. Beth is spending significant time on her publicist gig, at her laptop in our bedroom, and in NYC, where a couple times a week Sasha's people put her up in a SoHo pied-à-terre. Sasha's debut single is certified Gold, and she's rising up the Pop and R & B charts.

My hands are still full with Evan, especially when he hangs out with Katie, who routinely ransacks the Lamont house like a berserking Hun while Evan watches, shaking his head with indulgent disapproval.

Action-packed playdates are the norm. Christa refuses to employ Brianna Shulz as a babysitter, no doubt afraid to further expose Katie's over-the-top personality to the world. She claims it's because Brianna's a dumb redneck, but I don't believe her. Like a hoarder with clutter blindness fearing guests, she knows once people see how crazy her kid is, she'll have to acknowledge it, too. So the extent of Katie's socialization is due mostly to Evan, Beth, and me.

We've settled into three playdates a week. Despite, or perhaps because of, Katie's crazed behavior, Evan has grown to like her. As Thomas the Tank Engine would say, he feels "very useful," puffing out his little chest as he teaches her how to draw stick figures with his Sharpies, how to build with Legos, and even how to talk. Her first word, in fact, is his name: EBBA. I see him drawn to her tot charisma, content to witness and be uncritical of her antisocial behavior, much like I once enabled and continually forgave Tristan, the hapless alcoholic train-wreck lead singer of Stereoblind. Similarly, Evan forgives. He seems to have willfully forgotten her scratching him. It helps that she's not hurt him again, perhaps due to my presence and distinction as the only adult who calls her on her shit; when I shout "No, Katie, not so fast," or something, she looks at me with a mixture of confusion and toddler rage. But she usually listens and begrudgingly obeys, as Evan nods sagely, backing me up. I vacillate between pride at Evan's magnanimity, and fear that he's too passive. Sometimes I wish he'd hold a grudge or even be a bully.

Trip and Christa never intervene in Katie's meltdowns, even as she hurls crockery, shreds Trip's lesson plans, and pushes over bookshelves. They cite *The Indigo Challenge*, a child rearing book that discourages creating "a house of 'no.'" When not extolling the virtues of the absurdly "laid-back" "Indigo Way," Christa remains vocal about her dried-up sex life but only in Trip's absence. She does spare him that indignity. In weak moments, I've been tempted to answer her intimacies with some of my own, to open up about my suspicions of Beth and Paul, but this will make me further indebted to Christa, dependent on her to guard my shameful secret, the touchstone to rage I'd much rather not give voice to, especially around Evan.

Plus she's been pissing me off. To his face, she regards Trip with contempt disguised as *just kidding*, rolling her eyes, calling him "Gomer" and "Goober." Trip shrugs everything off with an empty laugh quite unlike his resplendent guffaw of yore. He affects being consumed by his work, unaffected by her disrespect, but I don't believe him.

Another benefit of being unmedicated is heightened perception, which, while it can feed back on itself and bloom into paranoia, it can also reveal the unquiet mind of a loved one. In Trip's heavy features I recognize the pressure of depression kept at bay. Although I see more of him than I have in years, I miss him. Yet at the same time, I confess, the Lamonts' misery and drama are welcome distractions.

Spray, spray, scrub, scrub, scrub, spray.

Bring it all on. Please. The more activity, the more distraction, the more opportunities for schadenfreude with Trip and Christa, the better. I'm hoping this kitchen cleanup will keep inconvenient thoughts—images of my wife and Paul fucking, for instance—in check. Shoveling snow, taping plastic over the drafty windows, and bodyguarding my son from a psycho-tot work well, but perhaps wielding poison on primordial ooze will satisfy a need to enact malice.

If only I could scour my own ever-widening inner ooze with Clorox. I'd upend this bottle and swig away. For a med-free moment, it actually seems a grand idea. I lean back on my haunches in the middle of the kitchen, my head spinning dreamlike, and consider. Wonder what bleach tastes like. Just a tiny sip.

A "someone's walking over your grave" shiver passes through my body.

What the fuck is wrong with you? I ask myself, suddenly stiff with realization. *Get your shit together.*

I rise from the floor, unsteady on my feet, as if drunk, chemical burn in my throat. I grip the countertop as blood reaches my brain. And there's Evan, hovering in my peripheral vision, a man behind him. Trip? Are they back already? I rip the respirator from my face and toss it to the countertop.

No . . . it's just . . . phantoms. Welsh ghosts, the kind you only see in the corner of your eye, but you look and they vanish.

Another caustic breath and I'm back to work on the edges of the breakfast nook. Fuck the respirator, which digs into my flesh anyway. Under the kitchen table, I'm a kid in a fort, hiding in the half-light. Lego pieces litter the tiles. Toss them into the living room, and *spray, spray, spray.*

The Legos are little touchstones to newly raw emotions for my son, for my own childhood, and I'm missing Evan as if he's been gone for months, not hours. The whole "giving Evan what I never had" impulse has morphed from sweet possibility to ill-thought-out, selfish fantasy. How could I do that? Saddle him with the co-responsibility to redeem something in my life?

A sob lurches from my gut. Fat tears gush from me, stream down my face, *plop, plop, plop* on the grime. The Clorox bottle rolls away, nestles against a wayward magenta Sharpie. My stomach heaves, half-digested coffee and bile bubbling up. I'm crying, full-on, for the first time in years, filling the kitchen with gulping breaths.

From far away, the gummed-up gears of my rationalization machinery creak, and out seeps a sad old man version of my voice, perhaps my father. I don't know. Several people, a composite character, like in a dream.

"She was grief-stricken, sonny. Drunk. Likely a toot of coke burning the back of her throat, no doubt offered by coke-enthusiast Paul. And damn, did Beth love that stuff back in the gravy-train days. You remember, yes you do. That simple double-snort giving her temporary immortality, immunity, not to mention blind lustiness—key word: *blind*—an evening's worth of time travel back to her single years, no strings attached, a promise of relief for a few hours, a narrowing of focus to the now. People say they want it, the 'power of now' and all that, but they never consider that once you're there, untied to the past or future, you may surprise yourself, meet a new version of yourself, an uncaged, insatiable Id. You're free of pain, sure, but also responsibility. No worrying about bringing home the bacon, no oppressive sense of duty—to Billy, to you, to the kid, to herself, even. Sounds good, right?

"Truth is, monogamy is *unnatural*. Face it. You know it already. Just face it. After fourteen years of the same old, same old, she wanted some new cock, some rock star cock, rock star cock that wanted her. She wanted to fuck someone successful, someone flush, someone whose failures didn't remind her of her own failures.

"She loves you and all, but she needed someone who hasn't cleaned the tiles after her food poisoning, hasn't watched her vagina accommodate a baby's head. That's what she needed, in that moment, to get past the pain. And you, with all your baggage, all your knowledge, could not give that, then or ever. And you know, sonny, his rock star fuck style, likely Viagra and cocaine enhanced, no doubt uncorked the new lustiness you've been enjoying these last three months."

Another voice, closer, louder, younger, says: "Fuck that. Fuck trying to understand. What are you going to *do*? He's coming here tonight, to enjoy your hospitality, maybe pinch your wife's ass when you're not looking. *What are you going to do?*"

"Don't do anything," the older voice says. "You'll ruin this great connection you and Beth have. She's still grieving, and you're there for her. And of course, there's Evan . . . Your main job is to give him what you never had: stability. Bringing this to a head will do damage."

"Fuck that. *What are you going to do?*"

"Shut up," I say.

The sobs slack off. I shudder. I haven't cried since Evan was a toddler, since pre-Zoloft days, since I lost him in the park. Two years ago. I should've cried before now.

Wet, heavy sigh. I am as wrung out and poisoned as my *Toy Story* pajama rag. I breathe deep and savor the sharp funk of dying mold spores and Clorox mist, freeing me from the racket of my mind. Mold calls. Back to the mold. Thank you mold, my worthy and all-encompassing adversary.

I grab the spray bottle and crawl from under the table, stagger to the trash can, toss the *Toy Story* pajama rag away, and tear Evan's pajama top in half to create a couple more.

Ripping the cloth reminds me of Beth recently ruining a few of my shirts, laughing as buttons flew. Fucking on the stairs, on top of the washing machine, like kids.

One shirt she'd made ribbons of, then asked me to use it to tie her to the bed posts, face down. I never would have predicted Beth McNeil, alpha female, would even entertain this position, but apparently—*what the fuck do I know?* The more I know, the less I know. The notion that I don't know her as I thought I did induces a vertigo both exciting and terrifying, like looking over the edge of a cliff and realizing you are so much higher up than you thought, so much farther to fall. I sink to the floor again, another Welsh ghost flickering in my peripheral vision. I look and there's nothing, but in my mind I see Billy.

A few weeks ago, after we'd killed a bottle of red, thrashed on the bed, and lay entangled, Beth turned away from me, coiled into a ball, and cried.

"Billy, Billy, Billy . . ." she cried.

"I miss him, too," I said.

But that's a lie. I do not miss him. I resent him, even in death. Especially in death.

~

Scrub, scrub, spray, spray, spray, scrub, scrub.

I'm muscling into the tile. A crow caws just outside the window, and when I look up, as if to answer him, pain shoots up my right forearm. I jerk my head back, crying *ah* and *fuck.* A nail head has ripped my rubber glove, and the exposed, pale meat of my hand is pink with blood, quickly going scarlet. Some former tenant, maybe Ricky Shulz himself, nailed down a piece of warped linoleum, and my weight on the soggy floor has made the nail stick up.

I've torn a gash, about a half-inch long, into the heel of my palm. Pain radiates quickly, and I'm on my feet, holding my wrist, sobered from my fume-drunk.

"Motherfucker! Motherfucker!" I stomp the slick floor.

I throw my Clorox bottle out the kitchen window at the crow, whose superior instinct tells it to flee skyward before the projectile even leaves my hand. Still, this emboldens my body, and the flicker of possible future regret snuffs out. I'm stomping the blood-splotched lino-leum, turning the kitchen into a massive bass drum, yelling *fuck* over and over, shaking the crockery in the cabinets, the appliances all rattling in concert with me, my voice distorted like an overdriven, tattered speaker cone. Words pour out in a slurry stream, punctuated by stomps.

"Fuck this place! Fuck it! I miss our old life! I hate this house! I hate this town! I hate having no money no rich fucking family I hate motherfucking Paul . . . You dare fuck my wife. I hate Beth . . . hate our fucking friends, shittiest parents ever!"

"Uh, hello?"

It's Brianna, cheeks red like the tips of her lank hair. She's standing in the kitchen door in a knit brown toque, hoodie over a belly-revealing black tee, low slung, too-big jeans, and huge blue snow boots. Her eyes are wide, disgusted, yet also mesmerized. She's seeing everything: blood on the floor, my injured hand, and who knows what kind of pure crazy on my be-slimed face. I'm unmasked. In three months, this is the first time I've felt her full attention on me. Hazel. Her eyes are hazel.

"You OK?" she says, frowning, her nose wrinkling. "I heard . . . I thought . . . Want me to get somebody? My dad?"

"No, no, no, no, no," I say, trying to smile, heaving a breath. "I'm OK, Brianna, just . . . hurt my hand trying to get rid of this mold."

"I thought I cleaned all that up." She folds her arms over her chest.

"You missed a few spots, just a few. And . . . it grows."

"Oh. Sorry. You sure you're OK? You shouldn't be breathing that stuff."

"I was using my respirator," I lie, pointing to it.

She nods, knows I'm lying. "I'm heading over to the café to get trained," she says. "I could, like, send my dad over? Or Mrs. Lamont?"

"No, no, no, no. Christa's got her hands full. Your dad, too. Big day tomorrow. You working?"

"Yeah. Waitress. Hope the rain won't . . . you know, spoil it? My dad says? If they'd let him dredge the creek? It wouldn't flood. But the DEP won't let him dredge the creek since before I was born. He's pretty pissed . . ."

There's a pause, during which echoes of my rant boomerang back into the room.

How much did she hear? What she must think.

"Uh," she lingers at the door. The raw-boned teenager in her wants to run, the child still visible in her rounded cheeks wants to help me in some way. I strip off my glove, groan, and she frowns at my hand. "That looks bad . . ."

"I'm OK. I've had worse." Hell, yeah. So badass. I reach for the paper towels, rip off about five, and wrap them around my hand.

"OK," she says brightly, relieved to be let go. She turns to leave, remembers something, turns back. "Is Paul Fairchild really coming over tonight?"

"Yes. He is."

"Is he staying?" She steps into the kitchen. "I love his music. I got all of it online for, like, nothing."

"He'll be thrilled. And yeah, he and his wife'll be staying over . . ."

She nods vaguely and hums a few bars of "Kiss My Ring."

"Catchy tune, for sure," I say. My hand is throbbing heavier now. "You know, we're playing a gig . . . a show . . ."

"I know. My dad? He told me. That's so cool." She gasps and I look down. The paper towels are heavy with blood.

"Oh, look at that," I say, tossing the towels away, tearing off more. "Of course this would happen today, of all days . . ." 'Cause, you know, I'm such a loser.

Brianna steps back outside. "I hope you feel better," she says, like I'm getting over a cold.

first aid

"**H**ey hon," Beth is saying into the answering machine. "Hello, hello, hello, hello, pick up the phone, pick up the phone . . . Damn. I was hoping to catch you. Where are you? Hm. Well, we missed the noon movie so we're gonna get some stuff at Target, like batteries and supplies, in case we lose power, and some fresh sheets for the futon, and then we'll catch the two p.m. of *Piglet's Big Fucking Movie*. Guess that puts us home around five-ish. Hope your clean-up's going OK. Thanks again for doing that. Wish you were here with us. The kids are in good form, they're adorable . . . Katie just keeps screaming *Ebba* in every store. It's hilarious. Call me when you get this, let me know if you need anything from Target, like razors or socks or anything. I know you need underwear. Love you, bye."

I'm screening Beth's call, my brain numb from beer and Clorox, my body hollowed out from crying, bleeding, and shouting. I'm on the futon couch, where Paul and Melora will sleep later, my hand throbbing in a tatty beach throw pressed into service as a guest towel. It still smells of Coppertone, the towel, from a trip to Christa's family's place in Ocean City, pre-kids, about six years ago. Christa and Beth in one-pieces, walking ahead of Trip and me on the beach, Beth jumping up and down as a pod of dolphins swam beyond the breakers. She was like a little kid, perhaps the happiest I'd ever seen her.

The blood is clotting at last. I'm polishing off my third Rolling Rock when Christa pulls into the driveway. The radio weatherman drones on.

"A flood warning is in effect for all of Ulster, Columbia, Litchfield, and Dutchess counties," the weatherman

says. "This system is moving fast from the west, bringing up to five inches of rain an hour. The combination of
this and the northerly moving storm, plus the prospect of
heavy snowmelt, will make for extremely hazardous conditions. We recommend stocking up on batteries, bottled
water, and canned goods. Power outages and flooding
are expected, especially in areas along waterways. Do
not drive across flooded roads. Those living near streams
and rivers are advised to seek higher ground . . ."

Christa stomps in from the kitchen with a brand-
new, cellophane-wrapped Red Cross first-aid kit in a
white plastic box.

"Jesus, Grant, what the fuck happened?" She's standing over me in gray paint-spattered sweatpants and a
holey, black Run DMC T-shirt, green eyes bulging, hair
tamed into a tight ponytail. She smells of sawdust.

"I'm OK, I'm OK," I say, holding up my left hand as if
she's going to strike me.

"Brianna said you fucked up your hand. What the
fuck? It smells like a public pool in here."

"It does, it does. But the mold, he hath been
vanquished."

For the second time today, a woman looks at me like
I am crazy. Because I am, a little.

"I cut myself on a nail," I say. "In the floor."

She kneels in front of me, grimaces at my hand, and
frowns. "Let's get you to the ER."

"No, no, no, no . . ."

"I'll pay for it, I don't care. Let's go. Chop, chop."

"It's not that, Christa, fuck, it's not the money! Just
leave me the fuck alone. I'm fine."

She sits back on the rug, cocks her head at me, and
nods, as if something just became clear.

"Got any more of those beers?" she asks, pushing
a sweat-darkened lock behind her ear. "I sure as fuck
could use one. Goddamn Biblical rainstorm coming

for my opening day, we just started a war, and now . . .
you . . . with your shit."

I jerk my head toward the kitchen. She goes in and
hoots at the stench and the blood on the floor. Bottle
caps hit the linoleum. Returning with two Rolling Rocks,
she hands me one and drinks deep on the other.

"Looks like *Friday the 13th* in there," she says, and
burps. "Brianna says you were bleeding like a stuck pig,
yelling, freaked me right out." She plops on the futon
next to me and cracks open the kit. "And Jesus, Grant,
you reek like Newark. And your eyes. Have you been . . .
crying?"

"Speaking of reek," I say, "you got serious BO, you
know. And ass-breath."

"Fuck you. Let me see your hand. Does it hurt? I've
got some Vicodin. I already took one this morning."

"For what?"

"Nerves."

"You pop those things like they're Tic Tacs, girl."

"You want one? Or two?" Before I can answer, she
produces a bottle from her hip pocket. "These are great
if you want to get fucked in the ass, by the way."

"Noted."

She tips two pills into her palm. I open my mouth
like a Catholic taking communion, and she places them
on my tongue, her fingernails grazing my taste buds.

"There you go, the body of Christ," she says, leaning
close as I wash them down. "Down the hatch. Now let's
see that cut." She peels away the towel and sucks in her
breath.

"It's not that bad," I say. "You suck as a nurse."

"Trip usually handles the injuries," she says, popping
a Vicodin. "Katie slices herself open on a daily basis.
He's like a battlefield medic."

Indeed, Katie's been to the ER several times already,
been stitched up twice after banging her head on

countertops while running pell-mell through the Lamont kitchen. Amazingly, no one's called Child Protective Services. Yet.

"Listen, Grant," Christa says, "you gotta get out of these clothes. I can't see straight from the smell. Really. Go take a shower, and fucking burn these clothes."

"Fine." I kick off my Timberlands and head upstairs with my beer. "You can leave, you know, get back to work," I say from the second floor. "Beth called, says they're running late, home around five. Ish. Thanks for checking on me."

"No siree," she shouts up as I drop my flannel in the hallway. "You ain't rid of me yet. Anyway, Ricky and Brianna've got it covered . . . two peas in a pod, those yokels." She's following, picking up after me, depositing my shirt and foul socks in the hallway hamper. Like a mom. She steps out of her clogs. "I got the same old battle-axe waitress that worked there when it was the Mt. Marie Diner, she's getting double pay training Brianna, making sure everything's square. Liz, that's her name. Liz. She may be a Nazi, but she's my Nazi."

I'm stepping into the claw-foot tub and under the '80s-era shower massage when I hear Christa outside the bathroom door, voice raised against the shower and the hum of the old fire hazard space heater. "And my cook is Johnny-on-the-spot, this people-pleaser bi kid Armando just graduated from CIA. Very into the locavore thing, got some great menus for the weekenders and the townies. This one's gonna fly . . . Everything OK in there?"

The water feels amazing. The Vicodin is kicking in. No more throb in my hand, plus a gentle release of a vice around my chest that I didn't even know was there. The spray caresses me with thousands of tiny fingers. A laugh bursts from me.

"Everything OK?" Christa pokes her head into the bathroom.

"Everything is so OK," I say, soaping my torso. "Want to join me?"

It's a joke. But then it isn't. I can feel Christa on the other side of the shower curtain, her presence expanding and contracting like respiration. It occurs to me she should see my newly skinnier body. My hipbones.

"You won't believe how skinny I am," I say into the steam. "I've dropped like ten pounds."

"Oh, I've noticed. You're a rail, baby."

A faint, shrill undertone hums at the edge of my mind. But warmth and giddiness overwhelm it. Little wet tongues French-kiss my bedraggled nerves. My cock stirs. Water buffets the little flap of skin on my cut, but I feel only pleasurable jolts up my wrist, into my forearm.

Christa pushes the curtain aside. She's naked from the waist up, flush spreading from her cheeks across the tops of her breasts, each with small puce-colored areolas and surrounding goosebumps. For a woozy moment I feel like the nipples are looking at me, appraising me like big, sad eyes.

She's not as fleshy as she once was, so my assumption of how she'd look naked, compiled from knowing her for over a decade, doesn't correspond to the reality. But she's beautiful, an underfed Rubens model. Her familiar face aglow atop a body that is all new information and open invitation, thumbs at the elastic of her sweatpants, eyes mischievous like a drunk teen's, checking me, asking me.

"Hey," I say, only half-surprised, swaying. My eyes roam over her. "Look at you."

"I could use a shower, too," she says, in a tightly wound version of relaxed talk. "And you need some help there." Then, in a shaky whisper, "Your call."

"You do stink," I say, dimly wondering if maybe this will ease my jealousy. I decide it will. I am receiving payment on a debt. Any second now, the jealousy that's been tormenting me will subside. "So . . . yeah, come on."

She pushes her sweats and underwear down, kicks out of them, and steps into the tub. Her entire upper body flushes a rosy pink as she squirts a dollop of Head & Shoulders on her hands.

"Head down," she says, pretending to be annoyed at my dumb-faced ogling. She grabs my head with soapy hands, forcing my chin to my chest. "We gotta get this stink out of your hair." I close my eyes, place my hands at her waist, and bow as if in tribute, which is not far off. For the first time in about thirty years or so, someone else is washing my hair. My mind swirls with memories of warm water, summer bath time, bitten fingernails massaging my scalp, the backs of my ears.

She lathers, rinses, then melds into me. My hands roam her breasts but are happier at the small of her back, the cleft of her ass.

She's running her fingers over my lower abdomen, my hipbones. "There they are . . . This is called the iliac crest, you know," she whispers, daughter-of-a-doctor-like. Her ponytail falls from its scrunchie, hair going dark in the spray. With one hand she pulls my face to her upturned lips, her tongue fat and exploratory; with the other, she reaches between my legs.

I'm hardening in her hand, and she moves against me, snaking her tongue around my ear, emitting little grunts of assent, lifting one leg onto the rim of the tub as my fingers find razor stubble and soft heat below. She presses into my hand, meeting my rhythm for a con-centrated minute. The pleasure-pain from my wounded palm spikes as the torn flesh scrapes her manicured pubic hair, her stubble. She squeezes my cock just shy of pain, shuddering, convulsing away from me like she's been scalded.

She steps out of the tub into a cloud of steam. The word *mistake* is forming in my forebrain when she grabs my hand. The bathroom is sauna-hot from the space heater.

For the first time today, King commences barking. Christa slams the yellow terrycloth-covered toilet seat down and sits on it. An echo of my son's name resonates deep in my brain, staunching the flow of blood to my half-hard-on; he has yet to get in the habit of putting the seat up, and his aim is awful, so that rank toilet seat cover, having soaked up a lot of pee, is overdue for a wash. This is how my mind is calibrated. These thoughts are like cavalry barreling down a hillside, riding on the benumbing effect of the Vicodin. Christa sees me deflating and grabs me with redoubled intent, brings me to my knees in front of her. She pulls on my drooping cock, guiding it to her.

I'm barely hard enough to penetrate, but she's very wet, and once inside, I'm stiff and freshly mindless, especially when she gasps and throws her head back, sending a wet tendril of hair into my eyes. I will be coming soon. We are dripping water everywhere, goose-pimpled, flesh-slappy and grunting, my knees going raw on the tiles. I'm just beginning to clock her distinctive grip, my mind awash with Vicodin, alcohol, and bleach, when the rubber-band-pulled-taut feeling stretches through my abdomen. I pull out and come on her belly. The toilet tank rattles, sending spare rolls of toilet paper, stacked ill-advisedly on the tank lid, to the floor.

"You didn't have to do that," she says as I fall back on my haunches.

"You never know . . ."

"No," she says, grabbing a hand towel. "I know."

My cock is shriveling as I reach for towels, wrapping one emblazoned with SpongeBob around my waist. I'm suddenly modest and compelled to apologize for the brevity of the fucking but also for not saying no, for further complicating our lives. Hands trembling, I reach inside the tub and turn the faucets off. The spray has gone cold, all the hot water in the rusty basement tank used up.

We stand to dry ourselves, our movements louder now that I've silenced the shower. Everywhere is evidence of Evan—his toys, his little robe, his Mr. Bubble, his Johnson's Baby Shampoo—all materialized alongside Beth's hairspray, gels, eau de toilette. I avert my eyes, inhale the scent of a fresh towel for distraction, and pull on my robe as Christa steps back into her sweats.

"I gotta get back," she says, in that faux-chill voice, as if we've only just had coffee.

I nod, my mouth very dry and my mind hungry for another Vicodin. My hand is throbbing, dripping blood again.

"I still think you need a stitch or two," she nods at my hand and re-scrunchies her hair. The ordinariness of her tone annoys me.

I frown and shake my head *no*.

Her eyes are full on me, pupils heavy black, the angles of her face accentuated by her hair plastered wet against her scalp. With clammy hands, she turns my face to hers, smiles sadly, and says, "This never happened. Don't get all freaky on me. I get a one-time pass. Trip and I discussed it."

"You discussed *this?*" My voice is thin and scratchy and I hate the sound of it.

"Not specifically. Not with you specifically, because . . ."

We're friends. Were friends.

"We'd discussed Chris Cornell, actually," she says with a forced laugh. "But that's never gonna happen. You and Beth never talked about a free pass? Even as a kind of joke?"

I shake my head. Somehow I always knew if Beth wanted a "free pass," it would be for Paul. No discussion necessary. She'd never mentioned her attraction to him, and I'd never pushed her to admit it. Easygoing as I was.

The only other woman with whom I'd seriously fantasized about a "free pass" was flame-haired Shirley Manson from Garbage.

"I'm not gonna tell, you know," Christa says. "It wouldn't go over well."

I nod.

"I can keep a secret. You?"

I nod.

"If he wants to fuck one of the teachers at Mt. Marie Elementary," Christa says, "I am fine with that. I've seen those trailer trash gals give him the hairy eyeball. Or he could fuck Claire Danes. That's the 'free pass' we discussed for him."

I doubt you'd be OK with either of those situations, I think.

"Don't you get a pass?" She's adjusting her bra. Her eyes are huge, verdant, eerily calm.

"I should," I say, grasping at a wavery feeling of righteousness. "I'm pretty sure she fucked Paul."

"What?" Christa says, clearly excited.

"I . . . think she fucked him when she stayed with them in January. I found a Trojan wrapper in her stuff."

"You're talking about when Billy died?"

"Yeah. When fucking Billy died."

"A Trojan wrapper?"

"Yes. It's under the bed as we speak, three months later."

Christa nods, unsurprised, which galls me. "You haven't said anything?"

"Not yet."

"She was pretty bad off, you know."

"Of course I fucking know. One reason I haven't said anything."

"It was probably nothing," she says. "Like this."

I am both insulted at her repeatedly disparaging our sex, and mildly comforted at her willing it to be nothing.

"And she seems so much better these last few weeks," Christa says, letting a bit of icy jealousy spill out. "Like her perky old rock chick self. The girl with everything. How *does* she do it?"

I grunt.

"You could just let it go," Christa says. "Like we'll be letting this go . . . Right?"

"I just have a hard time thinking that Paul, my kid's godfather, would do that, would let it happen . . . or would make it happen, or . . ."

"Maybe you should talk to Fuckface Moneybags himself," she says. "Seeing as you guys are gonna be gigging together. Or maybe you should just tell him to take that ten grand and shove it up his ass."

Easy for her to say. Now that Christa's talking money again, dialing in that entitled tone, I'm even more eager for her to leave.

"You gonna be OK for the big dinner at our place tonight?" she asks. "Trip's really doing it up. Boeuf bourguignon."

His name again. Is it always going to make me nauseous with guilt? "I don't know," I say. "I don't know. You better go."

She bends down and kisses the top of my head. "Mm," she says. "Now you smell good."

As she turns to go, she says, "It was nothing, Grant. It was fun. But it was nothing."

~

"Papa!" Evan says as he runs to the porch and leaps into my arms. "Look at the ghosty air!" He is much heavier than he was this morning, or maybe I am still a little drunk and weak with shame. His weight sends pain up my arm from my cut, which I've bandaged in gauze from Christa's kit. The pain is welcome, although maybe it's time for another pill.

In the hubbub of returning from the mall, no one's noticing the bandage. Trip and Beth pull Target bags from the Camry, each glancing to the darkening late afternoon sky, big bellied clouds bearing down on us, swallowing the mountaintops. King is still barking.

A slushy snowball hits the back of Evan's head and splatters, drenching us both. Katie is screaming with delight in the driveway. "Ebba!" she yells, then laughs. Amazing aim.

"Katie!" Evan says, furious. I want to hurl her into Stony Clove Creek, which is significantly higher than a few hours ago. But I can't even yell my usual *No, Katie.* She stands waiting for me to do it, disappointed that I'm not. But I can't.

"Ebba!"

Evan turns to look back at his friend's upraised eyebrows. His body relaxes as he offers his usual wordless forgiveness. Katie absorbs it like sunshine and bolts toward the road. Trip drops his bags in the muddy driveway and gives chase.

I fucked your wife, old friend, although just barely. I'm sorry.

"Goddammit, Katie," Beth says, smiling ruefully as she watches Trip give chase. I welcome my usual annoyance at Trip not saying *no* to his daughter, but then I think to myself, *And* you're *the model parent today?* You're *the faithful friend and husband?*

"Bad word, Mommy," Evan says, feigning exhaustion and disappointment.

Beth's dark eyes meet our son's and they share a moment of secret, quiet laughter. She shrugs and he shakes his head. This is a frequent little dance between the two of them, a role reversal game they love, and it is, at this moment, killing me.

"She's always keyed up after a movie," Trip says from the street as he scoops Katie into his arms.

"And a huge Coke," Beth adds, kissing my freshly shaven face. "Missed you," she whispers.

"Me too, Papa," Evan says. I brush ice from his collar. "Missed you."

"You smell good," Beth says. "You clean up nice. But your eyes . . . you look . . . high."

"Allergies, I think . . ."

"You've got allergies since when?"

"Maybe the Clorox."

"You wore your respirator, right?"

"Oh yeah. I'm not an idiot."

Trip gathers his bags as Katie clambers like a monkey to his shoulders, leaving muddy footprints on his coat. "You missed a great flick . . . not," he says.

"It was good," Evan says. "Piglet! Piglet!"

"I can't believe this weather," Trip says, scanning the evaporating snow.

"Heard from Paul?" Beth asks.

I shake my head, and she rolls her eyes, pretending, once again, to be put out with Paul Fairchild. Then she sees my hand and gasps.

"It's OK," I say. "I just cut it on the kitchen floor when I was cleaning. On a nail. A hidden nail. Which I fixed."

Trip comes over with Katie. She stops nuzzling him and joins in the group focus on my hand.

"That looks bad, G," Trip says. "That's a lotta gauze."

"It's OK," I say, uncomfortable with his concern. "Really, I've had worse. Christa came by, fixed me up."

"God help you," Trip says. Beth laughs.

"You sure you're OK?" she says.

"Yeah. A scar to remind me of, uh, this, uh . . . day. And she left me some Vicodin."

"Oh, lucky you," Trip says. "That really brings out the best in her."

"What's Vicodin?" Evan asks.

"Grown-up ouchy medicine," I say.

"Let me kiss it," Evan says, and I do.

"Much better," I say, my eyes burning.

"Speaking of my better half," Trip says, "I gotta go check in, make sure her new staff hasn't killed her yet."

Yes, please go. Go.

Thunder rolls over the mountains. Stray drops pelt the ground.

"Better hurry!" Beth yells after him. "Let me know if you need any help whippin' up that dinner."

Trip gives a thumbs-up as he race-walks down Shulz Way, his laughing daughter riding him. Katie grabs fistfuls of his hair like it's a horse's mane. "See you guys," he calls over his shoulder. "Whenever El Padrino decides to grace us with his presence."

"Padrino," Evan says, though he seems a little less enthused about the imminent arrival of his erstwhile hero. My Paul jealousy still burns at his name, however, squelching my tears for the moment. I conjure the image of the Trojan wrapper, the talisman that connects me to my righteous rage. But that rage, usually invigorating, is significantly watered down.

Beth sighs as she heads inside with her loot. "I am beat," she says. "I gotta lay down before they get here. We got some new videos Evan can watch while we, uh, take a nap?" She flashes me a lascivious glance.

"I'm feeling pretty beat, too," I say. "That Vicodin . . . knocked the, uh, stuffing out of me."

"Stuffing!" Evan says. Behind us, rain is falling more steady, drops fat as frogs. "You don't have stuffing, Papa! The Scarecrow's got stuffing. But he doesn't got a brain."

"Well," I say into his hair, "I've got a brain."

You wish, asshole.

"Do you . . . got courage?"

"Uh . . . yes."

Liar.

"Do you . . . got a . . . broken heart?"

"You mean a heart. Just a heart."

"No. A broken heart. Broken. If it's broken, I can kiss it, too."

Before I can say anything, he burrows his face into my shirt and kisses my chest.

chapter 16

floodgates

I'm on the porch with Evan, chewing my lip, my mind a riot, the churning Stony Clove Creek and the steady rain a perfect soundtrack. Trees on the flooded banks—mostly youngish birches—sway in the current. Rain spritzes us from the sodden, now-snowless yard.

We're waiting for Paul and Melora, due any second now. I've been out here since we got Paul's confused call from a gas station ten miles away; although we'd told him numerous times we have no cell service, he didn't process that info, got lost, and doubled back to a Citgo on Route 28, where he charmed them into letting him use their phone. Beth reiterated the directions, rolled her eyes yet again in exasperation as she laughed and said, "Fucking idiot," polished off her beer, put on the kettle, took her pound cake out to cool, and sent Evan and me to the porch to wave Paul down just in case. I'm holding our biggest umbrella, closed and pointed down like a walking stick. Beth is sure—because she knows them so well—they will have no umbrella of their own, and I'll need to run and shield them from the rain. But I've already decided not to do that.

Several possible scenarios play out in my pressure cooker mind; confrontations, reckonings, violence. But it will all need to be away from the kids. I'm the one who protects them from chaos, not the one who causes it. Ha. Should've thought of that before engaging in a bit of chaos in the bathroom today.

But it was nothing.

So maybe I'll have my reckoning with Paul when the kids go to sleep? Or maybe we just eat some boeuf bourguignon, drink the expensive wine Paul and Melora will no doubt foist on us, run through Paul's absurdly rudimentary oeuvre, and I just let everything slide, like the old medicated me. Especially now that I'm not in much of a place to judge.

I'd been wondering since Beth's "lost weekend" if a tryst of my own would make me feel better, ease some of my Paul envy, blunt my rage, maybe even help me forgive. But my sloppy afternoon fuck with Christa—*nothing, it was nothing*—hasn't helped at all. I still harbor hate for Paul, resentment for my wife, and now more loathing for myself. And, on top of it all, I'm embarrassed at being a lousy lay. Plus, I still feel owed. What will it take to pay that debt, if not that?

Every word I say comes out tinged with vague hostility. I've been trying not to speak, still blaming the Vicodin for my poor social skills. Christa left me three, and in just a couple of hours, I've taken two. My hand does not hurt.

I hear the distinctive rumble of a car crossing Stony Clove Creek Bridge, then the hiss of wheels on blacktop. My pulse quickens as a sleek black Saab, windshield wipers slapping, speeds down Shulz Way, passes the house, skids to a stop, backs up, and turns into our driveway. The engine goes dead, and the interior lights swell on, revealing the blurred shapes of Paul and Melora behind the windshield.

Evan tightens his grip. I look down at his shiny green raincoat dappled with cartoon frogs, plus matching boots and fisherman-style hat. From Target. He is quiet, tightly wound with anticipation, focused inward. He's unfazed by the weather, the dire radio reports of flooding, the strange, steamy dusk. I keep hoping the distraction of his affection—his Jedi mind trick—will work on me as before. But since he leapt into my arms, babbling about Piglet, no such luck.

I'd also thought he'd bolt into the downpour to greet Paul, but no. He'd rather be with me, which gives me a ripple of pleasure.

As Paul and Melora gather their things in the front seat, Brianna, who's been watching from the living room window of the trailer, drags King out into the rain on a leash. Shielded beneath a lavender umbrella, she walks directly to the stone wall separating our driveways. She's wearing an orange spaghetti-strap top, her bony shoulders curved inward in contrast to her eager stride. She's waited for Paul's arrival to walk the dog, and she's in luck. Paul, in a black leather pea coat and trilby hat, climbs from the car, without an umbrella, and Brianna and King hop over the wall. Melora sits in the yellowy glow of the Saab as Brianna introduces herself while holding the umbrella over Paul, who smiles and ducks under, an unlit Marlboro Light between his lips.

Evan looks to the folded umbrella at my side, then up at my face. I meet his big doe eyes, tapping the umbrella against my foot. I expect him to suggest we run into the rain to help shield them, to take their bags, to reunite, but he doesn't.

Brianna walks alongside Paul, jerking King along. The waterlogged dog hates the rain, pulls in the direction of the trailer, desperate to be inside. Brianna pays King no mind, sheltering Paul as he pulls a guitar case and a wheeled suitcase from the backseat. The roar of the rain and the rush of the creek mute their conversation. Soon, Paul, Brianna, and King are moving up the flagstones to the front porch of Shulz House.

"Hey, little man!" Paul shouts from the steps. "Hey, rock star. Looking good! Foxy parka!"

"Hey," I say. "Hi, Brianna."

Brianna nods.

"That was an adventure," Paul says. His face is swarthy from St. Croix, a little fleshier than last time I saw him. "I feel like French-kissing the ground," he says. "For real."

"Hi . . . Padrino," Evan says, reaching out his hands, hesitating, like his body remembers but his mind is no longer sure. Paul lifts him and kisses his cheek.

"Damn, you're heavy, little E!" Paul laughs. "You got so big! I can't take it! You'll be lifting me before too long. How you like this crazy weather?"

"I like it OK," Evan says. "Rain is good."

"Unless you're driving through it! I'm telling you," Paul says, taking in the farmhouse. "I like these digs. Looks like something out of *Hee Haw*. Or, you know, *Deliverance*."

Paul squeals like a pig and laughs. He looks at Stony Clove Creek. "That's no creek. Beth said you lived across from a creek. That is no creek, that's serious whitewater shit."

"Beth must've lied," I say. Once again, badmouthing Beth gives me temporary anxiety relief, like a puff on a cigarette.

"My dad says it wouldn't be so bad if they let him dredge," Brianna says. "With his backhoe? He says it never used to flood when he lived here as a kid. But the DEP . . ."

"Oh, this is exciting," Paul says. "If we lose power, we'll tell ghost stories, right little man?" He shakes Evan. "Or, what is it? Alien Man. We'll play Alien Man!"

Evan's eyes bug out. "Alien Man!"

Melora honks the horn.

"I'll go get your wife," Brianna says and runs back to the Saab. Paul glances at the umbrella at my side.

"Didn't want to deprive your fan of a chance to get up close and personal," I say. Evan reaches for me, and I take him.

After a few seconds of scanning my face, Paul frowns for a micro-second of *fuck you*, then nods. "That kid, what's her name? Betty Ann?"

"Brianna."

"Anna?"

"BRIANNA."

"Yeah. Says she downloaded all my stuff, even some old rough mixes from *Bodega Perfume*. All on Limewire!"

"What's Limewire?" Evan asks, energized by the Child Whisperer's retention of something he mentioned on the phone months ago, i.e. Alien Man. I can't decide if this is contrived on Paul's part or not.

"It's a thing where people go on the Internet," Paul says. "You know what that is, right?"

Evan nods and twists in that way that says, *put me down*. I do.

"Well, people go on the Internet and go on this Limewire and share songs," Paul says. "And I didn't know my songs were on there."

"Is 'Kiss My Ring' on there?" Evan asks.

"Apparently."

"For free," I say.

"Whatever." Paul laughs and pulls me into an embrace. "Good to see ya, Grant. You doin' OK? Seem a little tense. You ready to rock?"

I nod and break free.

"I'm ready," I lie.

Beth comes out smiling broadly, kitchen-baking scent trailing her. She's barefoot in cuffed indigo 501s and a snug red vintage cardigan over a camisole, her hair ponytailed with a silver clip I'd given her for her birthday a couple years back. Her lips are plump red, her eyes ever-so-slightly heavy-lidded, indicating she's had a nip or two of the bourbon she was pouring into the tea to make hot toddies. She is breathtaking. For a magic moment, I think about nothing but that.

"Hey good lookin'," Paul says, crash-landing me as he pecks her cheek. "Damn."

"Shut up, I'm a hag," Beth says.

Brianna and Melora step up. Melora's vampire-pale face, quite the contrast to her husband's, pokes out from a hooded black raincoat, high-end designer-y, cinched tight at the waist. She looks Xanaxed out, leaning on Brianna for support.

"Brianna," Beth says, "what the hell are you doing out?"

"I was just walking King."

Beth frowns for a millisecond at my unopened umbrella, then accepts a double cheek kiss from Melora, who then gives me the same, a big masseuse hand at my flank.

"Hey, skinny," she says.

"He does look skinny, right?" Paul says. "Like from back in the day."

"Country livin'," I say.

"Come in, come in!" Beth says. "Hot toddies all around! Swiss Miss for Evan! Thanks so much, Bree!"

"I was just walking King."

Thunder claps over Mt. Marie. King strains against the leash, knocking Brianna off balance. She relents and lets him lead her back to the trailer.

~

Paul's sipping a hot toddy while Evan shows off his Sharpie art, which papers an entire wall in the living room: stick figures, hearts, swirls, blobs, and spaceships, on paper and cardboard. My instrument cases, stacked in a corner, are similarly covered with silver Sharpie designs. Paul has acquired a muffin top of flesh at his waistline. As ever, he is dressed down in threadbare black jeans, red high tops, and a pea-green sweater with a moth hole at the elbow. The only clue to his affluence is the chain attached to his battered biker wallet and linked to a belt loop. It gleams silver.

Melora drops to the futon, tugs at her leather skirt, kicks off her flats, and points her black-stockinged toes. She's allowed herself to appear wealthy, which is refreshing. She shuts her eyes and sighs dramatically, rubbing a ceramic mug, rolling her head to loosen neck muscles.

Like Paul's, Melora's hair is dyed a deep, unnatural black, which fades into the background in New York City, but glares in the low-ceilinged, homely Shulz House, especially against her stark white, artfully mussed dress shirt.

Beth tidies the kitchen while I lean against the doorjamb, tipping more Maker's Mark into my hot toddy, watching my son and his godfather.

"This is some people running from a spaceship," Evan says. "Those are black stars."

"Is that smoke?" Paul asks, gesturing with his unlit cigarette.

"Yes! From the rocket, see."

"So, if I understand you correctly, Alien Man's rocket is going to Planet Robot, where Alien Man's wife, Alien Lady, is imprisoned by Bad Robot. Alien Lady can't get away because she lost a leg."

"A arm and a leg."

"An arm and leg, yeah, got it."

"But Alien Man is gonna get her back," Evan says. "He ex-scaped from Bad Robot's wife. She's got bad magic."

"Does Bad Robot have bad magic?"

"Yeah. He's a robot, and he used to be a man who became a robot because he fell apart from the Big Thing smashing him. Now he's 'lectric. He and Alien Man were friends. But not anymore! Not since he pee-trayed him."

A thick silence descends on the room. My heart races as I drop to a chair. Once again I wonder how my son knows things, and whether he thinks he's making this up from his own imagination or from . . . his life. Our life.

Beth stares at her mug. Beside her, Melora looks impatient, trying to follow Evan's story like it's in a foreign language. Which it sort of is.

"Who betrayed whom?" I ask before I can stop myself, my voice shaking. The bourbon is warm in my gut.

"Bad Robot pee-trayed Alien Man. They were friends. Now they anemones."

Everyone laughs a little at Evan's malapropism. No one corrects him.

"That is some trippy shit," Melora says, scanning the room. She pats the futon. "Is this where we're sleeping? Like old times."

"Yep," Beth says, rallying with the change of subject. She takes the Maker's Mark from me and tops off everyone's tea. "Welcome to *Lifestyles of the Poor and Obscure*. Just like you remember it."

"We stayed in a place in Majorca that was about the same dimensions as this room," Melora says. "Remember that, babe? Casa de something-or-other? With that amazing vino."

Paul says nothing, his sloped shoulders still as he stares at Bad Robot and Alien Man. I imagine him feeling vaguely guilty, looking at my son's drawings. I hope to hell he is. I hope a little spot of rot is opening in his gut. Hard to say. Impossible to say.

"I know you guys are pooped," Beth says, dropping to the futon and pulling at loose strands on the cover seam. "So we won't stay long at the Lamonts. And I got some Sasha work to do."

"Sashaaaaaaaa!" Evan says.

"They good landlords?" Melora asks. Before anyone can answer, she says, "Paul, babe, we should look at some property while we're up here."

Instead of answering, Paul traces the ink with his fingertips.

"Paul. Babe . . . Pablo. Hello."

He nods slowly.

"Wanna see my own room, Padrino?" Evan says, pulling Paul's sleeve. "I got my own room, I sleep in my own bed cause I'm big now. I can be Alien Man, and you can be Bad Robot."

175

Paul doesn't move.

"Paul," Melora says sharply. "Paul."

"Oh," Paul turns to Evan with a stunned look, like the boy was just beamed in. "Uh . . . yeah. Yeah, hell yeah, I'd love to see your room. Let's go." He drains his hot toddy, hands the cup to Beth, and bounds up the stairs with Evan, apparently guiltless, free of the shame that's imploding in me like a sinkhole.

"True love never dies," Melora says.

"Aren't his stories . . . amazing?" Beth asks, her voice tight. "His imagination floors me."

"I guess." Melora yawns. "You only get them 'cause you're his mom. You know my thing with kids . . . No offense."

"You're gonna adore Katie," I say. Meanness brings relief.

"Paul says she's a terror. Should I take another Xanax before we go over there?"

"She's not so bad," I say, deeply glad to know Katie Lamont, and hoping she'll be in fine form. "And how does Paul know? He hasn't met her."

"Beth keeps us posted."

"I didn't say she was a terror," Beth says.

"Whatever." Melora sighs. "Doesn't matter. Maybe Christa'll slip the rug rat a mickey. I know some parents who do that. But whatever, let's get over there and get our feast on. I haven't had any of Trip's cuisine in too long. Remember those Thanksgiving dinners he used to whip up? Jesus."

Very close thunder rattles the windowpanes. Lights flicker, the floor rumbles, and a loud snap cracks the air outside, followed by a boom. Beth, Melora, and I look at one another. Melora cackles.

"Whoa!" I hear Paul say upstairs.

"Shit!" Beth says.

The back door shakes under someone's knuckles.

"Who's that?" Beth asks, getting up.

I open the door to Ricky in a loud yellow poncho. He barrels into the kitchen.

"Everything OK?" I say. "What was that boom?"

"You guys got phone?" Ricky asks. "My phone went out. Jen's still at the library, wanted to check in with her, get her to come home. They shoulda closed already."

I pick up the cordless. It's dead.

"The grid's going down," Ricky says as Melora glides into the kitchen. Intoxication has always made Melora strangely graceful when everyone else gets clumsy.

"You must be Ricky," she says, extending her hand.

He shakes it. "That your Saab?" he asks.

She nods.

"It do OK in the rain?"

"I guess. I don't drive. Native New Yorker."

"Surprised you guys came up, what with the storm and all."

"We're adventurers!" Melora's eyes go wide, actress-y.

"Good for you," Ricky says.

"They overstate that stuff, though, right Ricky?" Melora says, stealing a quick glance at Beth. "The left wing media?" Clearly, Beth has told her Ricky's a Libertarian.

"Absolutely," Ricky says. "I don't know how many times I've heard the weatherman forecast doom just so folks'll buy up all the batteries and stay tuned so his advertisers'll be happy."

"Your daughter was so kind to escort us," Melora says. "Beth, shouldn't we get Ricky a hot toddy?"

"Nope, no thanks," Ricky says. "Hey, Grant, how's that hand? Brianna told me about it. Sounded bad."

"Hey," says Melora. "you've got gauze on your hand."

"You noticed!" I say. "It's OK, Ricky, thanks for asking."

"What happened?" Melora asks.

"I was doing housework. You know, living the dream."

Paul and Evan bound down the stairs and into the kitchen. "What was that boom?" Paul asks.

"Boulders," Ricky says.

"Boulders?" Beth gasps.

"Yep. Boulders. The creek's so strong now it's moving boulders like they're pebbles. Sounds like thunder but louder. Shook my trailer. Took down a tree on the bank right across the street there. You hear that crack? That doesn't happen all that often . . . Hey, you're that Paul guy."

"Nice to meet you." Paul shakes Ricky's hand and grins wide, baring his tooth gap. "You must be Ricky Shulz."

Ricky is dazzled, despite himself.

"That a L.L. Bean, that poncho?" Paul asks.

"Uh, yeah, my, uh, wife, she got it for me . . . about twenty years ago, if you can believe that."

"Smart woman. I gotta get one. Melora, babe, that's what I want for Christmas, a poncho like that."

"It does keep me dry," Ricky says.

"Ricky," I ask, in part to distract from his budding man-crush, "you think it's safe to walk over to Trip and Christa's? Ricky?"

"In the words of the immortal Han Solo," Paul says, "'Never tell me the odds!' Right, Ricky?"

Ricky laughs, which is a rare thing. His coffee breath closes the space between us.

"We could just drive," Beth says.

"A couple hundred yards?" Paul laughs. "What kinda country folk are you, anyway?"

"I do not want to get back in that car," Melora groans.

I'm wanting very much for Ricky to advise us to just not go. It's too dangerous. The road's going to get washed out, etc. Please say it.

"Oh, I'm sure it's OK," Ricky says. "You guys being *adventurers* and all. Like Paul here says, it's just a couple hundred yards. I know they got a big to-do planned. Christa talked about it all day, Jesus she never *stopped* talking about it. Wanna know what you're having, down to the last detail? I can tell you."

"That's our Christa," Paul says. "She means well."

"Anyway," Ricky says, conspiratorially, "I'd hustle if I were you."

"Hell yeah," Paul says. "Into the breach!"

"Can we borrow an umbrella?" Melora asks Beth. Beth gives me a weak grin.

~

Thankfully, when we all step onto the front porch and gaze as one into darkening twilight, the rain has slacked off from a dark curtain to a drizzle. The creek roars on, parallel to Shulz Way, more ominous now that we can't see it. Paul lights up the Marlboro he's been sucking on. Melora carries a canvas tote in which several bottles of wine clank. Beth is holding her still-warm pound cake, shielded with a plastic bag, against her chest. Evan clings to her raincoat. My feet drag as my head swims with Vicodin and liquor.

The air is thick with pressure. Ricky drives off to the library to get his wife as we all begin the walk to the Victorian, sheltered under three umbrellas, lighting the blacktop with flashlights, stepping over broken tree limbs, skittering frogs, and brimming potholes.

Whiskey-mouthed Beth huddles against me beneath our umbrella, while Paul and Melora grasp each other beneath theirs. Evan has his own, a green one that matches his Target ensemble. He is delighted with the frogs in the street, while I'm thinking about a Biblical plague, wondering if locusts are due tomorrow, wondering if this augurs comeuppance for all.

Just before we get to the Lamonts, Paul says, "I wanna check that river out." He leaves Melora, tosses his cig away, and walks to the shoulder of the road, where a rusty guardrail protects passersby from an incline that normally leads about ten feet down to the edge of the creek. But now the water reaches the very edge of the road, splashing against the lip of the cracked pavement.

"What the fuck, Paul?" Melora calls. "Don't . . . just don't!"

"I'm fine, babe, don't fret," he says, his voice faint against the water.

"Not a good idea, Paul!" I yell as Beth gasps. I move in his direction, but she clasps me tight, almost drops her cake, and roots her feet to the pavement.

Evan stands still and silent beneath his frog umbrella, his flashlight beam pointing toward Paul, illuminating the raindrops.

I shine my light on Paul. He's leaning over the rail, one foot off the ground, his fingertips in the current.

I break free of Beth and rush to him. The women are screaming, but I can't make out their words over the roar of the creek.

I grab Paul's coat and jerk him away. His trilby falls off his head and disappears into the black water. His flashlight tumbles to the road, cracks, sputters out. I pull him back to our group.

"What the fuck is wrong with you?" I yell. "You can't do that kind of shit in front of a kid!"

"Hey! Hey, hey, hey!" Paul says, twisting away from me. "Fucking let go of me, Grant."

I do.

"My hat, my favorite, favorite hat," Paul says, his voice pitched high, adrenalized. "You're buying me a new one, Grant, you are buying me a new hat."

"Jesus, Paul," Melora says, a voice in the dark, thick with disgust.

"Your hat?" I shine my light in his face like a cop. "Who gives a shit about your hat? You fall in that water, you die."

"Fuck you." Paul is half-laughing with surprise at me. He cleaves to Melora, whose face is hidden beneath her hood. "Take that goddamn light off me, Officer Friendly," he says. "I was fine. I was. I was totally fine."

"Chill out, boys," Beth says. "That was pretty stupid, Paul."

"And you know stupid, right Beth? Grant, take that fucking light off my face, OK?"

Beth tightens against me. I leave my flashlight beam on Paul's face.

"OK," I say. "Next time I just let you drown, how's that?"

"I was fine, big daddy, I wasn't gonna fall. Light, please."

"Setting a fine example—again—for your godson, huh?"

"Do as I say, not as I do, Little E!" Paul says.

No response. Only the roar of the water.

"Oh my God," Beth says. "Where's Evan?"

I shine my flashlight in the space where he was. He's gone. I shine it into the birches on the roadside opposite the creek. Nothing. Toward the creek itself. Only churning black.

"No," I say. It's been two years, but suddenly The Junkie Incident is happening anew. "Not again, not again, not again."

Beth drops her cake to the pavement and runs to the guardrail, umbrella in hand, screeching Evan's name into the dark. She is louder than I've ever heard her, primal and chilling. I run past Paul and Melora, toward the Lamonts' house, calling Evan, Evan, Evan! The glow of Trip and Christa's high-intensity motion-sensitive floodlight burns behind some trees.

The rain intensifies, back to heavy, thick sheets, drenching me, like a mighty hand pushing down. The roar of the creek rises.

"Evan!" I'm running up the slight slope of the Lamonts' lawn.

"I'm here, Papa!" Evan calls. He's about twenty feet from me, standing in the hazy light on their porch, but I can barely hear him.

"Stay there!" I run back to my wife, who is teetering at the water's edge, shining our flashlight over trees in the current, trembling and screaming. Paul and Melora are fumbling in the dark at the other side of the road, calling Evan's name into the swaying birches.

"I found him, I found him!" I'm yelling as I run, and Beth's light turns toward me. Then she's in my arms.

"I found him," I say, breathless. "He's OK, he's at their porch. Waiting. Guess he got tired of our bullshit."

"Smart kid," Paul says behind me.

"Smarter than you think," I say. "Smarter than you . . . that's for sure. . . . Asshole."

"My fucking cake," Beth says, both angry and giddy with relief. "Goddamn you, Paul."

"Oh, right," Paul says. Then he sings a line from Nirvana's "All Apologies": "Everything's my fault."

I nod, but no one sees me.

chapter 17

dinner with friends

"Come in, come in, come in!" Trip says. He's in regulation khakis, Oxford button-down, and a long white apron emblazoned with the face of Justin Wilson, aka the Cookin' Cajun. "Looks like your umbrellas weren't much help. Chris, throw me down some towels!"

"Hey there, Trip," Paul says. "Looking lean and mean, sexy as ever. Smells amazing in here."

"It's the George Hamilton of rock!" Trip says. "Hey, there's this new invention, called sunscreen?"

"Eat yer heart out . . ."

Melora goes in for the overlong hug with Trip. "I love, love, love this house," she says. "This is what we need to get, babe, an old Victorian with good bones. We could weekend up here."

"Sounds like a plan," Trip says, fake smile crinkling his sad eyes. "Hope you guys are hungry. Chris! Towels!"

"Ebba!"

"Good God," Melora says. "What was that?"

"That's my kid," Trip says. "She loves Evan. How you doin', big guy?"

"OK," Evan says, a little shaky from our walk over.

"I dropped my pound cake in the street, Trip," Beth says. "I am so sorry."

Somehow, we've all tacitly agreed not to discuss the walk over. Thankfully, Trip's not interested.

"Bummer," he says. "But not a problem. We've got some kind of sorbet, some Entenmann's something or other, some whipped cream. Some critter will be very happy to find that cake, I'd wager."

"I want to see a critter before we leave," Melora says, taking in the foyer, the dining room set off to one side, the quaint living room to the other. "Don't you, babe? Want to see a critter?"

"Careful what you ask for," Trip says. "Hey, speaking of critters . . . Chris!"

"Ebba!" Katie is bumping down the steps on her bottom, Christa behind her with some folded towels, clomping in heels she's not accustomed to.

"Look what the cat dragged in!" she says, eyes landing on all but me. She's poured herself into a little black dress.

Katie plows through to Evan and wraps him in a hug, lifting him off the ground an inch or so as Christa doles out towels to everyone. Katie musses Evan's drenched hair with her little ravioli hands, screaming with glee as Beth covers and towel-dries his head. Evan laughs, which makes me want to find a bathroom so I can cry. Christa kisses everyone on the cheek, including me, cooing tinny pleasantries, thanking Paul and Melora for the wine, the labels of which she inspects like an expert.

Paul kneels down to Katie, whose face immediately darkens. He squints into the thick tangle of black hair over her eyes. As ever, a diaper rides up from her jeans and over her belly button. She's bursting out of a black CBGB T-shirt, frowning in Paul's face.

"Wow," he says, impressed. "You're all rock star."

Amazingly, Katie smiles through her willed frown and says, "Grrr."

Melora flattens herself against the foyer wall, rattling a mirror. Katie senses fear, extinguishes her grin, and jerks her dark gaze Melora's way. Melora shudders. Christa barely hides a smirk.

"Paul, Melora," Trip says. "This is our daughter, Katie. She'll be three in two weeks."

"Big girl!" Evan smiles.

"Ebba!" Katie says. She rattles off some staccato Chinglish gibberish.

"She wants to show me something upstairs," Evan says.

"That's what she said?" Christa says.

"Perfect," Trip says. "I gotta check on the boeuf and crack open this wine, but then I got a surprise for everyone, especially you, Grant."

My heart jumps to my throat.

"You've gone gay," Paul says to Trip.

"Very mature, Paul," Trip says as he heads back to the kitchen. "All of you into the living room, pronto. Chris, hon, get some glasses, pretty, pretty please."

Christa sighs dramatically and follows Trip into the kitchen, relieving me from having to not look at her. She seems completely unfazed by our afternoon indiscretion, which is both relieving and annoying.

I wonder if Trip somehow knows, if he will be killing his wife with one of his high-end blades, then returning from the kitchen with a gun, with which he will kill me.

Thunder booms again, and the lights flicker as Katie leads Evan upstairs. They laugh at the rattling windows and yell *BOOM* to each other. Paul watches them longingly, then follows his fellow adults to the living room, where the flat screen sleeps and Trip's bedding remains in a pile behind the couch. The stereo is on low, an LP of Stevie Wonder's *Songs in the Key of Life* humming along. "Sir Duke," one of the most joyous songs ever, rises defiantly through my dark thoughts and the dismal weather.

> *You can feel it all over*
> *You can feel it all over people*

"My favorite Stevie album," Melora says, shaking her boyish hips a little before reclining on the couch.

All agree it's a classic from a classic period. It reminds me of my childhood, of walking the streets of my North

Carolina neighborhood in the summer dusk, dumping quarters foraged from my mom's change bowl—a ceramic thing I made at camp—into the Kiss pinball machine at the Quickee Mart. "Sir Duke" spills from car radios, apartments, front porches. White folks, black folks, Cuban immigrants, everybody loves the song. Mom is spending the night at her boyfriend's again. I'm glad about that. A reprieve from her tempestuousness and impatience, a break from walking on eggshells, placating her anger at me, at the world, at the alcoholic boyfriend/replacement for my dad. She's left me five dollars to go to Burger King, which I will instead spend on pinball and Pixy Stix. I'll cook some Campbell's Chicken & Stars later and watch *The Midnight Special*.

Paul hoots, stirring me from my reverie.

"I would love to be able to make an album like this," he says, uncharacteristically modest. "Someday, maybe."

Yeah, right, I think, enjoying the exquisite bob-and-weave of Nathan Watts' bassline. *This is art. Not a jingle.*

Christa comes in with glasses for all. She pours the wine, sniffing and swirling it.

"You a sommelier, now, Christa?" Melora asks. "Take a correspondence course or some such? You should meet this sommelier we know, lives in our building. He's the real deal. He recommended these vintages. Pricey stuff. But you can probably tell, right?"

Before Christa can respond, Trip comes out of the kitchen carrying a shoebox overflowing with papers. He grimaces at his wife for a nanosecond and holds out a glass, which she fills, smiling meanly.

"Turn that off, will you?" he says, gesturing to the stereo. She does, with a cartoonish pout.

Trip takes no notice of her and swigs deep as he sits in a wingback chair, the box on his lap. He steals a quick, nervous glance at me and unfolds a dog-eared, multi-paged document.

"Everybody comfy?" he asks.

Everyone insists they are and please get on with whatever.

"Check this out," he says, breathing deep.

From: Grant Kelly, 214 Avenue C Apt. 3C, NYC, 10009, USA. To: Trip Lamont, c/o Chateau de la Napoule, Avenue Henry-Clews, 06210 Mandelieu-la-Napoule, France. June 22, 1989.

"Oh, I know what this is," I say, relieved not to be found out but afraid of being consumed with shame.

"I dug 'em out," Trip says, smiling. "Some of our letters. Ye Olden Tymes. I copied a couple of mine before I sent 'em to you back in the day. Made carbons, actually, like Kerouac. They didn't have a copier at the chateau. It was like being in a time warp."

"Letters?" Melora says. "You guys wrote letters?"

"Oh yeah," Trip says as I squirm. "I got into this writing workshop at this incredible chateau near Cannes in eighty-nine. Chateau de la Napoule. *Oui, oui.* Grant here badgered me to apply. Got a scholarship, actually."

"I remember you telling me about this, honey," Beth says. "You guys had a nice little correspondence there for a while."

I nod.

"Pre-email, pre-wives," Trip says.

"Oh yes, it's our fault they stopped," Christa says.

"Thirteen years you've kept these?" Beth asks.

"I'll never throw 'em out," Trip says. "Ever."

"Well go on, go on," Paul says. "I do loves me a good letter."

"You've never written me a single letter, babe," Melora says to Paul.

"Just an album's worth of songs," Paul says, feigning hurt. "But that doesn't count, I guess . . . Poor li'l Melly, no one gives her enough attention. Just a Barney's charge card. Give her a sec, she'll bitch about that."

"No one knows what those songs are about," Melora says. "The way you write, who the fuck could tell? They could be about anything."

Their bickering gives Trip energy. "Grant here was the letter-writing king," he says, perking up.

"Yeah." Beth grins. "I've gotten a few. I knew exactly what they were about. Pretty steamy."

"You're making me ill," Christa says. "Go, Pops."

"OK," Trip says. "Here goes:

> *Trip, Trip, Trip . . . Hope the workshop's*
> *fun. As promised, I'll bring you up to*
> *speed on some cool stuff.*
>
> *I'm sitting here at Scenic Ave. C, killing a*
> *Foster's. Salsa in the street, Dominican*
> *kids running around shirtless, scream-*
> *ing "fuck you!" Hot as hell, I am stewing*
> *in my own juices, taking a break from*
> *listening and listening and listening to*
> *mix 1, mix 2, mix 3 of "What the Funk Is*
> *Up?" Very Chili Peppers, and Hugh, our*
> *guy from Polygram, is talking like—I shit*
> *you not—"This is the single, this will rule*
> *the airwaves next summer, first college,*
> *then crossover, we've got 100 grand to*
> *spend on promo and this is the one" etc.,*
> *but at this point I don't have a fucking*
> *clue. It sounds to me LIKE SHIT, really*
> *tinny, my bass wimpy but my bad atti-*
> *tude may be because I've heard WTFIU*
> *so much and Tristan rejected a couple*
> *verses I wrote. No sharing. But I digress.*
> *Tristan and Stan say next album for my*

song, and Hugh defers to them, the Len-
non-McCartney—HA—of Stereoblind.

"Whatever happened to that asshole?" Paul asks.
"Tristan. What a dick."

"They lost their deal in the post-*Nevermind* blood-
letting," I say. "They tried to 'grunge up,' let their mullets
grow out, stopped washing, got flannels. Nobody bought
it. This was a couple years after I quit. Tristan hit bottom,
cleaned up, got married, works in in human resources
for some company in New Jersey. Terribly happy."

"Best part's coming up," Trip says, draining the wine.
Droplets fall on his stubbly chin and Justin Wilson's face.
"So glad you documented this time, Grant. Check this
out:

> *Yes, Electric Lady Studio is amazing,*
> *ultimate pinch-me-so-I-know-I'm-not-*
> *dreaming experience. It's underground*
> *so it does feel like a rock n' roll batcave*
> *complete with computers—EGAD—and*
> *some digital stuff . . . producer Clive says*
> *computers are future of recording. God*
> *I hope not . . . haven't heard anything*
> *digital yet that I like. Gimmie that warm*
> *analog mush over clarity. Words to live*
> *by.*
>
> *Other words to live by, especially for you,*
> *as you are no doubt getting laid a lot:*
> *keep them condoms close at hand.*

Christa gasps. "No," she says. "No. You're not going
to read about condoms. Not condoms. About fucking
AIDS? Beth, you don't want to hear this, do you?"

"Actually," Beth says serenely, "I do."

"Me, too," says Melora.

"Me three," says Paul.

Trip glares at his wife, draws a deep breath, then carries on, louder.

> *Yet another old friend—Chuck, you don't*
> *know him, bartender at King Tut's Wah*
> *Wah Hut—has AIDS.*

Smiling Chuck. Such a sweetheart, so funny. The first of many casualties from my circle. I haven't thought of him in years. Like a surrogate big brother to me when I first moved from North Carolina to the East Village. Gave me a biker jacket he'd bought on the street. Wasn't his style, he'd said. Fit me perfectly. I sigh, and Trip stops, raises his eyes to me. I nod and he continues.

> *He's in Beth Israel with pneumonia and*
> *those awful spots on his skin. But he*
> *was still all smiles when I visited, which*
> *I can't grasp. Remember when all we*
> *cared about was herpes? Almost seems*
> *quaint now. Almost. Be careful.*

"Ha!" Christa says.

We all flinch from Christa's fake laugh. A heavy silence descends. Paul gets up and refills Trip's glass, emptying the bottle. Trip drinks. My breath is shallow, like my lungs are filled with fluid. Evan's and Katie's footsteps resound just above us, carefree, heartbreaking. Thunder booms again, closer.

Trip continues, laboring over the jocular tone of my long-ago letter, slurring from the wine.

> *Speaking of condoms and whatnot I met*
> *a girl if you must know.*

"Oh shit!" Beth says.

> *She's 28 but looks like she's in college. Her*
> *name's Beth McNeil and she's really, really,*
> *really beautiful . . . kind of a punk rock*
> *Diana Rigg, with the eyeliner and black*
> *pegged jeans—zipper in the back!—and*
> *Chelsea boots and . . . a great ass, like the*
> *best I've ever seen, a 10 out of 10.*

"Enough!" Beth says, her face darkening. But she is smiling.

"No way," Trip says. "My house, my rules."

Christa seems ready to weigh in on that supposed fact but refrains.

"Go on, go on," Paul says. "I'm loving this. Captive audience, always a good thing."

Trip steals a quick, appreciative look at Beth and continues.

> *She's also got a Lauren Hutton gap*
> *in her front teeth, which I do like very*
> *much. We met at CB's. I step outside for*
> *a bit of Bowery air, and there's this girl*
> *leaning up against the streetlight, bum-*
> *ming a cig from Tristan. (We were there*
> *to see the Spin Doctors.) It was hot n'*
> *sticky (the weather, ha) but she was*
> *sporting this blue bolero-type jacket over*
> *a Ramones T and those slim trousers,*
> *boots, etc. SHE should've been onstage.*
> *Beer tucked under her jacket. I hear her*
> *laugh, and it made my heart swell like*
> *the Grinch when he hears the Whos of*
> *Whoville on Christmas Day. Kind of a*
> *Kathleen Turner thing, that laugh.*

Melora does a bad imitation of Beth's distinctive, grosgrain laugh.

"Fuck you, Mel," Beth mutters. Melora smirks.

"But wait, there's more," Trip says.

Beth groans.

> *She holds out her hand, says, "I know*
> *you, you are hot shit on a stick. I saw you*
> *guys play at the Cat Club, Easter week-*
> *end. Great show."*

"That's not what I said," Beth says. "I said you were hot shit, but not on a stick."

"Jesus, who cares?" Paul says. "Carry on, my wayward son."

Trip smiles.

> *Tristan introduces her. Beth McNeil,*
> *freelance publicist, here checking out*
> *the Spin Doctors, who have the Golden*
> *Buzz going. She touches my Trash &*
> *Vaudeville shirt for a few seconds and*
> *asks where I got it and is it dry clean*
> *only? But these are just place-holder*
> *words, because I swear she's looking*
> *at me and those peepers are not saying*
> *anything at all about my shirt.*

"I remember that shirt," Beth says softly.

> *I love the way she says my name. Kind*
> *of hoarse. She was borderline rude to*
> *Tristan, not even looking at him while*
> *she and I chatted about—get this—early*
> *'70s-era AM radio pop singles and K-tel*
> *records and variety shows and The*

Bionic Woman. *He huffed and threw his cig butt at our feet and stomped off. That was a first—a lady preferring me to the mighty Mr. T.*

That's it for now. My hand is killing me and I hope you can read all of this. I'm happy for you and can't wait to read your novel, can't wait to pick up that hardback at St Mark's Books and see your mug on the back flap:

Booker Prize-winner Trip Lamont's work has appeared in The Village Voice, The New Yorker, *and* Harper's. *He was selected as one of* Time *magazine's 1990's Fifty Most Influential Writers under 40.*

Trip stops and drinks.

By the time you get this, you'll be getting ready to head home and I'll be getting ready to hit the road—we've got some dates opening for Faith No More in California, where this KROQ DJ plays the hell out of our EP, bless his funky soul. FNM are on Slash and they've got a new singer and they're huge on the West Coast, so that should be fun.

Hoping you and I can get at least a little quality time before I split. Can't wait to hear how the rest of the workshop goes. Wanna play you some of my new tunes and sit here in this very tenement, where it all began, sharing a brew or three as everythang expands before our very eyes from Scenic Ave. C to a big, bad, wonderful, lusty, rock-and-roll, story-filled world, which apparently awaits us with open arms and legs . . . till then I remain yers, Grant.

Trip folds the letter tenderly and places it back in the box as we all sit in silence, buffeted by the familiar sounds of toddlers knocking over chairs and who knows what else, plus the whooshing of the wind and rain at the bay window. Somewhere a tree branch is whacking the siding in an irregular, increasingly loud rhythm.

Christa reaches for another bottle and corkscrews it open while Beth squeezes my hand and bites her quivering lip.

The oven timer goes off, beeping insistently. Trip sighs.

"Damn," he says. "I was gonna read a carbon of one I wrote to you."

"That's enough nostalgia, don't you think?" Christa says. "And I gotta go see what Katie's destroyed. This book I'm reading says to redirect aggression in the moment."

"*The Indigo Challenge?*" I ask, grateful for a fresh topic.

Christa laughs condescendingly. "God, no. That book's been debunked, don't you know that? How could you not know that? I'm onto *Sutras to Satisfy, Nonviolence in Parenting*. It's amazing."

She kicks off her shoes, revealing fresh raw spots on the backs of her heels, and runs upstairs as everyone heads for the dining room.

Trip presses some crinkly folded carbon copy paper in my hand. "Put it in your pocket," he whispers, his sour breath on my face. "Read it later. It's from ninety-two. Last letter I sent you. Pretty classic."

"I've got the original in a box somewhere," I say.

"'Course you do." He nods and lurches toward the kitchen. I pocket the letter and head for the dining room.

"Punk rock Diana Rigg!" Paul says as he sits between my wife and his. "That's pretty choice, Grant."

~

We're passing rolls when Ricky's headlights shine through the bay window. In seconds he's at the door and Christa's letting him in. The wind has picked up, blowing twigs and rain into the foyer. Katie and Evan, enjoying chicken nuggets at a kiddie table next to us, gasp in unison as Ricky stomps in and stands dripping in the dining room doorway.

"I barely made it over," he says breathlessly. "That damn creek may take out the bridge. Firemen are on the other side, too scared to come across, told me to tell you to stay put."

"This is awesome!" Paul says.

Katie yells something that sounds a little like "awesome."

"We're not going anywhere," Christa says. "We'll have a sleepover if we have to. Where's Jen?"

"She's in the truck there, pissed off I drove over. She was gonna stay at the library all night. That's high ground."

"Are we high ground?" Beth asks.

Ricky pauses. "More or less," he says. "When this house was in my family, my great aunt said the creek never breached the banks onto the road. They had this place for three generations, from when it was built—"

The lights flicker.

"You all got supplies for when the power goes out?" Ricky asks. "That generator I hooked up all full? Floodlights working?"

"Got it covered, my friend!" Trip says from the table. He is officially drunk. He jabs his fork into the meat on his plate and holds it up like a Viking. "Ricky, hey, Ricky man, you want some boeuf bourguignon?"

"Yeah, my chef Armando picked this beef up locally," Christa says. "We're gonna serve it at Katie's Café!"

At the mention of Armando's name, Trip's face falls.

"Uh, no thanks . . ." Ricky says. "Gotta get home, check on Brianna and King. Batten down the hatches. You guys be careful when you head back over to the house, which I'd do soon if I was you. Road may wash out, too."

"Guess the weatherman wasn't pulling our leg after all, huh Ricky?" Melora says from the table.

"Hell yes he was," Ricky says from the door. "This is actually a lot worse than he said it would be. Because of all the sediment in the damn creek bed—"

The truck horn honks, and Ricky bolts into the rain.

Christa shuts the front door and sits back down, across from me. "Knew I shoulda upped my dose," she says. "Pass the potatoes, please, and a Xanax and an extra Effexor if you got one."

Trip laughs dryly and shakes his head just as the lights go out, plunging us into blackness.

Katie screams. It's a chilling, monkey-house-at-the-zoo cry. I've heard her scream a lot in the past three months, but never like this, never from *that* place.

"Katie, for fuck's sake!" Christa says in the darkness. "This is the only thing she's still afraid of. The dark. Like, the *only* thing."

Katie screams again. The hairs in my ears tremble.

"Oh God, kid," Christa says, her voice tinged with fear. "Stop."

Evan is silent. The music—Chet Baker's version of "Embraceable You" on LP—has abruptly stopped. The humming in the walls, of which I'd previously been unaware, ceases. The storm's volume rises in the new quiet. Beth's hand lands on my shoulder.

perfectly broken

"Shit," Melora says. "I knew this was a mistake. Knew it, knew it."

Paul flicks on his Bic. Seated on his lap, clinging to him, is whimpering Katie. He's humming what sounds like Sonic Youth's "Cool Thing" into her hair.

Christa grabs a hurricane lantern from a cabinet. She holds it next to the Bic and Paul lights it, sending a warm halo and the scent of kerosene around the room.

Evan makes his way under the table and into his mom's lap. She's crying softly.

"It's OK, Mommy," he says, wiping tears from her face. "We're gonna be OK."

Trip snatches Paul's lighter and uses it to light his way as he stumbles into the kitchen. Doors slam as pots and pans cascade to the floor.

"Goddamn him," Christa says. Her voice is louder, fuller in the dancing shadows. "It's no wonder . . ."

"You OK in there?" I call.

"FINE," Trip says angrily. "I'm good. Generator switch is in here somewhere. Where the fuck is it?"

"No wonder what, Chris?" Melora says. "Do tell."

Christa draws a breath. "So," she says, staring at the slab of meat on her plate. "No kids for you guys, huh? Too bad. Paul there's a natural . . ."

Melora's eyes are hidden in shadow, but her body tenses into a kind of frown. "Well I got *pregnant* a few times, but that's the easy part, right?"

"There's kids here, you guys," Beth says.

And very nervous adults, I think.

"Evan there's my kid, sort of," Paul says, stroking Katie's hair. Evan says nothing.

Christa laughs. "Really? That wouldn't surprise me, actually."

"Ha," Paul says. "That's not exactly what I meant, you know . . ."

"Christa," I say, squelching an impulse to ball up my cloth napkin and shove it in her mouth.

197

"I'm not saying anything"—she laughs thickly—"but . . . you all know . . . what I'm *saying*. No shame in spicing things up, right? For old married couples."

"How 'bout another glass of wine, Christa?" Melora says icily. "Wash down some more meds."

"Kids present!" I say, my voice much louder than I intended. I'm using my kid as a human shield, for fuck's sake.

Christa's face prunes up in disdain. "You must get a free pass, huh Melora?" she says, like she's conducting a sadistic séance, and a malevolent, drunken spirit has overtaken her. She shoots a conspiratorial look my way. "If anyone deserves a free pass, it's the wife of a rich rock star!"

"We should go," Beth says.

"I'm not a rock star," Paul says. He always says that. This time, instead of annoying me, it sparks a welcome rage.

More rattling and cursing in the kitchen.

". . . or the wife of a"—Christa drops her voice to a stage whisper—"failed novelist. I get a free pass. Free pass! Where's Chris Cornell? Free pass!"

Beth stands, Evan grasping her neck, his face in her shirt. She gazes into the black of the foyer. "Goddamn it, Trip," she shouts, "we need light! Like now!"

"Or the husband of a . . . unfaithful publicist," Christa drones on. "*Especially* the husband of an unfaithful publicist . . . He deserves a free pass after all the shit he's . . . Look. Let's be honest here. All is fair . . . and all that. No big whoop. It's nothing."

Beth stiffens.

"Yeah, Beth," Christa says. "Bathroom quickie. Today. Me and your man. The rent's cheap for more than one reason, y'know. We're getting like a hippie commune, right?"

My heart somersaults as the chandelier over the table ignites and Chet Baker slurs to life on the turntable.

*Just one look at you, my heart grows
tipsy in me
You and you alone bring out the gypsy in
me . . .*

The generator is rattling to life under the lean-to in the Lamonts' backyard. It is quite loud, its racket nestling into the rainfall. Beth charges into the foyer with Evan in her arms. The floodlights shine through the glass panes on the front door.

"Success!" Trip yells from the kitchen, pathetically joyous.

"Christa, you are a piece of work," Paul says, half-laughing as he gingerly places Katie on the floor. She clings to his shirt, mewing in protest.

In the foyer, Beth is pulling down Evan's rain gear and hurriedly dressing him in it.

"Oh, you know what I'm talking about Paul." Christa smiles, blinking in the light. "Don't pretend. No more fibbing. You know. Padrino. And Grant knows. He knows. About when Billy died. You and Beth. He knows. No secrets in the country. Truthin' time, baby."

Melora looks over to her husband, and in that instant I know she knows, and I know it's true. What little boeuf bourguignon I've eaten rises in my gullet. My face is hot, and my heart pounds so hard it hurts.

Melora's face twitches. My eyes flash to Paul's wide-eyed blue stare, his subtle, guilty smile, the slight shake of his fake-blackened hair. He's calculating, meandering into a shrug, perhaps a reflexive thing he does when busted; he's hoping I'll say Christa's full of shit, delusional, but all I do is nod and stand, my head swirling from wine and heavy blood flow. Paul puts up both his hands, as if I'm going to hit him, as Beth pulls her raincoat from the coatrack, which falls to the floor.

"FUCK!" she screams.

My wife opens the door to the downpour. Stony Clove Creek roars, boulders clashing. Evan stands rigid beside his mother, his face hidden beneath the brim of his rain hat. He reaches his hand up, either to support her or to be supported, or both.

I'm up and at the door, beside my wife and son. Evan reaches for my pant leg. Rain pelts my face. The motion-sensitive floodlight illuminates the front yard and a strip of the road, which is flowing with water. Stony Clove Creek has breached its banks. The dense thicket between the Victorian and Shulz House dances wildly in the rain, formerly dry ditches filling with water, maples and birches groaning, branches cracking and falling.

Beth turns to me, her brow creasing. "What the fuck, Grant?"

"I'm sorry, it's . . . we need to talk . . . you and him, you and . . . fuck. I know. I know."

"I . . . I don't know what to say . . . I . . . it's nothing . . ."

That word again.

"We'll talk about it later," I say, my voice trembling as I tip my head to Evan. The sight of him somehow blocks my panic, fills me with a humming clarity.

"You should sit down, Beth."

"No, I gotta get out of here, I gotta get out of here, I gotta get out of here."

"Not now. Look. The creek's overflowing."

"The woods," she says. "I'll go through the woods . . ."

She drops Evan's hand and walks to the edge of the front stoop, relaxing in the weight of the rain. She turns her face up and opens her mouth. Her hair clip tumbles to the steps, loosening a cascade down her back.

"Mommy!" Evan calls from the doorway. Katie runs to his side and yells her version of *mommy*.

"Stay right there, Beth," I say. "Don't move. We can't leave."

Paul and Melora are beside me, throwing on their coats.

I turn my head to look at Paul, the cords in my neck tight, snapping. He holds up his hands as if to say *Calm down*. I can almost hear him say it: *Calm down, Hoss*.

"We're leaving," he says, as If I asked him a question.

Trip runs into the foyer. "What the fuck? Where's everybody going?"

"We're going back to the city," Paul says. "Now."

Melora nods.

"Good idea!" Christa yells from the dining room. "Great fucking idea, Padrino! Run, you fucking coward!"

"She's just drunk, guys," Trip says feebly.

"No," I say, heat rising in my gut. Evan looms in my peripheral vision, his dark eyes wide and glistening. "They should go, Trip. Now."

"But . . ." Evan says.

"I don't think so," Trip says, swaying in the foyer light. "I think . . . it's a bad idea. Remember what Ricky said . . ."

"No, we're going," Melora says. "That redneck is dumb as a rock. We'll be all right. Our car can handle this . . ."

Paul and Melora hustle past Beth, across the yard and into the street, two fuzzy shapes in the downpour making splashy footfalls. Melora's flashlight winks in the black.

"They're crazy," Trip slurs. "That is not a good idea."

"Stop!" Beth yells to them, then doubles over, crying, "No, no, no."

The water rushes over Melora's and Paul's ankles as they walk back toward the farmhouse. Then they're just a flickering light in the blackness.

"Stop!" Evan yells. "Papa, tell them to stop."

Beth steps back to the doorway, drenched. Evan and Katie both throw their arms around her legs.

"Tell them to stop, Grant," she says, eyes downcast as water puddles around her feet.

"They can't hear me," I say. "They'll be OK . . ."

No, a voice inside me says. *They won't.*

Trip has wandered back to the dining room, where Christa still sits. I can hear them talking.

"You're just gonna sit there, I guess," Trip says to his wife.

"I let the cat out of the bag, Trip."

"What cat?"

"At fucking last. I couldn't take it anymore. Him with that smug-ass smile, everyone thinking he's so fucking cool. He's a fucking asshole. In *my* fucking house."

"And you're perfect, I guess," Trip snarls drunkenly.

"No, I'm not, I'm a bitch, a crazy-ass bitch, right? Isn't that what you want to say? Say it. Fucking say it, Daddy."

"You think I don't know . . ."

"Hey!" I yell. "You two shut the fuck up, will you?"

Katie squawks her version of *shut the fuck up.*

"I gotta get out of here," Beth says again, her voice quaking. Evan is still as a statue.

Katie runs to the stairs. She flicks her big eyes at Beth, then at Evan. She barks something in her strange patois.

"Come, Mommy," Evan says. He pulls Beth to the stairs. "Katie's room has a fort."

"Go," I say. "Go. That's a good idea. Evan, get Mommy some towels, will you?"

The trio mounts the steps as I head back to the dining room.

Trip stands over his wife, swaying.

"You think I don't know," he says again, darkly amused, "that you're fucking that kid Armando. Everybody knows that. Your fucking waitress Liz told me you two spend a lot of time in the stock room, says her husband cheated on her, nobody said anything, she feels sorry for me. She hates you, by the way. I just hope you're using a fucking rubber."

"Oh, look at you, Columbo, you're so smart," Christa says, in an ecstasy of rage. "Armando just wanted to see my tits, that's all. He's the only person interested in them, and he's a fag. And that Liz, ha! That's the pot calling the kettle . . . she's a whore, that one. You want the lowdown, I'll tell you, I don't give a shit. I bought this fucking house, all this fucking property, put up with all your shit, that goddamn kid . . . I don't care anymore. Beth got her free pass with Paul and I deserve my free pass, and I got it with your best friend over there, your pen pal."

Trip swivels, almost falls, and squints at me as if my face is a spotlight. He crumples over and lurches to the sofa in the living room, plopping onto the couch, where he puts his head between his knees and vomits on the rug.

"Fuck, Trip!" Christa yells. She grabs a wastebasket, stumbling over herself, and shoves it under his dripping chin to try to catch the last of the puke as it spasms out of him, filling the room with a noxious, sour odor of wine, beef, and bile.

A car horn honks outside, followed by shouts.

I run to the window. In the glare of the floodlights, I see Paul and Melora's Saab stalled in front of the Lamont house. The creek has swelled to the tops of the wheel wells. Melora's window is down, and she's trying to open her door against the current, but it's too strong.

"Help!" she yells, barely audible over the water. "Oh God, help! Fuck, fuck, fuck!"

"What's that?" Trip says from the couch.

"Paul and Melora," I say, my body a riot of impulse: *stay, go, stay, go.* "They're . . . the water's . . ."

I run to the front door. Trip is beside me in a cloud of puke smell. "I fucking told you," he says. "Fucking told you. Nobody listens to me around here."

A light flickers in the woods beside the house. It's Ricky, bursting through the thicket, a coil of yellow rope around his shoulder.

"I tried to stop 'em," he yells. "Soon as I heard them start that car, I tried . . ." He moves to the edge of the rushing current swirling around the mailbox.

"Come on," I say to Trip.

"What the fuck?" Christa says, barreling into the foyer from the living room. "No way, no way, no way. Beth, get down here!" She grabs her husband's sleeve.

"Let go of me, Chris," he says. Through the puking and the adrenaline, Trip is beyond sober, actually more alert than I've seen him in months.

Beth descends the stairs, the kids behind her. I meet her eyes, full-on.

"They're gonna drown, Beth," I say.

"I fucking said so," Trip says.

"These guys want to go help," Christa says. "I'm telling them no."

"No, don't, please," Beth says. "PLEASE."

"See?" Christa says. "Listen to her! She's the smart one."

Evan's eyes are wide, his chin trembling.

In the yard, Ricky's yelling to Paul and Melora. Paul has pulled himself out through his window and is on top of the Saab, reaching his hand down to Melora, who is screaming. The car is filling with water. It moves sluggishly in the current, ever closer to the now-raging creek. Ricky has tied the rope around an old growth maple at the edge of the Lamonts' driveway. He throws the rope again and again, but Melora's trapped. Paul tries to get her out while also trying to gain purchase on the slippery top of the car, his engineer boots scrabbling. Several times, he almost falls into the water.

I run to Ricky. Trip is right behind me. Christa and Beth shout in protest from the front stoop. I turn to the wives.

"Stay with the kids," I yell. "Just stay with the kids!"

The rain has slacked off a little, but the creek rages on. Ricky is calling encouragement to Melora and Paul. He glances over to Trip and me, then back to the Saab.

"Give me the rope," I say. "I'll tie it around my waist and grab her."

"That is not a good idea, Grant," Ricky yells, his eyes focused on the car.

It's the first time he's called me by my first name.

"You're stronger than me," I say, "but I'm heavier than you. I'll wade in and grab Melora, and you and Trip can pull us back."

"What about Paul?" Trip yells.

I hadn't thought of Paul.

"I'll get him second," I say.

Ricky frowns, thinks for a second, then says, "Take your shoes off so they don't fill with water."

I do, my toes sinking into the sodden lawn. I grab the rope out of the floodwaters, wind it around my waist, through a couple of belt loops, and tie it in a double knot. The moment I step in the water, my jaw stiffens and my knees lock up. It is, by far, the coldest water I've ever felt. I look over my shoulder at Trip and Ricky. Behind them, Beth and Christa stand on the stoop, the kids at their feet. All watching.

"Careful, Grant," Ricky says. Trip is behind him, biting his lip, the rope in his fists and coiled around his forearms. They look like they're getting ready for tug-of-war.

The force of the creek is beyond what I expect. I stumble, then regain my footing on the asphalt about two feet down, leaning into the flow, reaching my hands out, both for balance and to catch Melora. Twigs and branches hit me and float on. It occurs to me now that I am risking my life, but this registers only for a brief, clear second. Then I have one impulse: grab her.

The interior lights are still aglow in the Saab, and now I can see Melora. She's submerged from the chest down, grabbing at Paul's hand, pulling herself up with the seat belt, gasping for air.

"Melora!" I yell, my voice thin in my shivering jaw. "Take my hand!" I'm about five feet away, making slow but steady progress, praying the current doesn't increase. The closer I get to the car, the stronger the current and deeper the water. Paul nods at me quickly, his face contorted. He reaches once more over the edge of the roof and grabs his flailing wife. He pulls her up, his neck all tendon and muscle. I heave myself toward them, falling, grabbing the door frame to keep from being swept away.

With her husband's help, Melora pulls herself through the window. I reach for her as Paul releases his hold. She grabs me and pulls herself out as I totter and scrabble at the side-view mirror for support. Our combined weight roots my feet.

The water rises to our waists as my hands grasp fistfuls of wet clothes and slick skin. She's panting in my ear, clawing at me in blind terror, and kneeing me in the balls.

"Don't drop her!" Paul yells, belly down on the Saab roof, gasping. If I didn't know who he was, I would not recognize him, with his hair wet against his head, eyes wide, lips raw. He's afraid. I've never seen him afraid.

He reaches to me unthinkingly, and I consider grabbing him, although his weight could spell disaster for all of us. I'm about to reach for him anyway when a calculation flits across his eyes and he waves me off.

I nod.

The creek swells and rises to my chin. Melora's head goes under and she flails, knocking my legs out from under me. Paul is shouting something as Melora and I struggle to keep our heads up. Water gushes down my throat as I cough reflexively, fighting the urge to let Melora go, save myself.

A sharp pain shoots up from my waist. They're pulling us back. Paul recedes as my feet touch asphalt, and I'm able to concentrate on keeping Melora in my grip. In the glare of the floodlight, I see Beth's silhouette alongside Trip's and Ricky's. She's helping them gather us back in, her arms glistening. Christa stands with the kids in the doorway, her hands over her mouth.

I move over stray river stones, sediment, then grass. Melora kicks and thrashes, coughing as she grips my clothes and hair. We tumble into Beth, Trip, and Ricky. A loud crack splits the air, followed by a splash upstream and a boom. A felled maple slams into the back of the Saab, sending Paul into the murk, his hands grasping at floating debris for a few moments until Stony Clove Creek swallows him.

part three

june 2003

Rolling Stone

Paul Fairchild, Six Ray Star Frontman,
Drowns
Fairchild, 41, was planning Six Ray Star
reunion show at Nike HQ

by Andy DeWilde
April 2, 2003

Six Ray Star guitarist and songwriter
Paul Fairchild, who penned the alternative rock hit "Kiss My Ring"—now
universally recognized as "the Nike
anthem"—drowned Friday in the hamlet of Mt. Marie, New York. He was 41.
Fairchild and his wife, Melora Thompson, became trapped in their car when
a creek flooded during a heavy downpour. Thompson was pulled from the
car by Grant Kelly, former bassist for
Stereoblind ("What the Funk Is Up?")
but Fairchild was swept away. His body
was found by local residents the next
day. Fairchild had been visiting with
Kelly, a recent émigré from Manhattan,
who was to replace Six Ray Star bassist
Otto Grunther in an upcoming reunion
concert at a corporate Nike event in
Portland, Oregon.

Along with The Jon Spencer Blues
Explosion, Pavement, and Blonde
Redhead, Paul Fairchild's quartet, Six
Ray Star, came to prominence in the
post-Nirvana, pre-file sharing, New York
City indie scene of the 1990s, releasing
an EP, *Pledge* (Matador, 1990), and
three albums, *Bodega Perfume* (Matador, 1991), the classic *Peppercorn*
(Warner Bros., 1993), and *Turpentine*
(Warner Bros., 1996), before disbanding
in 1999. Fairchild's quirky, distinctive
songs—he called them "slacker punk"
and "popcore"—have since been used in
a variety of media: commercials for Nike,
Royal Caribbean cruise lines, Wran-
gler jeans, Nissan, and various video
games. "They don't play me on the radio
anymore 'cause I'm old," Fairchild said
unapologetically in an *Adweek* interview,
"so licensing is a perfect way to get my
songs out there. Radio is all about selling ads anyway, right? Same as it ever
was."

Fairchild grew up in Baltimore, moving to Manhattan in 1985, where he
earned a name as a magnetic front man
in proto-grunge rockers ScuzzPup and
Bovril. With Six Ray Star, he found a
more tuneful template and developed a
following that included celebrities like
Matt Dillon, Steve Buscemi, and Lili
Taylor. Asked about his band's breakup,
he told an interviewer, "Nervous exhaustion, or whatever you call what happens

when four guys take a lot of drugs, fly on too many planes, and drink like Vikings, which we are not. None of us wanted to end up like Kurt."

In recent years, Fairchild and Thompson had been living in the Christadora building on Avenue B in the East Village, where Fairchild was recording solo material on a Mac. He is survived by his wife; a brother, Carlos Fernandez; and his parents, Luis and Rosa Fernandez, of Baltimore.

chapter 18

return to sender

D'Angelo Manse
Ocean City, NJ

Grant Kelly
244 East 7th #5E
NYC 10009 USA

8-12-92

Hey Grant,

Coming to you from a ridiculously quaint little room in Christa's family's "weekend place."

The book is going well I guess. Changed title from Aftermath *to* Shadow World. *Still keeping the asteroid-hits-Earth angle with everything happening on the Island of California.*

Having this palatial place to myself is a little weird, especially with the photos of The Blonde D'Angelos—and the painting of Papa Damien—all staring me down every time I turn a corner. They all look like angry merpeople, pissed off they can't go back to the ocean.

Anyway the solitude is a welcome change from Christa's craziness made worse as

*Digital Café has kept her from joining her
family in the Caribbean BOO HOO.*

*I am lucky of course that she's OK with
me bailing. It was HER idea I come to
Casa D'Angelo and get out of her way
so I can finish the umpteenth draft of
my book before classes start up again at
Hunter. What a great idea indeed.*

*Still please do check in on her if you're
walking through Gramercy. I worry.
Her mom's mental collapse haunts her.
(Mama D'Angelo medicated into submis-
sion these days. Creepy.) As you know,
one never knows one's DNA inheritance,
although C seems OK all things considered. I guess I got lucky with Ward &
June Lamont aka my mom n' pop. Thank
God they are so boring. If a writer is
made by his childhood I am fucked.*

*Enough about me. I have been thinking
about you and hoping the demos are
going well. As I said before . . . leaving
Stereoblind was the right thing for you.
Your songs are better, and the Stereoblind crew is intimidated. Fuck that
noise. Especially since Tristan talked to
you like that onstage. That "it was the
cocaine talking" bullshit is pathetic. And
blaming the lousy reception for the first
record on your bass playing and your
"look" is beyond obnoxious. (Tristan is
going bald, have you noticed? He hates
your hair.) Your funky plunk junk MADE
that record and esp. the single.*

*I cannot believe they rejected that tune
"Words Fail Me." That is a hit. A HIT I
SAY. And now it will be in my head all
day.*

*I'm sure you'll get a deal and be fronting
your own band, touring and selling beau-
coups of albums within 18 months. That
is my wager. Meantime the proofreading
gig sounds good. Put that spelling B
brain to good use. Becawse yew kan spel
gud. I caint.*

*Happy Anniversary, by the way. Two
years! And they said it wouldn't last. I'll
say it again: yours was the Best Wedding
Ever. Such an amazing day. Everyone
enchanted into good behavior: Tristan
not being a dick, Billy clean and sober,
your mom in her hippie getup actually
NOT pissing anyone off with the constant No Nukes stuff. And Beth's parents—both of 'em so hale and hearty.
It was all magic. Thanks for singing
"Words Fail Me."*

*I was thinking of that night you two
came into Digital Café. Both of u soaked
from that August rainstorm, laughing
like kids. When you left Christa says,
"Those two are gonna grow old together
just like you and me, Pops. And our
babies will grow old together." She may
be crazy sometimes and that freaked me
right out but I think she's right.*

*I gotta fly and get back to work. Always
a pleasure procrastinating with you—
something we perfected back in Scenic
Ave. C days. I know you're planning to
go to VA to check in on Beth's folks and
I know you'll have your hands full, but
pls know you can call/beep me anytime.
Give Beth a hug for me. Bet you're glad
you're not on the road with Stereoblind
when she needs you. This is the important stuff.*

Onward ho. (Ya 'ho!)

*Rgds,
Trip*

~

For the first time in weeks, I'm not crying after reading
what Trip pressed into my hand the night of the flood, the
carbon of the letter he'd sent me way back when, typed
on his Smith Corona electric, when he was pretending
to be Asimov or Vonnegut, making carbon copies "old-
school style," documenting everything for a future date,
like his heroes did, with no notion that the future may
not care for his words, for recordings of his life.

I'd been like that with my music: *of course* people will
want to hear it. One hopes and hopes in a fog, assuming
some god or goddess, some Fate, will smile. We were
like compulsive gamblers, but our capital wasn't money,
just boatloads of blind hope, excitement over possibility
eliciting streams of dopamine from our brains, making
us clueless as any drunk, junkie, or religious fanatic.

In my mother's prefab barn, the late spring heat,
unseasonable even for Goldsboro, has turned the letter
paper crisp. I gingerly place the three double-spaced

pages back on the card table and hold them down with a palm-sized piece of petrified wood I'd given my mom when I was ten or so.

Trip knew this letter was a touchstone to Ye Olden Tymes. I think that's why he gave it to me the night of the flood. He'd wanted to read it aloud, but his boeuf bourguignon was calling. Now, of course, I wish he had. Perhaps it would've cast a protective spell. Everything would've remained unspoken, Paul would be alive, I'd be ten grand richer, and my marriage would not be wrecked.

We haven't talked, Trip and I, since I fled Mt. Marie six weeks ago, so I can only guess what his motives were for reading letters aloud that night. Maybe he believed the letters would offer light. In those moments before we all sat down to dinner, he decided to act. He knew my marriage was in trouble, just as I knew his was, and he wanted me to recall the "me" of the letter, the "us" that existed before Paul and Melora, before Trip's and my dreams were unfulfilled, before our wives had become otherwise engaged. He wanted to revivify our dreaming selves, our un-disappointed selves, our better selves.

Or maybe he wanted to assert to Paul and Melora that our lives were once rich and special, and while we didn't publish novels or become rock stars, our creative abilities were on par with his. Here was proof. We'd been quite complete before he slouched into our lives.

Or maybe he was just drunk, medicated, and unmoored, beyond reason or explanation. Someday I'll ask him. If he will talk to me.

~

The first time I read the letter, I'd only just arrived here, sleep-starved, still damp in my bones from the flood, and stinking of the Greyhound that brought me south the night after Paul drowned. Back at Trip's, just after Paul vanished, I'd changed out of my soaked clothes, squeezed into an ill-fitting pair of Trip's chinos, and pulled on a sweatshirt that smelled of him. I'd retrieved the soaked letter from my sodden jeans pocket along with my wallet. But I'd not looked at it until I got here.

That first morning, I peeled apart the wet layers, read it, and wept. I stopped reading several times and almost destroyed it, but Trip's words held sway. He'd always wanted his writing to hold sway. Plus, I'd disrespected him so deeply and felt, frankly, that I should take my lumps and honor his work. So I spared it. And now, every couple of days, I read it and time travel.

The occasional moments of time-transcendence, in which I am back in those scenes Trip describes, before everything went to shit, are worth the pain of coming back to the dull ache of this strange exile. The accompanying tears have purged me somewhat. Evidently, I needed a lot of purging. But today, no tears. At least not yet. It's still early, the mid-morning sun peeking through the dingy curtains of my one window.

When I first arrived, it seemed I had an inexhaustible supply of unmedicated tears. Having been dammed up by Zoloft for several years, they tend to flow easier than ever these days. Walking the Goldsboro streets, I see twenty-somethings hanging out, and I weep. I see couples in love, and I weep. Happy fathers and sons pass me and I think of my Evan, whose earliest memories will be indelibly traumatic, just like mine. That thought in particular makes me weep. I'd so wanted to protect him from that, to give him a sense of safety like I never had, to protect him from, at the very least, death before his very eyes. But I failed.

I think about the night of the flood. I replay moments again and again, rewriting the story in various ways, redirecting the players, the angles, and the outcome.

Most often, I am heroically jumping into the water, swimming with superhuman strength until I find Paul,

and miraculously, my adrenaline—not spent after all—
pumps me full of energy. I beat the odds, find my footing, pull his unconscious body from the creek, give him
mouth-to-mouth, and become famous as the lifesaver of
the great Paul Fairchild, indie rock star, original "alter-
na-hunk." My son is so proud. And this selfless action
connects me to a wellspring of magnanimity, and I'm as
forgiving as Jesus, able to let all betrayals slide. Similarly, I'm forgiven my transgressions.

I can't keep these fantasies afloat for long. As much
as I'd like a psychotic break with reality, I have, sadly,
retained my sanity, and the memories, the images of
what actually happened, torment me.

~

The immediate aftermath of Paul's disappearance was
all desperate hope, each of us bolstering one another's
vision of him somewhere downstream, pulling himself
out of the creek by grabbing a branch, or washed into
someone's front lawn, gasping but alive, or maybe onto
a bridge on Route 28. Outside the halo of the Lamonts'
floodlights, we couldn't see anything, even with our flashlights, so running into the pitch-black rain was pointless.
For hours, we posited various scenarios in which Paul
was OK but unable to get back to us for one reason or
another.

*We shouldn't give up hope until we know for sure, we
shouldn't give up hope.*

We had little recourse anyway. We were prisoners,
cut off from the highway by a waterlogged bridge strewn
with debris and mud and unable even to get to that
bridge due to washed-out roads.

We were in a frozen frame of film, an extended
now, wherein reactions to drunken revelations, and fallout from Paul's death, waited in the distance. No one

entered the swirl of emotion kicked up at dinner, and no one mused aloud about Paul. We tacitly agreed to circle it until we knew.

Each of us picked up the phone several times, hoping for a dial tone that wouldn't come for days yet also glad it was not there to deliver us back to our timeline. I even prayed for the continued hypnotizing drone of the generator. As soon as we were back on the grid, we'd be startled awake, and payment on our life-changing night would come due.

Not long after the water took Paul, Ricky had headed back through the dark to his trailer to wait out the storm with his family, making his way via Maglite through the woods. We found out later that Jen forbade him to leave again, lest he get himself killed helping the idiot New Yorkers. Stony Clove Creek had edged right up to their deck, flowing under Ricky's pickup, but it did no serious damage to their property, or, for that matter, Shulz House and, thank God, the Camry. This struck me as a kind of insult, like waking to find the sun shining after the worst day of your life, which is what happened.

~

When they pulled Melora and me from the water, Trip clicked into action, confidently administering first aid to exhausted, confused, jabbering Melora, stripping her out of her clothes, pulling one of Christa's flannel nightgowns over her shaking, ghost-white body. He wrapped her in a quilt and guided her to the living room sofa, all the while talking low and calm, mindful of shock. She muttered madly and even laughed a little until Christa gave her a couple Valium and she passed out.

All night, Trip refused to leave her side. Melora provided him with focus, and he took full advantage, screening us out. He spoke little and looked no one in the eye, just sat and listened to the weather band on his camping radio. Meanwhile, the storm lashed the house, flung branches at the roof as we moved with clumsy deliberation in the flickering lights.

Christa expressed a ridiculous, strong conviction that Paul was OK. She related a false-sounding story about him telling her once that he'd been a champion swimmer in high school and she just knew in her bones he was fine, probably hiding in the bushes right now, watching us worry, the bastard. Ha, ha. After a couple hours of this, she ran out of steam and spent most of the night in her and Trip's bedroom with the door shut. I looked in on her several times, made sure she hadn't vomited in her sleep and choked. Each time I checked, she was face down on the bed, breathing heavy in a medicated stupor.

Beth focused on the kids. Although trembling throughout, she snuggled down with Evan and Katie in Katie's canopied princess bed. Katie, unfazed by everything as long as the lights stayed on, fell right to sleep. Evan remained awake for some time, snuggling his mother, talking nonstop about Padrino, suggesting scenarios in which Paul was safe and on his way back to us. I stood outside the doorway and listened as Beth nodded and appreciated, but did not agree with each scenario.

"Padrino's got a boat," Evan said.

"Maybe he does," Beth said. "We don't know."

"Or he can swim and get back like that maybe. Or . . . a eagle grabs him and they fly, they fly and fly."

"That would be amazing."

I knew from the strain in her hoarse voice she was coming apart inside, but I couldn't go in. If my eyes met either my son's or my wife's, I would break, of that I was certain. A deliberate softness in Evan's voice told me he knew how fragile his mother was, too, that he was making up these stories for her. *Too soon,* I thought. *Too soon for this.*

The bandage on my wounded palm had washed away, so I redressed the purpled cut with the Lamonts' extensive and, due to Katie, much-used first-aid kit. My hands trembled and would keep trembling for hours, but due to Vicodin and still-pumping adrenaline, I felt no pain.

I went several times to check the Lamonts' generator, even though I knew it didn't need checking. It was the best, if not the quietest, money could buy. On one of those unnecessary trips outside, raindrops pelting my face, I saw light over the soft peak of Mt. Marie. Dawn coming, pushing through the gloom.

A comforting certainty rose in me: *I must go.* If I stayed, if I looked into anyone's eyes, my mind would shatter and I'd make everything worse. Plus, I let a man die in front of my kid, moments after damning revelations my kid heard.

Go, I thought. *Go.*

I thought of the certainty, the sense of accomplishment, even the good humor a suicide feels when he makes his final decision. I wondered if my dad had felt similarly that day he sent me to the pool by myself, knowing I would be the one to find him when I returned.

I had tried, but I was no better than him: unfaithful, irresponsible, incapable of providing a safe environment for my kid. Bad parent. Self-absorbed. Faulty wiring.

Best to get away before Evan did any more modeling after me, before he looked at me and grasped the knowledge that I am not who he thinks I am. The thought of that crystal recognition, of seeing my son's eyes sharp with disappointment, terrified me.

Even though Paul had waved me away—I think—I could have grabbed him, but I didn't. Evan saw that. Does he know that action may have killed all three of us? Or does it look to him like I just let his godfather die? And did I?

From my thoughts and into the wet darkness around me, a familiar presence coalesced. Death hovered.

"I remember you," I murmured to the rain. I flashed on my father, Death enveloping him as I stood and watched; I thought of Billy, and Beth standing over his body as Death worked its wiles on her.

My father's death had given my mother permission to do what she wanted with my inheritance; Billy's death gave Beth permission to consummate a lurking passion for Paul.

Paul's death was granting me license to leave.

Death suspends the "rules." That to which we've bound ourselves loosens its grip, and/or we are imbued with temporary dark energy with which to pull away. Part of me, in fact, was already gone.

Bad times do not bring out the best in everyone, apparently. Unless the best in me is what is pulling me away, to protect my son.

~

Back inside, I turned off the chandelier and slumped to the floor in the dining room, my head between my knees. I listened to the song of the pounding generator pistons, the incessant rainfall, and the crackle of the repetitive, Stephen Hawking-sounding weather band in the next room. I wondered if I'd ever hear silence again. As the room lightened, pain rose in my arms and traveled down my sides, into my legs and my rope-burnt back, muscles overstretched in Melora's rescue, drained of endorphins, now beginning a rising whine of complaint. My hand wound joined in, growing warm, throbbing beneath its fresh bandage.

And yet I drifted into a twilight dream, a dream I've thought about so much it has gained the patina of half-reality:

I'm walking down Shulz Way behind my father and another man on a bright, hot summer day. We're headed toward Shulz House, away from the Victorian. Instead of his usual shape-shifting from old to young, corporeal to shimmery ghost, Dad is solid, very much as he was when he killed himself. His companion is similarly dense, shorter than my father. Both wear white coveralls, like house painters. They're talking, but I can't hear their words over the generator, which, despite the clear sky of my dreamscape, is pounding on, and three times its normal size. King stalks the machine like it's prey, his fur ruffled. My father's companion points at the dog, and the two men laugh, their voices echoing over the mountain like yodels.

I am the shape-shifter in this dream, at once a child, then the same age as, then older than these adult men, who glance over their shoulders to make sure I'm keeping up. Yet when they look back, their faces are blurred. It is hard for me to keep pace, and I'm not sure why until I look behind me and see Evan, who is pulling on Ricky Shulz's rope, coiled again around my waist. Evan is trying to leash me to a clothesline stretched across the road. But the rope has a lot of slack and, to his frustration, he can't gather it up quick enough. He calls to his mother to help—"Mommy, Mommy"—but I can't hear the words, I can just read his lips. Anxiety of being tattled on spreads through me.

I'm eager to get away from my son, who is intent on exposing me to Beth. For doing what? I don't know, but it's bad and it has something to do with these men and what they wish to show me. Something in Shulz House, something exciting they want me to see. They're like the gang leaders, and I am limp with surrender, drifting on a current, passive, although I don't want to be. Or do I?

We're in the dim shadows of Shulz House. The crow that cawed at me when I was bleaching away mold yesterday—or decades ago—perches on the window above the sink. It turns its head upward. The dropped ceiling I'd scrubbed with Clorox is gone, rafters exposed. My father and his companion turn their full attention to me, fumbling with the rope at my waist, their faces still obscured, their heavy hands welcome on my body.

I look to the rafters and see the rope fly into the air, tossed by my father's companion. It misses, and my father says, "Now you know why I didn't do it this way. Labor intensive."

"Well," the other man says, his voice familiarly low, "this isn't like you think. If you can tie a decent knot, you're good to go."

Good to go, good to go, good to go. It's good. To go.

The generator runs out of gas, and the silence jerks me awake.

~

The morning was clear and sunny, birds everywhere, the air thick with petroleum scent. The heat wave continued. I walked outside, my dream slipping away from center stage but hovering in the wings, beckoning me . . . elsewhere.

The receded water revealed Paul and Melora's overturned Saab in the creek bed. About six inches of creek sediment covered the road. Standing on it, I felt a tremor and looked down Shulz Way to see a fire engine approaching. The bridge had held. We were one step closer to reengaging with the world.

Trip, Beth, and a still-shaky Melora stumbled out of the house to the commotion of the fire engine. Christa and the kids slept on. The engine pulled into the branch-strewn driveway, and the volunteers disembarked to check on us. Beth, her voice shaky with hope, asked if they knew about Paul. None did. The chief said someone needed to report him missing. Several folks had gone missing. The sound of Paul's name on my wife's lips, spoken with tenderness, tightened my gut and sent my mind whirring back in the direction of escape.

Trip, still avoiding eye contact with me, insisted he go alone to the police station. Beth helped a still-Valium'd Melora back to the sofa and tended to her.

When Trip returned from giving his missing persons report, he went straight upstairs. As I stood in the foyer, I heard him talking to Christa. He said Katie's Café was "toast." Stony Clove Creek ran alongside Mt. Marie's Main Street and had jumped the banks there, too, coursing through businesses, including the Mildew Mart, Greta's General Store, and Katie's Café. He said everything was ruined. Everything.

"It's all gone," he said evenly, no trace of rancor or sadness.

Christa was silent.

I went to make coffee for the volunteers. Turns out about five feet of water had risen in the Lamonts' basement. Sodden cardboard boxes, most filled with Christmas stuff, floated under the basement lights.

The volunteers were all locals I'd seen in Greta's General Store, the Mildew Mart, and fishing Stony Clove Creek; Ricky Shulz's tribal companions, with ruddy faces, mud-crusted boots, grimy, well-worn work clothes, and, with the exception of a muscular woman with slicked-down, dirty-blond hair cinched into a ponytail, all were bearded. Most I'd never said hello to, just nodded. I tried to rectify that, each utterance made with a lot of effort, hollow like bad acting, which it was. They tramped in and out of the kitchen, uncoiling hoses, threading them down the basement steps, tracking river mud everywhere, nodding to me as they worked. They laughed and ranted, comparing notes. All were from higher up the mountain, and all had made out OK, staying in, hunkered around wood stoves, mindful of the weather. Like Ricky, they talked derisively about the Department of Environmental Conservation.

"Damn DEC. Cleaning up their mess. Again."

"God forbid they let us dredge that fuckin' creek. God forbid some poor little fish habitat gets disturbed by my mean ole backhoe."

"They don't give a damn about the fish. They just wanna break balls, be big government, nannies getting paid off our backs. A little flood here or there, they don't care."

As the pumps groaned and whooshed and the refueled generator pounded on, the kids finally awoke and came down for Eggos and OJ. The bustle of the firemen and Katie's happy cluelessness held Evan's attention. If he understood all the implications of Christa's revelations, like "quickie," "free pass," and "unfaithful," he wasn't letting on. I prayed he wasn't as sharp as that.

The rest of us milled about zombie-like, drinking coffee and giving each other wide berths, none of us speaking much, just conveying absolutely necessary information.

Trip headed outside and shoveled sediment from the lawn into a wheelbarrow, grunting loudly, his jaw set tight. Christa, heavy-lidded, finally came downstairs in big green waders and threadbare overalls, hair pulled into a ponytail and held down by a red kerchief. She barely acknowledged us, slipped on some kitchen gloves, and headed into the basement, which was down to about two feet of dark, cold water. She pitched in. She said very little, just hunkered down in the murk, sifting through dripping garbage, filling contractor bags.

The flood had turned the Lamonts' front yard into a big wet sandbox. The kids begged to go play in it, Evan with words, Katie with various vocal sounds and hand gestures. I let them out, following closely. Ricky was driving up and down Shulz Way in his truck, setting his plow blade to the silt and debris like he'd done with the snow, his blade crying against the pavement.

Jen and Brianna appeared with a casserole, walking the edges of the road. King followed them, ecstatic in the tangles of branches and mounds of dirt washed up on the pavement, jumping like a mountain goat from felled tree to displaced river rock, barking cheerfully. Jen and Brianna deposited the casserole on the porch, brushed off everybody's appreciation, muttered strained words of hope for Paul, nodded to assorted firemen, and quickly retreated to their trailer, King at their heels.

Ricky rolled down his window to ask after Melora, but that was it. An aura of morning-after shame clung to him. He'd wanted to save Paul but couldn't. Like me, his derring-do was spent entirely on Paul's wife, because, I told myself, Paul had wanted that. In any case, like me, Ricky knew Paul was dead. He wasn't going to entertain otherwise.

Our efforts had linked Ricky and me, on a subtle, nonverbal level. A twitch of his chapped lip was as good as a paragraph.

As Ricky and I spoke, I saw Beth take a steaming mug into the side yard. She let her coffee go cold as she stared at Mt. Marie, a light breeze tossing her hair. She and I had talked of going back to Shulz House, though neither of us wanted to. We'd negotiated in monosyllables, talking as if from a preordained script: Shulz House had no generator and more importantly, Evan was reluctant to leave Katie. So let's stay here for now. In limbo. Not talking.

Yet I felt drawn to Shulz House . . .

"I'm outta here," Ricky said, raising his blade. "Let me know if you need anything. We're pretty well stocked. Looks like it'll be awhile 'til stuff's back on."

I nodded my thanks in a cloud of Ricky's exhaust. I turned back just in time to see Beth hang her head and cry. I couldn't hear anything over the racket of machinery, but I could see the familiar sag of her shoulders. They shuddered in a very particular rhythm.

She turned and walked back to the Victorian, giving me a furtive glance through a curtain of hair. Everything about her was small, coiled, protective.

Katie was normal as ever, even jocular in the depressurized air. Perhaps that was why Evan clung to her presence. And perhaps, like his parents, he instinctively knew that once it was just the three of us again, we'd need to adjust to the new versions of ourselves, work the revelations and losses into the picture somehow. I pray he didn't think that, but on some level, I know he did, and for that complicated bit of mind trouble, I felt responsible. I should have held my shit together for him, but I couldn't.

Evan watched Katie busy herself in the sediment. She dug holes and tried to engage him in play, saying, *Ebba, come, Ebba, come.* He did a little digging, but mostly he watched with a guarded smile.

~

A police car came to pick up Melora. As I led the officers to the door, the kids were transfixed. I stood in the doorway as the officers waited on the porch, kind and patient. Beth pulled Melora off the sofa and helped her dress in private. The two women emerged, Beth holding up Melora, leading her as if out of a bar. The officers opened the back doors to their cruiser, solemn and gentlemanly, and off they all sped.

A makeshift morgue, I would find out later, awaited them. This was where Melora identified Paul's bloated body, in private, as per regulations. It had washed up in some shallows half a mile downstream. It all took about a half hour, after which the police drove her and Beth back.

When the cops returned with Beth and Melora, I was still in the front yard, digging holes alongside the kids. We could hear Melora keening in the backseat before the car pulled into the driveway. Beth got out first, cast me a long look, and nodded.

The kids stood as still as lawn ornaments. A combination of relief and dread washed over me; Paul's death would make it easier for me to leave, but would my leaving be the *coup de grace* for my marriage? I couldn't say. I could see nothing clearly but flight.

The real world returned; light shifted around us, sharpening everything. Beth helped Melora from the patrol car. Melora wailed and gasped, hunched over a black plastic bag bulging with Paul's clothes. I wanted to go and offer help, but I couldn't make my feet move. On the far side of the lawn, Trip stood motionless, watching, held in place, like me, by the ripples of grief expanding from the two women.

Just before they reached the front door of the Victorian, one of Paul's engineer boots tumbled from the bag and thudded to the flagstone walkway. Melora took a sharp breath and stiffened as Beth snatched it and stuffed it back in the bag, patting the plastic as if it was a living thing. They disappeared inside, and I released a long breath.

The cops came over and told me about Paul, filling me in on details about the morgue. They were eager to talk about it. Trip had filed a police report, and they went over everything with me, all of which were correct.

"So you pulled his wife out?"

"Yeah."

"You?"

"Yes. Me. Ricky and Trip helped. And my wife."

"That sounds like something Shulz would do."

"Your wife helped?"

"Yeah. She did."

"You're lucky, you know."

"Yes, sir. I do know."

"We got five fatalities. Two are people who tried to drive over flooded roads. Never do that. Don't drown, turn around."

"Gotcha. Thanks for . . . you know."

"Sorry for your loss."

And off they went.

"Padrino's dead," Evan said, watching the squad car disappear around the bend. His body collapsed into itself a little.

"Dead," Katie repeated, hands sunk in silt. "Dead."

"Yes, he is, honey," I said, kneeling down, my knees creaking.

Evan's eyes went to the creek. "Drownded?" he said.

"Yes." I took him in my arms, and he sighed but did not cry.

"He's with Uncle Billy," Evan said into my shoulder. It wasn't a question. Then: "You saved her, Padrino's wife. I saw. Padrino was happy when he drownded 'cause she was OK. Muh-roar-a."

"Trip and Ricky and Mommy helped me. We did it together."

Evan took this in and said, "But you." I held him to my chest for a minute and felt his breath rise and fall, steady, deep.

Trip put down his shovel and came over. He watched Katie. She looked up and met his eyes for a long, grave moment. Finally, gaze still on his daughter, he said, "We gotta talk, Grant. Not right now, but . . . we gotta talk. As soon as she gets done in the basement, Christa's heading to New Jersey to her folks'. She's leaving the kid here. Brianna's gonna look after her while I'm at work, and I'm putting her in the hippie daycare in Woodstock."

I nodded, thinking it was time to get Evan into some kind of program, too. Past time. Flower Children Daycare had a goofy name but looked good in the brochure.

With Beth's Sasha income and our ludicrously low rent, we could almost afford it now. If Trip didn't evict us.

"But you and me"—Trip headed back to his mounds of dirt—"we gotta talk."

"Talk," Katie said, then went back to digging herself deeper into a hole. Evan watched her with a blank stare, leaning into my legs as I squeezed his shoulders. Lucky Katie: removed from the gravity of everything, focused on just digging ever deeper into the wet river soil, not caring what may be buried in it.

~

The fire department left, Christa set the kids up with a video, and I headed over to Shulz House under the pretense of "checking on things." But I just wanted to get away, and the farmhouse exerted a pull on me. As I approached, images from my dream played across my mind to the rhythm of Ricky's generator.

The Camry was OK. Water had only risen to the wheels, which were coated in mud. But the interior was dry and still smelled of my family.

I entered via the kitchen door and there, in the half-light, stood Ricky Shulz.

"Hey," I said.

He nodded and looked at the ceiling.

"Everything OK?" I asked. Too loud.

"My dad," Ricky said. "He offed himself in here, you know. Hung himself on the rafters there. Under that drop ceiling."

None of this surprised me. I felt like I'd known all along but merely forgotten.

"Oh man, Ricky. When?"

"In eighty-one. I found him. He'd gambled us into a hole. Got out of his mind, did it while I was at school and my mom was at work trying to get us out of debt. Fucker."

I resisted an impulse to tell him my own story. He turned to me.

"I was just checking on things," he said. "Making sure everything's OK. There's water in the basement, but it'll go down. Water heater and furnace are out, but I'm sure Lamont'll replace those."

"Oh. OK. Thanks."

"This house is solid. Always has been."

I nodded.

"We couldn't have saved Paul, y'know, Grant. I know you're thinking maybe we all could've pulled both of 'em, that you could've held on to 'em both, but I really don't think so. I do not think so. No. Even with Beth helping—and she is strong as an ox, that girl—you'd be dead, and so would Paul's lady, along with Paul. That water's strong. Strong as hell. Hell, we almost lost our grip as it was."

He held up a rope-burnt palm.

"Thanks, Ricky. I appreciate that." At the time, it seemed quite normal that Ricky would be so clued in to me.

"I knew you were thinking it," he said. "Am I right?"

"Yeah."

He looked at me closer.

"You OK there, Grant?"

"Actually . . ." A wave rose in me. I let it crest and crash. "No, I'm not OK. I feel like . . . if I could get away . . . I might be OK. Everybody might be OK. I feel a little . . . crazy. Fucking crazy."

He nodded as my words hung between us.

"Jen did that to me once," he said. "Split for a couple weeks when Brianna was like four or five. Did what she had to do. And I think she mighta cracked if she didn't take off for a little while, get herself a little personal liberty. I don't know exactly what she did, who she was with. I got an idea, but . . ."

"I'm sorry, Ricky."

"No. I had it coming. I was a bit of a rounder, y'know, like my dad. With the booze and speed. The apple don't fall far and all that. I was no angel, and she had to get some wild oats sowed before she could settle down to being a mom for our kid. And that made me do the same. I settled my ass down. Turnabout's fair play, y'know. I guess."

He sighed and let his broad shoulders droop.

"Look," he said, "being married's hard. No two ways about it. You know it, I know it, the wives *definitely* know it. Looking after a kid's hard. I found that out when she left. But we did OK, Brianna and me. Kids are so resilient, more so than folks want to think these days. And I had to clean up. Had to. Wouldn't have if we'd just, you know, talked it out or whatever. And my Jen came back, ready to nest and all, got her library science degree, and we're good. But it's hard sometimes. Still. Twenty years."

"Yeah," I said. "It is. . . . We got problems, Ricky."

"Well hell, who doesn't?"

"Big problems."

"That's no secret, you know."

I looked at him and realized: *you live in a small town, Grant. People talk.* I wondered what, exactly, he thought our problems were and how he knew, but I didn't ask. He does live one hundred feet away.

"Do what you gotta do," he said, heading for the door. "I got your back."

"But my kid," I said, my voice cracking. "My little boy. He's . . . he's really everything to me. I don't know if . . ."

"That may not be the best thing for the tyke, him being your everything and all. No offense. Listen, I get what you do, I see what you do. You are devoted to that kid. Got all those dad bases covered. Anyone sees you guys, knows it." I began to protest, shaking my head, withering under his praise. I was about to tell him I do not have a pot to piss in financially, but he cut me off.

"He knows the score, that kid, he's smart. Damn smart. He'll be OK. If you're shaky, see to that. Don't worry about your family. I'll keep tabs on 'em, and my girl's dying to look after your boy and that Katie. She ain't afraid of nothin', my Bree.

"You can call and check in. But"—he frowned—"you make sure you come back."

~

I grabbed our cash stash—$152—consulted the Trailways schedule, and left a note in the kitchen, where I knew they'd come looking for me when I didn't return.

> *Dear Beth,*
>
> *I'm going away for a while. I'm getting the bus to my mom's. I am sorry. I know between Brianna and Trip, and maybe Flower Children Daycare (finally) Evan will be taken care of when you go away for work. I can't be around right now. I feel like I'm going to lose my mind. I'm in no position to look after a child.*
>
> *We need to talk about everything but not now. You, me, where we're at, what's happened. Your thing with Paul, my thing with Christa. It was a mistake and I wish I could take it back. I wonder if you wish you could take back what happened between you and Paul.*
>
> *I have known about you and Paul since it happened. I wish I'd brought it up months ago, maybe it would have kept*

*all this shit from happening. I know you
were bereaved and stressed and probably fucked up, but it still hurts. Even
with Paul dead, it still hurts. Maybe that
makes me an asshole.*

*Please burn this when you're done. I'm
having a hard time believing last night
happened, and even though I hated Paul,
I didn't want that. Right now I can't get
any clarity, and I need to get away for
that. I will call from Goldsboro.*

I love you.
Grant

I left the note on the kitchen table, stuffed some clothes in a backpack, and headed into Mt. Marie. If any-one saw me walking past the Victorian, I'd say the back-pack was for supplies I was going to get in town. But everyone was inside.

My walk revealed roads cracked, buckled, and sunken in, edges scraped away by the deluge. The creek had gouged out the ground beneath the pavement, caus-ing cracks everywhere. The water was still higher than usual, not yet back to its usual benign babbling. Where there had been thickets of trees parallel to Shulz Way, wet furrows of naked clay glistened. Split tree trunks lay piled amid boulders newly delivered from upstream. Birds clamored mockingly, riotously. In my twisted mind, they were celebrating humankind's temporary demo-tion, nature's cruel, capricious disregard. I hated them but also agreed.

A shadow passed over me, and for an instant I thought it was my bald eagle friend. My spirits lifted a little as the silhouette of a big bird glided between me and the sun. But when I shielded my eyes from the glare, I saw the telltale wing tips: spaces between the feathers meant this was not my eagle. This was a scavenger.

The vulture dropped to the road about twenty feet ahead of me, raggedy black wings beating as it picked up a fish washed onto the road. The bird settled for a moment, then registered me with a twitch of its russet, featherless head, and took to the air again, wheeling into the yellowy green of the maples, its meal in its talons. Farther ahead, other vultures circled the creek. It was a good day for them.

Closer to town, generators hummed and diesel engines rumbled ever louder. Only one car passed me as I crossed the branch-strewn bridge, under which many more trees lay washed against the pilings.

As Trip said, Mt. Marie was trashed. The water had receded, and the plows had removed the silt, but Greta, Scotty from the Mildew Mart, and the old codger from the pharmacy were all shoveling mud out of their businesses. The air was thick with exhaust from all their generators running, making the usually sleepy town loud as a steel mill. I wondered if the droning racket was lulling folks as it had me.

The same first responders who'd pumped out the Lamonts' basement were pitching in, and there was much hubbub, even conviviality. The Mt. Marie Rotary Club had set up a tent with food, water, coffee, and shovels, and were offering to help anyone who asked. Jen and Brianna were there, engaged in lively talk with townsfolk. People had come in from the surrounding hamlets to see the aftermath of the Flood of '03, and Mt. Marie was actually hopping, oblivious to the rock star who'd drowned twelve hours before.

Katie's Café, however, was not hopping. The exterior clapboard walls, freshly painted white, were stained with about two feet of brown from the creek overflow. I didn't bother looking inside. Brand-new picnic tables Christa had set outside were gone, washed to the outskirts of town, and the glass on most of the windows was broken. No one was tending to any of it.

To my surprise, as I watched the incongruous bustle of the devastated town, the southbound Trailways pulled in, almost on time, rolling over stray detritus in the road. I bought a ticket, took a seat in the back, and fell promptly to sleep, the toilet sloshing beside me. I didn't wake until Port Authority Bus Terminal in Manhattan, where I transferred to a Greyhound train that would take me all the way to Goldsboro, North Carolina, where I've been now for six weeks.

Why here? I needed to go where I don't owe anyone anything, where, on the contrary, someone owes me and cannot turn me away.

chapter 19

southern comfort

I'd worried that the rising heat of the North Carolina afternoons would put me in constant memory of my childhood, but more recent experiences play on a loop, elbowing those deeper memories to the edges of my thoughts. Not exactly a blessing but a perspective shift I'd not expected.

My mother, with whom I've not spent significant time in almost twenty years, gives me space to sleep, read, and occasionally idly strum a guitar she purchased for me at a yard sale, a surprisingly decent '60s-model Harmony arch top with dead but serviceable strings.

I'm also working, making money for the first time since Evan was born. In addition to continuing her job in the records department of the hospital, my mother has launched an eBay shop, selling yard sale and thrift store finds. She has a discerning eye and a flair for the business; she writes compelling copy for her wares and racks up impressive sales. Yet she still refers to it as *the* eBay.

She calls her shop AzaleaTreasures, and I am her first employee. I photograph, list, and ship items—somewhat mindless work I can do even saddled with depression. It takes up enough time to qualify as a part-time job, and she's been paying me fifty dollars an hour in cash, the majority of which I send back to Mt. Marie to help cover Flower Children Daycare and Brianna charges, which are significant.

The exorbitance of my salary, I like to think, is to offset my mother's deep-buried guilt over raiding about twenty grand of inheritance money my father had, to everyone's surprise, squirreled away in a trust to be accessed on my eighteenth birthday. (Money likely acquired through drug sales but still, a shocker.) She'd used the money to fund a T-shirt business with one of her boyfriends. Vice squad arrested him on opening day for dealing pot, the store failed, and she used the remaining cash for drug dealer boyfriend's bail, a generosity he rewarded by leaving the state. Luckily, she'd held onto her job at the hospital.

I discovered the truth about my inheritance a couple years later when, as a seventeen-year-old, I was snooping through her desk, looking for loose change for bus fare, but instead found bank statements with my dad's and my name on them. When I asked about it, she confessed to using the money to fund the T-shirt shop—Totally Tees. A fight ensued, during which she would not apologize. She'd done it for me, she claimed, as an investment, a way to make the money grow. Wasn't her fault her beau was a scofflaw. She'd make it up to me, she said, if I stopped being such an asshole. Then she slapped me.

This episode had been the final push to get me to Manhattan, in search of rock stardom.

We'd spoken only intermittently in the intervening years. She'd attended a couple of Stereoblind concerts when we came through town on the wings of "What the Funk Is Up?" and she'd come to my wedding. We spoke on Christmas and her birthday, or rather, usually left answering machine messages. She visited her grandson when he was one but hadn't made a return trip. His utter helplessness made her nervous, though she wouldn't admit it. Prior to my seeking distance and shelter from my fucked-up life in Mt. Marie, I'd begun to think my mother and I were settling into permanent estrangement.

~

Mom raps at the door. I can smell the coffee.

"I need you to pack up some stuff for UPS," she says. "Please."

I open the door, and my mom walks into the prefab barn holding my usual "I Am Not a Morning Person" mug filled with Folgers. She places it, a Yoplait, and a spoon on the card table next to Trip's letter. She sizes me up.

"You look good," she says flatly. Her bright blue eyes focus on my outfit, clothes she bought me at Belk's: stiff, new Lee jeans and a white, long-sleeved tee. First time in decades she's bought me clothes.

"You OK, Grant?" my mom asks, her accent elongating syllables into a familiar rhythm. I'm staring into space over my mug. "Your coffee's good and hot. Drink it. We got work to do on the eBay. I left some stuff to ship and stuff to photograph and list in your room. Some humdingers. Come on."

I nod and do as I'm told, still mildly stunned by my mother's engaged self.

In the last month, I've almost acclimated to her new personality. Age and solitude have mellowed her. She makes me less jumpy, which is taking some getting used to.

In her early fifties—about fifteen years ago—she stopped dating men and found she preferred being alone. Ironically, or perhaps not, she looks better than ever. She eschews makeup, lets her hair go snow white, and does Pilates, making her body wiry and taut. ("Come do the Pilates with me, Grant," she says. I demur.) She has acquaintances, mostly younger women who adore and idolize her, but no close friends.

The Internet is perfect for my mom, as she is more in control of relationships, and her eBay rating speaks volumes in her stead. The love she gets in user feedback lights her up like nothing I've ever seen.

These developments make me think that maybe she wasn't cut out to be a wife or a mom, just as I've been thinking I wasn't cut out for marriage or procreation. My DNA hums this song to me almost constantly.

She was so miserable when I was a kid, before and after my dad's death. She'd been drawn to alcoholic dreamers, doomed, grandiose narcissists who drained her of energy, leaving her exhaustedly yelling, snapping, routinely slapping me until I left home for New York City. But now she's radiant, off cigarettes for years, a healthy, lone, content she-wolf.

Maybe she's forgiven herself her trespasses. She certainly seems at peace. I am ambivalent about this, but I admit her paying me so well for the eBay work helps assuage my need to see her remorseful about her shitty parenting. And it's not like I've been the stellar parent; my own mistakes have softened my heart toward her. I am my mother's son.

~

After the flood, I'd called from a Pennsylvania rest stop to say I was en route, visiting her for the first time in a decade. Surprise. I told her Beth and I were "having serious problems," and she simply said, *Come on, you can stay in the cabin*, end of discussion. The "no questions asked" part annoyed me at first—*as ever, she does not care*—but now her lack of inquiry is welcome.

The first day, after I'd slept for twelve hours on a brand-new single bed, I simply said, *I had to get away*, and she nodded, like that was all she needed to know. We didn't dwell, and she didn't judge, either out of grace or apathy, I'm not really sure.

She was, however, demonstrative about her prefab barn, i.e. "the cabin," bought with eBay money. I prefer this sad little space, where I am safe from the three territorial rescue cats—Otis, Leopold, and Loretta—who stink up her house. Otis routinely attacks my ankles when I venture inside to work on eBay listings in the room where I once slept, hid, and became a musician.

~

I talk on the phone with Evan every other day, when he gets home from Flower Children Daycare at three p.m. We keep it light and short. He seems to get it, somehow. He asks when I'm coming home. I just say soon. And he says OK. Then he tells me about his day and what Katie's up to. They attend Flower Children Daycare together, and Katie is making an impression. Kids—and, I'm guessing, teachers—love her and are terrified of her. Evan talks like he is her manager.

"Katie's talking good now," he says. "She broke a stick, a big stick, she's really strong. Right next to Molly, she broke it and Molly cried but she's OK and Katie turned it into a big gun and Miss Luna said 'No guns in school' and Katie threw it in the woods. Like a . . . a . . . spear. And then she said all her days of the week. 'Cept for Tuesday."

Then he asks about the cats, whose exploits always provide ample distraction.

"Otis has been hiding under Grandma's fridge for a couple days," I say. "Totally normal. And Leopold brought Grandma another dead chipmunk as a present, and Loretta pooped in the bathtub again."

"They're so bad," says Evan.

"Yeah, but Grandma likes them."

"I like them, too. When can I see them?"

"Soon."

Underneath his outwardly "normal" tone, a dark harmonic in his voice conveys nonverbal subtext. He's wary, never fully engaged, talking atop an undercurrent of strain that's subtle enough to brush aside, at least on the phone. But that information—the subtle stuff—echoes in me constantly. I wonder if it's real or if my shadowed perspective overemphasizes or even invents it.

In any case, these conversations broke me down until a couple weeks ago. Now I can handle it better, although

I wonder if I'm giving myself an ulcer. My stomach trouble is intense and frequent, to the point where I'm not eating a lot and my clothes hang on me. The thought of heading north, or of my family heading south to see me, provokes even more gut pain.

Beth and I rarely say more than perfunctory, tight-lipped hellos, exchanging mostly need-to-know information about our son and various bills. If we keep paying the monthly minimum on our credit cards, we'll be free of debt in thirty years. Sasha's album is a hit, though, so Universal has extended Beth's contract, which means decent money for the next six months, a new computer—a Mac this time—and more trips across the country to handle press for her employer, as Sasha wows the talk show circuit and *SNL*. Her follow-up single, "Kiss Me You Fool," is in the running for the Song of the Summer of '03.

Beth's bearing up well. As with my mother's attitude, I am of two minds about it. On the one hand, part of me wants my wife to be so devastated she can't get out of bed, but another part is perversely impressed, as ever, by her focus. She does have a kid to feed and clothe. And she'll be needing lawyer fees for our divorce. So she works on.

We keep putting off deep discussion of our situation. Her voice still evokes waves of anger, shame, and dull sadness, sometimes even lust. But everything is so raw-edged, I don't address it, for fear it'll morph into rage, and I'll lose my shit. She feels the same reticence.

We'd tiptoed into the thick of everything right after I arrived here, but we soon stepped back. Those first few conversations were excruciating.

"So," I'd said into the phone. "You fucked him."

After a pause, a whispered, defeated: "Yes."

Sitting down, trembling, stabbing in my gut. "How many times?"

"Does it matter?"

"Yes."

"I don't know, two? I'm just so sorry, it was nothing. Please let me . . ."

But I'd hung up. The questions bearing down on me—was he better than me, were you pretending I was him those months you were so hot for me—evaporated into vapor but gathered form like clouds destined to rain again.

The next day, she'd called back and asked to be allowed to explain. Before she could begin, I laid into her. "I gotta know," I said, riding my rage like a wave, "where the fuck was his wifey when you guys were . . . uh . . . together? Fucking. Sleeping together."

"She was in their bed, I guess, I don't know . . . Maybe out. They have . . . an understanding . . . And I was so . . ."

"Let me guess," I said. "You were wasted and grief-stricken, I know. I know. And he took full advantage of that opportunity. What a guy."

Then she just cried and I sat and listened, mollified by her layered grief but only enough to shut up, not to change my mind.

"And you fucked Christa, right?" The words shot out of her, a razor lifeline.

"Yes. Once. When you were at the movies that day. It was nothing."

"Right, well, I don't want to know anything else about that," she said, collapsing back into despair. I thought perhaps she'd want to know it was an embarrassing memory, but kept quiet.

"It's better she's not here," she said, sharpened. "Some friend."

"I'm sorry," I said, sounding mostly irritated. "I really am. I'm sorry for it all."

"I am too, Grant." Her voice was oceans away. "We fucked up."

Long, heavy pause, during which I apologized again and again in my mind but not aloud. Finally, she said, "Did you get the box?"

I hadn't, but the following day a box arrived via FedEx from Mt. Marie, a box I remembered packing into the U-Haul on East Seventh. I'd written "LETTERS B 2 G '89–'95" on the sides.

I have not yet opened it.

~

In my absence, Brianna has become a nanny for Evan and Katie and is good at it. She transports the kids to and from daycare, then stays with both of them while Trip and Beth work. As often as not, it's Brianna I talk to when I call. She fills me in. Trip works late every weeknight, ostensibly to grade papers, plan lessons, and help challenged kids, but I suspect he's mainly getting time alone, and what he's actually doing with it, I cannot say. He's been only cursorily communicative with Beth, and she hasn't been pushing for anything more. He hasn't spoken about evicting us, which mystifies me.

When Beth's away, Brianna stays over at Shulz House, sleeping on the futon downstairs and looking after Evan. She's called me a couple times to check in, sounding much more together than before, rising to this new challenge like it was meant to be.

"Mr. Kelly, it's Brianna."

Heart in my throat. It was nine p.m. I knew from my At-A-Glance calendar that my wife was wrangling paparazzi on an LA video shoot with Sasha.

"Everything OK?" I gasped.

"Yeah, just letting you know that Evan read a whole book. *Go Dog Go!* That's pretty awesome for a four-year-old, you know? He read it to Katie. Thought you'd want to know. Awesome, right?"

"Wow. Thanks." Mixture of pride and sadness that I'd not been there for this milestone.

"And he potty trained her."

"Who? Katie?"

"Yeah. Y'know Mr. Lamont? He's pretty blown away. It's frickin' awesome."

"Have you seen Ms. Lamont? Christa? Does she know?"

"I call her to, you know, fill her in? On Katie. Just like I call you. Haven't seen her, though. She's staying in New Jersey, you know. Is that far from where you are in North Carolina?"

Didn't they cover geography in homeschool?

"It's about seven or eight hours," I say.

After a pause, "When you coming back? . . . Are you coming back?"

"I don't know."

"You don't know when or you don't know if you're coming back at all?"

"I gotta go, Brianna. Thanks for calling."

"No prob. One more thing I gotta tell you."

Before I can reply, she says, "Your family? They miss you."

Evan, sure, but Beth? She only misses the old me, not this new, unmedicated, enlightened-through-pain version. She says she wants to work things out, whatever it takes. Minus a time machine, I don't see how that's possible.

Let's talk about it later is my stock answer. She has no idea who I really am.

I don't think I want to work things out. Why set ourselves up again for more hurt down the line? Why set myself up for yet more failure? Why not just divorce and work out some kind of custody arrangement in which Evan will come visit me in some hovel? And Beth and I, as individuals, will be free of the burden of monogamy, which we're obviously not suited for. And what's good enough for fifty percent of American marriages is good enough for us, yes? What has turned out to be a great decision for my mom is likely a great decision for me and for everyone: lone wolf-hood.

~

As ever, Otis, a tabby only recently free of mange, attacks my leg when I enter my mother's house. He latches onto the stiff denim of my pants, takes a ride like a burr, and doesn't pull in his claws until I'm assessing the items I'll be shipping: a pair of vintage Lucchese cowboy boots, cherry black, probably a size 8 (original Luccheses were made to order, no sizes), going to Miami, and a beige fringed vest, size M, looks like it was originally sold at The Limited in the seventies, going to Brooklyn. Both bought by my mom for next to nothing at a yard sale. As I'm rooting through Jiffy bags, the doorbell rings, the same ding DONG of my childhood. Except now the chime is answered by three sets of cat paws scurrying in all directions.

Who could it be at ten a.m.? My mother has already run off a couple Jehovah's Witnesses, so it's not them. Maybe UPS? But they almost always come after noon.

"Grant!" my mom calls from the door. "You got a visitor."

I walk in and there in the living room stands Christa, looking tired and sad, but also solid, at the tail end of a mission. Leopold and Loretta walk gingerly toward her, feline curiosity spiking their fur. Somewhere, Otis lies in wait.

"You want some coffee?" my mom asks Christa. "You look bushed. Just made some."

"No thanks, I'm caffeinated to the gills," Christa says. "You look amazing, Ms. Kelly."

"I'll have some, Mom, thanks," I say, in part to get rid of her. "Everything OK, Chris?"

She nods and holds up her hand, warding off my anxious tone.

"Christa, you are looking well, too," my mom says, ignoring me, beaming at Christa's honest praise. "What brings you to Goldsboro?"

"I was in the neighborhood . . ."

This is painfully lame, of course, but my mom nods, either sagely or cluelessly, I can't tell.

"OK," mom says. "Say, how long has it been since I've seen you?"

"Since Grant and Beth's wedding, I guess," Christa says, wincing in discomfort. She sneezes.

"Bless you," my mother and I say in unison.

It's like a dream. I'm standing agape, fighting impulses to both flee and hug.

"Thanks," Christa says. "Allergies."

"Cats?" my mom asks.

Christa nods apologetically, and we head to the prefab barn, leaving my mother. I've set up two old lawn chairs just outside the barn door, in the shade of a gnarled dogwood in full white bloom. The afternoon soundtrack envelops us as we sit, lawn mowers, birds, sprinklers spurting in rhythm.

"What the hell, Christa?"

"I couldn't sleep last night, so instead of taking Ambien, I went for a drive and just kept going. Your mom's listed in the phone book. You're so skinny."

I nod, looking for words as I take her in. Although sleepless, she looks better than last time I saw her, when she was knee-deep in black water in her basement. She's put on a little weight, filled back out, sporting jeans with blown-out knees and a snug black T-shirt, hair shimmery in the morning sun, split ends recently trimmed. She takes a deep breath and closes her eyes.

"You're lucky your mom's so spry," she says. "Mine's a mess. She's been keeping my dad and me busy. Fucking Alzheimer's. It's a good thing I showed up when I did. My brothers are useless."

"I'm sorry," I say. "But still, why . . . ?"

"I've been wanting to come down for a couple weeks. I just needed to see you, didn't want to call. Didn't feel right. I hope it's OK I came . . . I should've called. I don't want to make more trouble."

"No, it's OK. How long a drive . . . ?"

"Eight hours, but that's with a lot of pee breaks. Um, Grant, I . . ."

She's gathering herself to say something just as my mother comes out with two mugs of coffee.

"Here ya'll go," she says. I want to bitch about her not listening to Christa's decline of the coffee offer, but I bite it back.

My mom appraises Christa's knees. "Christa, I got some brand new Ralph Lauren blue jeans I think would fit you perfect. Factory seconds, but you'd never know."

"Thanks Mom," I say, sending code in my tone for *leave us*, which, thankfully, she understands. She heads back inside, striking up a one-sided conversation with Otis, quite audible through the screen door. She sounds very much like a crazy street person, albeit a happy one.

"What is it, Christa?" I ask.

Christa sips her coffee and says, "I'm just so sorry, Grant. That's the main thing. I wanted to tell you I'm sober; I'm off the Vicodin, and I'm tapering off the Effexor, which, they don't tell you when you go on it, gives me a constant motherfucker of a withdrawal headache, like a cocaine hangover. But I'd rather . . . I'm just . . . I'm trying to fix my life. Is the thing. Those meds were really bad for me. All that shit was. I'm seeing a new doctor now and he won't even prescribe Effexor, no matter how much free shit they give him. He says he's seen too many people who've had really bad side effects, some even worse than mine. People doing crazy shit, saying . . . crazy shit. A suicide, an almost-suicide. But the main thing is, I'm sorry. I'm owning all of it, not blaming the meds or anything. It was me. So much of what happened is my fault, and I'm sorry . . ."

"Wait," I say. "Wait. A lot of it is my fault. And Beth's fault. I mean, we're all blame-worthy. Except Trip and the kids."

At the mention of Trip, Christa tenses as if stung, then dives back into her speech. "I shouldn't have said all that shit at dinner, and in front of the kids, that was the worst, that led to . . ."

She buries her face in her hands and cries, and in that moment, my sorrow for Paul blindsides me. I reach over and clasp Christa's hand. A long-delayed remorse for Paul's fate washes over me; sadness over his death, over our one-time friendship, his friendship with my son, a sense of loss separate, for the first time, from my sense of betrayal.

I shrug it off and summon the hate, always at the ready, a salty-sweet taste like blood from a split lip.

This is Christa's and my first physical contact since we were naked in the bathroom, and a fresh memory of that scene flashes across my mind. It was my last sexual encounter, and probably hers, too; the embarrassment returns and I drop her hand.

Christa looks up and around at my mother's back-yard, too emotionally overwrought for pretense. "You OK here?" she asks. "Lotta shit went down here when you were a kid, right?"

"Yeah. I'm OK. I think I've learned a lot about myself here, actually."

"Like what?" she says, suspicious. "What have you learned?"

"I'm not cut out for the family thing, I don't think. I can't do it. I am my mother's son. My father's son. I think I finally get it."

Christa shakes her head and pushes herself out of the lawn chair with her fists. She paces for a few moments, then faces me.

"That is a crock of shit, Grant. A big, fat, fucking crock of shit. I love you, you know, and because I love you, I cannot let that stand. I'm sorry, I can't."

My head snaps back.

"You are *not* like your folks," she continues. "You think because you failed with the music and fucked up a couple times as a husband and parent that it's better for everyone if you just bolt, but that is a crock. Of. Shit. One good thing about your meds is they seemed to keep that kind of bullshit thinking at bay."

"At a price," I say.

"Yeah, I know all about that price," Christa nods bitterly. "When I did and said all that crazy shit, guess what? I wasn't depressed."

I flash on the night Paul drowned. "Christa, if I hadn't let them get in their car, Paul wouldn't be dead. That's the truth. I could've stopped them. My kid saw that. God. My kid saw that."

"You risked your life to save Melora. He saw that, too."

"Exactly! That was batshit crazy."

Christa sits back down, panting, flush spreading up her neck. She moves her chair to face me and changes tack. She's been thinking about all of this, driving south on I-95, threading it into a knot she is now untangling.

"Did it ever occur to you," she says, speedily, "that while you were wishing you had all that Paul had, he was wishing he had what you had?"

"He did have what I had for a few nights there."

"Not talking about that. Talking about your kid, your family. Don't be a dick. That Padrino shit was adorable, but Evan didn't love Paul like he loves you. How can you not see that?"

"Evan doesn't know me. If he did, if he knew the details, he wouldn't feel that way. I can't give him what he saw in Paul, and I can't give Beth what she saw, and, for all I know, felt, in Paul. And I let Paul die because of that. I am a horrible person."

"No. No, no, no. I was there, remember? I know what I saw."

"You were drunker than I've ever seen you. And drug crazy."

"Fuck you. I saw him wave you off. He made that choice. He did. He knew he was too much weight. What happened after that wasn't your fault. It was shitty luck for him. But he died saving his wife, which he could not have done without you. And in your twisted brain, that's bad? What the fuck is wrong with you? You're the only person I know who saved someone's life, Grant."

"Simmer down, please. You drove across three states to yell at me?"

"You're killing me here, Grant. You're so fucking blind with jealousy and all this other bullshit, you can't see anything."

"Well I'm not so great that my greatness kept my wife from hopping into bed with her rock star crush."

"Yes, that does suck, but listen . . . she was really bad off, and I'm sure she really regrets it. Her kid brother had just died, if you recall. Surely you of all people can understand that? Hello? She loves you, Grant."

"She says she regrets it, yeah. She says. But you know what? This has all been really instructive."

"Instructive? Whatever lessons you feel you've learned from this, you should also know this: Paul, for all his bullshit fame and dough, coveted what you have. He stepped over the line to get closer to it, yeah, but I bet he regretted it, too."

"Yeah, he was really tormented with remorse, must've haunted his beach time in St. Croix."

"For fuck's sake, Grant, he's dead. Dead. We gotta go on living."

"I am living."

"Yeah, in a fucking shed!"

"Christa. You are off your meds."

She swats away my comment. "You know who else covets what you have?" she says. "I do. I do." She hides her face again and sobs through her fingers. "I got so carried away, I took advantage. I . . . am so sorry."

"Christa. It's OK. I get it."

"Do you? I don't think you do. And you're surrounding yourself with just the people—or person—who won't call you on this shit. This is not a good place for you. She's clueless, same as it ever was. You need to get back to your family."

"Evan sounds fine on the phone. Getting along great without me. Beth, too."

"More bullshit." Christa throws her head back. "Has it occurred to you your son's keeping it together because you're not there and he thinks he needs to be the 'man of the house'?" She makes finger quotes, her face now beet red. "He needs you there now, in the wake of all this shit, and he'll need you there even more in the future. And not on a part-time basis. Who knows that better than you? You gonna let a trailer trash girl raise your kid?"

"Come on. Brianna's not that."

"I know, I'm just . . . my head is killing me, and you're not helping, you know, with your bullshit. Go home, Grant."

"I can't. I'm so anxious, you have no idea."

"Oh, I bet I do."

"I'll fuck up again. Like with the junkie in the park, like . . ."

"That could've happened to anyone."

"No. You're wrong there. Do you know anyone else that's happened to?"

Christa's lips tighten.

"Exactly," I say. "And! And! And . . . I am a shitty friend, too, don't forget that!"

I have been stockpiling my reasons. I hadn't realized it, but here they are, like items in a pile I can lift up and display. "I betrayed my best friend, and I'm supposed to go back and live on his land . . ."

"Our land . . . whatever."

"Yeah, whatever . . . I'm supposed to go back and do that? I betrayed him. In a house he owns. Co-owns. A house he gave me when I was in need. What kind of a friend does that? At least my wife didn't shit where she eats, you know. I did."

"Well I helped you there, and that is the cherry on top of my own little shit sundae, and I'm trying to get past the awfulness of it all. You're fucking reveling in it."

The "awfulness of it all." Again disparaging our indiscretion, again the mixed feelings.

"But for fuck's sake, Grant, listen: go back. He'll forgive you. It won't be the same, I won't Pollyanna it. But he'll forgive you. Not me, but you."

"Are you going back?"

She closes her eyes again. "No. We're done."

"What? So you're not practicing what you're preaching. God, have you got balls."

"I'm the one that's not cut out for this. Not you. We are not the same, you and me. Maybe I'm just not cut out to parent with Trip, and once we separate, it'll be easier. But supermom, superwife, whatever, I am not."

"C'mon, Katie loves you. Trip loves you, too."

"I guess. But maybe I should've listened to Mother Nature. I'm just not a natural. Beth is, and you shouldn't take that for granted. But I'm not. And I'm trying not to feel ashamed about that, because it's not like I'm bad or a freak. Not being 'Perfect Wife and Mom' isn't shameful. Not every woman is supposed to be part of a unit, living like the Huxtables or something. I can still co-parent, but best to do it separate from Trip. Better we realize it now. And I've thought all of this for a while, even before you guys moved up in January. I thought—and Trip thought—having a kid would bring us closer, and damned if we weren't gonna take that step. But the opposite has happened. And when you guys needed refuge, we both jumped on that to distract us from our problems even more. Like getting a dog."

"Three dogs."

"Yeah. Ha fucking ha. And Katie being so troubled? Turns out, it's us, Grant. *It's us.* She's just hypersensitive to our stress. Poor thing. And she really is better since I've gone. That is the fucking truth. She stopped shitting her pants and scratching."

She wipes tears with trembling hands. "I do love my Katie, and I'll help raise her, she'll want for nothing, but I'm staying in Ocean City to take care of my mom for a bit, and that is a fucking job, let me tell you. Trip is up for it, and Brianna, bless her, is actually a godsend, I gotta say. I'll visit, and Katie'll come stay with me at my folks' when things calm down a little. But I'm gonna buy Trip out. He'll own the land, all of it. And the restaurant, which insurance is covering. And he's fine with all that. He's much better without me there. More at ease. Getting himself back together. I think he's writing again. Sleeping better, he says. Off Ambien.

"So we've separated. We can get divorced in a year, New York state law. But you . . . that can't happen to you."

"She's right, Grant."

My mother is at the door to her back porch, all three cats sitting behind her, tails a-twitch, eyes glistening, watching the human man and woman in heated conversation.

"Everything she says is true," Mom says. "You and Beth are so much better at being parents than your dad and I were, and you're a good couple. Your dad and me . . . we . . . were out of our depth. I've made my peace with that. But I am not . . . good at . . . communicating this kind of stuff." She laughs hollowly. "It is not my forte, no sir. It's . . . painful to think, to talk, about failures, normal though they may be. That never changes. Unfortunately. I know you've had your share, but this one, your family, is still in play. And if you leave your family, I'd wager that'll haunt you. That much I know.

"You need to get back to your life, son. You are the best mistake I ever made, no regrets. My door's always open, and I've loved having you back in my life, but you should get back, get on that road. You don't need advice from me, of all people, but there you go."

She smiles sadly, turns, and heads back in, murmuring low to her cats as they entwine around her legs, eager to be fed and mothered.

~

Christa is napping in the prefab barn, and I'm handing Jiffy packs to the UPS guy when my mom approaches me with an envelope.

"So, you're off tonight?" she says.

"Yeah, after Christa gets on the road, I'll pack my stuff and get out of here. Can you take me to the bus?"

"I could, or I could do this."

She hands me the key to her Hyundai Accent. "This is yours now," she says. "I'm signing it over to you. It's a good car. 2002. Gets good mileage, should do well in the snow up there."

I gasp. "What? What about you? How will you get around?"

"I got a great deal on a Subaru Outback. Got it on the eBay. Guy is bringing it by tomorrow. Great price. I practically stole it."

I murmur a thank-you and fold her in my arms. She stiffens but doesn't pull back quite as quickly as usual. She breaks away and hands me the envelope.

"Here," she says.

Inside is a check for twenty thousand dollars, made out to me.

"I sold an 1808 atlas I found at an estate sale in Charlotte," she says. "Bought it for a hundred bucks. Sold it on the eBay for twenty grand. I've got a couple more, believe it or not. In a safety deposit box. I was going to leave this to you in my will, but you need it now, and I am not dying for a while yet, long as I keep up with the Pilates. If I'd known you were in trouble, I'd have done this before now."

"You sold *a book* for twenty grand?" I drop to her sofa, and a cat claw shoots out from underneath and digs into my ankle. Otis.

"Yeah," she says. "People just don't realize what they have. But I do."

chapter 20

flashback friday

It's approximately ten hours as the crow flies from Goldsboro to Mt. Marie. I'll be leaving around ten p.m., night driving. I bid farewell to a nap-refreshed Christa, clinking coffee mugs in the fluorescent hum of my mother's kitchen, dusk descending outside. Christa departs tearfully with a repurposed Belk's bag filled with various clothing items from my mom, including factory second Ralph Lauren jeans with intact knees. She'll stay off the interstate, she says, and take her time. Although she insists otherwise, she probably won't keep in touch, which is how it should be anyway. Aside from crossing paths when she visits her soon-to-be-ex and her daughter, Christa and I will never be friends again.

I take one last barefoot walk around my old neighborhood, nighttime dew condensing in the air. A hole opens in me where Christa's and my friendship had been. I try to fill it with images of happy times, but this action only draws more attention to the jagged edges and still-simmering guilt. I do it anyway: there we are, talking about "uncool" music and movies, and her scheme for a vegan BBQ restaurant, which I encourage to no avail; there she is, mildly tipsy at the Digital Café bar, sipping from a stash of absinthe, talking about Trip, back when she glowed from the light he bestowed on her; there I am, feeling buffed up from her praise of my music, her insistence that I could spin a snippet of melody on a hissy tape into a Big Fat Hit. She was always a Grant Kelly Superfan, even as I gained no satisfaction from my ill-advised solo pursuits. If there were a couple hundred thousand more like her, I'd be the star I'd always wanted to be.

I finally stop stalling and, after one last awkward hug from my mother, I head out in the Hyundai. Driving north is like driving back in time. Each time I stop to refuel or guzzle coffee, the air is a little colder, less springtime humid, and apprehension I've held at bay revisits me with renewed intensity. I listen mostly to AM talk radio and Christian broadcasting, both ludicrous and offensive, both raising my blood pressure almost as efficiently as caffeine, diminishing my need for yet another large, usually burnt, coffee. On the passenger seat is the box LETTERS B 2 G '89–'95, still unopened.

Outside a truck stop in Virginia, I call Beth on a pay phone. It's around two a.m., the darkest part of a moonless morning and cool enough for my breath to crystallize. A dilapidated textile mill looms across the service road, and the air is thick with honeysuckle and Dumpster. A fat raccoon waddles by, stopping to look at me sullenly, no trace of fear. In the nearby trash, his companion digs through a cornucopia of fast-food containers and who knows what else.

Only one of three pay phones works, and it reeks of urine. I enter the code from my phone card and take a deep breath through my mouth.

Three rings. In my mind, the action plays out in our Shulz House bedroom. One ring stirs her from sleep, the next, she's deciphering that it's the phone and not the alarm clock, one more as she clears her throat . . .

"Hello . . . ?" she says, panicked and confused.

"It's OK," I say. "It's OK. It's me."

"Is everything OK? What time is it?"

"Everything's OK. I'm in Virginia somewhere. Near Fredericksburg. I'm coming back."

"Oh!" she says, still a little confused. "When do you get in? Where? What bus?"

"No bus, I'm driving. Mom gave me her car . . . and . . ."

"What? She gave you a car? When?"

"Yesterday. I'll explain later."

"Is she OK?"

"She's fine, actually. I just needed to let you know I'll be there in about eight hours. Everything OK?"

She cries softly into the phone. "Grant, I can't wait to see you. I miss you so much. I can't wait. I . . . have something for you."

"What?"

"I'd like it to be a surprise."

"Uh . . . is it a good surprise?"

"I think so."

"OK. I've got a surprise for you, too," I say, my fingers tracing the edge of the envelope sticking out of the breast pocket of my jean jacket.

Why the mutual insistence on, and acceptance of, surprises? Staying in control. Afraid to unload too much too soon. We are still a leaky boat on the shoals, and we both know it.

A murmuring voice rises in the background. Evan in the bed.

"It's Papa," Beth says. "He's coming home." Then, to me: "Evan wants to talk—"

"Papa!" Evan is wide awake. "You coming back? You coming home?"

I almost double over at the sound of his excited voice. The dark strain I've heard for weeks is gone. I was not imagining it.

"Papa? Papa? Hellooooo?"

"Yeah, yeah, I'm here," I say weakly. "I'm here."

And I am. I am completely right there.

~

It will cost me a couple hours, but I give in to impulse and detour off I-95 and into Manhattan, bound for our old East Village neighborhood. Still in control, still dictating my own destiny, and procrastinating the inevitable confrontation with a life I left in shambles. My body hungers for physical contact with my wife and son, but renegade impulses in my mind strongly suggest going elsewhere, to a place where I can start over again with my car and my twenty grand, leaving Evan and Beth better off. This is the same shadowscape I've trod for weeks, not so easily obliterated. Despite my mother's and my friend's admonitions, the allure of escape remains.

I hit NYC at the tail end of morning rush hour. The Holland Tunnel is bumper-to-bumper, and the AM signal dies, so I switch over to "Modern Rock" station WLIR just in time to hear the propulsive bassline that opens "What the Funk Is Up?," i.e. my propulsive bassline. Wow.

The DJ talks over the intro: "Here's your Flashback Friday, going all the way back to 1990, with Stereoblind's 'What the Funk . . . Is Up?'"

Tristan's vocal rises in the mix. It's louder than I recall. Maybe this is a remastered version of the tune, or maybe I've lost some frequencies in my hearing and can't discern the chicken-scratch guitar as much. Whatever. It sounds great on the Hyundai car stereo, so I crank it.

I bob my head. I recall standing next to Tristan behind the mixing board at Electric Lady as Mark Opitz, fresh from producing INXS, spun the two-inch Ampex tape, smiled and said, "That's the take. This is a hit." He was right.

> *I'm lookin' at the sky, I say*
> *What the funk is up?*
> *I'm lookin' in your eye, I say*
> *What the funk is up?*
> *It's a psychedelic situation, an*
> *immaculate*
> *creation, making the entire nation say*
> *What the funk is up?*

Cringe-worthy lyrics. Just awful. I thought I could improve them, but what do I know? Maybe my less crude, more sophisticated efforts—rejected by Tristan—would've sunk the fratty ebullience that rocketed us to the top of the Modern Rock charts alongside The Cult, Tears For Fears, and Love & Rockets, and sent Stereoblind around the world and eventually to Lollapalooza.

My bassline holds up well. Muscle memory in my hands sets my thumb to whacking the steering wheel. My line propels the groove while also weaving harmonically under Tristan's croony-then-snarly vocal, which sounds alternately like a white dude affecting both hip-hop-speak and Bowie-isms. Distinctive, certainly. The guitar solo is still the weak link in the tune, but it is mercifully brief.

In three minutes and forty-five seconds, "What the Funk Is Up?" crossfades into "Seven Nation Army" by The White Stripes. As I make my way to the East Village, WLIR treats me to the current bands that are living the dream—and, possibly, a few of the nightmares—as I once did. Audioslave, Puddle of Mudd, and, still going strong, Red Hot Chili Peppers. The punky, post-Nirvana metal attitude of these acts makes Stereoblind seem "lite" by comparison, but onstage, we were an intense, well-oiled juggernaut, not to be fucked with, and I miss those days.

I pull up to a hydrant outside 244 East Seventh and kill the radio. I have no plans to get out of the car. A youngish couple I do not recognize comes out of our old building, gliding like ballet dancers—maybe they are—down the three-stepped stoop. I wonder if they're the new inhabitants of our apartment, and if so, should I apologize for the chicken bomb. They amble by, presumably to classes somewhere, or maybe walking each other to the subway where they'll kiss goodbye and each go off to the jobs that finance their Young Manhattan Life. Needless to say, I am invisible to them.

LETTERS B 2 G '89–'95 calls to me. I roll down the window to a perfect New York City spring day: a mix of exhaust, new leaves defiant in the diesel haze, and the frequent palate cleanser of river breeze. Spanish and English drift through the air, the creak and clang of greased machinery—men working under the street— groaning taxi brakes, and the flutter of pigeon wings. I pull the box onto my lap and tear into it.

At the top of a pile of letters Beth once wrote me is a Post-it note that reads "STILL TRUE." The letters, encased in cardboard, still retain the air of the very apartment below where I am now parked; a dry, old-wood-and-Murphy's-Oil-Soap scent with a tinge of Beth's own lavender and Chanel, and, somehow, her seafoam breath.

I reach into the pile and pull out a bundle tied with a red ribbon. I remember: Stereoblind was on tour, and she wrote letters longhand like diary entries and FedEx'd the bundles to various hotels. She was very choosy with paper and ink, writing with an expensive Cross pen on rag paper, which has barely aged.

June 28, 1990

My Love,

the waxing void the shadow ache
a thousand moments of bitter tears
lathering tongue boils for your honey
rusting symphony of lusty music
crying fingers moan frantic on sweat
petal mist
blood beats crushing want
head weak and shot through with raw
need
summer tenement moon smears our
dreamy sky

June 29, 1990

My Love,

Amazing. Dawn on a workday, and I am awake enjoying dream of you and me entangled, me reaching for you in a dark pool of water like velvet, you a sea crea-ture, a water mammal like a dolphin (but not) singing to me and me pulling you out and on top of me, and you become you and us making love. I came in my sleep, Love. Another first. Not even read-ing Judy Blume back in the day did that, and of course that is saying something, something that will echo through the day in my whole body as I shuffle papers, write copy for Proctor & Gamble, and water for you.

Question: what do I do now? As in this moment with 2 hours to kill and coffee and toast breakfast enjoyed and not able to drift back to dreamland where you are aquatic mayor shapeshifting loverman. What? I will walk the park in sporty new sneakers then walk all the way to work with a spring in my step, each step will be a different thought of you, all good or at least all delicious.

I love you madly. B

July 4, 1990

My Love,

*FIREWORKS. Watched from Christa's
rooftop, wished you were there, but you
know that. You would have made me
laugh and see everything differently,
which is your wont and which I do love.
Tonight I saw only through my own
lenses, and that was fine, but with you
it's Technicolor.*

*Christa is a hoot. I think I like her. She
never stops talking and most of it is
pretty funny but what is indeed funnier
is Trip, who is SHAZAM'd like Gomer
Pyle, a mess of adorable lusty love and
naturally I can relate to that. He will be
moving in imminently, and I foresee rug
rats. Gramercy digs are swank as you
predicted and you will be jealous but I
am still partial to our li'l love nest. But
when you get that record contract, we
will move on up to the east side to a
deluxe apt in the sky-hi-hi.*

*Fella name of Chris was there. Needs
publicist for record label he started out
of his apartment: Matador. Si señor. He's
got two bands—Teenage Fanclub (Scot-
tish, like Big Star meets Sonic Youth)
and Superchunk (Chapel Hill, loud college-y pop)—and he can't pay me much,
but I have a hunch he's onto something
like he can see the future, and I am sure*

*sure sure he will be interested in your
demos. Thinking about freelancing, and
if it's good I'll be able to quit my gig, and
we will get into any and all shows we
want. Yay. Also: free CDs.*

*Now off to think about what kind of
fireworks you are bringing home to me.
There was this big chrysanthemum (sp?)
looking one I especially liked . . . it went
on and on and on, till the tips almost
touched the tops of some buildings altho
that may have been an illusion. I am not
in my right mind.*

*I hope this finds you dripping with sweat
post show, which I can almost taste if I
bite my lip just so and concentrate.*

I love you madly. B

I retie the bundle, wipe tears, and pick out another,
an unfamiliar-looking envelope. It's new, dated April 10,
2003, almost a month ago. It had been on the top of
the pile but fell to the side. It's still sealed, with only my
name on it. Inside is a letter written on rag paper with
what appears to be a fancy pen.

April 10, 2003

My Love,

*That is what you are, still. I am sending
you these letters not to manipulate you
into coming home but to remind you of
a love I once took more time to express*

*and, in expressing it in these letters, I
feel I strengthened it, made it more real,
more tangible, and able to withstand so
much of what came after, although I fear
not everything.*

*I wish now I'd not boxed them up but
kept them close at hand like talismans.
But as you will know when you read
them—if you do, and I hope you do—they
can open a wound in the heart, and if
someone were to suggest that we don't
need any more wounds, it would be hard
to argue with them. And yet.*

*Tonight when I put our boy to bed I lay
awake listening to him sleep and wondering what to do, what to do, and something pulled me from bed and led me to
the box, I'm not sure what. It felt like a
benevolent presence is all I can say. It
felt like my brother.*

*Reading my letters to you made me
think and feel many things, not least of
which is what a double-edged sword is
email. The letters end right around the
time we all started emailing. What price
convenience indeed. I am so so so glad
you saved them. Thank you. They have
a distinctive power, yes? If I do say so
myself. Just as yours had, and still have,
on me. I read this strong lusty woman's
thoughts (me, that is) and want to cry.
And I do.*

I also say this: I am so sorry about what I did, which I understand casts even more doubt on your doubtful mind and causes me pain every day especially as it led to so much other darkness and hardship for all. I want more than anything now to get past this recent nightmare time and into a new chapter of our lives, a chapter where we are together with our boy. I don't know if I can restore what's been broken, but I want nothing more than to be allowed to try. I hope you want that chance too, because I am ready to give it. Our story—yours and mine—need not be over.

I read a great Lily Tomlin quote: "Forgiveness means giving up all hope for a better past." I like that, in part because it sounds cool and like you I love Lily Tomlin. I think it means to make an effort to not focus on anger—tho justified—and fear, which is challenging but is possible for me as I can see, especially through these letters, how expansive our story is, how strong our love was and remains and can yet be, and I've been drawing from it in my mind, and it helps to move focus away from our recent unchangeable past. For the most part we don't need a better past to hope for, so we can do this. That's how I feel. We can, it's just a matter of will we. I want to know how you feel. Want to hear the words from your dear, dear mouth. Or if it's better for you, in a letter.

*I am hope and lust and love for you all
at once, my Love. I feel you in my bones
and every stitch of every seam of my
raggedy heart.*

I love you madly. B

~

The maples lining Shulz Way are a deeper green, the
late morning air sweet and steamy. Silt mounds still line
the blacktop alongside snapped tree trunks and tangled
foliage, all bathed now in leafy shadow, monuments to
the flood. Passing the Lamonts' Victorian, I see no car
in the driveway; Trip teaching, Katie at Flower Children
Daycare, I assume. Evan, I know, is staying home with
Beth, waiting for me.

A chill runs through me as I pass the spot where I
saw Paul and Melora's overturned Saab. Somewhere
nearby, Paul took his last conscious breath.

I pull into the driveway behind the Camry, over potholes filled with fresh gravel. I drain the last of my water,
hoping it will calm my stomach, which still tenses and
aches, despite much Pepcid. My mouth is chalky and dry,
a mix of Altoids- and road-breath. The birches flanking
the driveway are fully greened now, branches bending
overhead, dripping from a recent rain.

A flash of yellow draws my gaze over the stone wall,
into Ricky Shulz's side yard, to King's tail wagging. The
dog's face is wide open, alert, his ears perked. I brace for
a volley of barks that do not come. He sits, regal, composed, watching, tail beating the rutted clay beneath the
clothesline, to which he is fastened. His gaze darts to the
porch, where Beth is rising from a wicker chair.

She walks slow, then almost runs to the car, hair tumbling, newly redarkened, I notice. A vintage rose-colored

sundress flecked with black dots clings to her, spaghetti straps loose over her rounded deltoids. Her arms are more sharply defined than a month ago. I'd forgotten how almost Mediterranean she looks in raw sunlight. We haven't been apart this long since my Stereoblind days.

I rise from the car, and she crashes into me, her biceps hard against my back, hands splayed over my shoulder blades, traveling down.

"Your ribs," she says. "I can feel your ribs."

"Where's Evan?" I say into her hair; rising scent, mixing with nearby lilacs, quickens and thickens my blood. My hands roam her waist, ass, lower back. Nothing beneath the thin sundress but skin, familiar curves and crevices, tight bands of muscle responding to my touch.

"He passed out," she says. "He'd been up since you called. So excited."

In a dim recess of my mind, I calculate the chances of Evan waking, and a wave of desire rushes through my torso, my heartbeat perceptible underneath my sternum and in the tips of my fingers. I maneuver Beth to the driver's side back door of the Hyundai. She places her hands over mine, seeks out my eyes. Her pupils are fully dilated, irises heavy brown, broad forehead lined from worry, breath coming faster, filling my nostrils, telling me she had coffee and maybe oatmeal for breakfast, then brushed her teeth with Colgate. Her mouth swells.

The skin on the back of my neck prickles. My thumb brushes her lips, she takes it in her mouth. I graze the gap in her teeth and she bites softly.

I pull the door open, push her hips onto the backseat, she gasps, nods. Quick look to the Shulz's driveway, which is empty. King is on his belly, contentedly chewing on what looks to be a cow's thigh bone, yet I feel his peripheral attention on us. With the Hyundai engine quieted, a cacophony of birdsong fills the air, a wood chipper howling in the distance.

I scoot in behind her, knocking cellophane wrappers and other travel trash to the floorboards. My senses heightened, I wince at the reek of the grilled cheese and coffee I scarfed down somewhere in Pennsylvania, and subsequent farts and BO. Beth either doesn't notice or doesn't care, responding to my hands, letting herself be thrown against the seat. The cool, damp sole of her foot knocks the side of my head and she gasps, says *oh shit sorry*. My head snaps back and I laugh. She returns my laugh.

I slam the door behind us and pull her to me, jerking her dress over her belly. A seam rips somewhere, appendectomy scar smiling at me, the scent of her desire darkening my blood. She's nodding and breathing quicker, hands at my cock, stroking, hardening it as I push my pants to my knees. One quick touch between her legs sends an electric jolt through her as my fingers draw back coated. Our pelvises find each other, and I sink in. We both yelp, our voices close and loud in the car, upholstery squeaking.

She is molten inside, hot almost to the point of pain. She contracts around me, humming low, fingers in my hair as I roam her breasts with my tongue. I grab her wrist, her Kegel grip on me intensifies. I'm holding her wrist against the car seat as her head lolls in a nod, her lips saying something that is a cross between *yeah* and *OK*. I grab her other wrist and raise it above her head, tendons tightening around the lump of her radius bone.

We begin a measured, let's-not-come-too-soon rhythm. After a few moments, she begins to buck fast and hard, but my hands leave her wrists and find her hips, slowing her down in the nick of time. A film spreads across the windshield. Beneath my palms, I feel her pelvic bones quiver, wrapped in cords of straining flesh.

The windows are fully fogged when, with a gasp of surprise, she cries out, a deep *Oh, Uh, OH*, directly into my ear as she shudders against me, her contractions coaxing my own cum, ambush style, like a sneeze.

Panting, she moves languidly against me, a cooling wave; I soften inside her, my fingertip tracing her shoulder, pulling her dress straps back over her now-slippery clavicle.

"I do like this car," she says thickly.

"Was that my surprise?" I ask.

"One of them, I guess. Was that mine? It was very nice indeed. I missed your hands."

I uncouple from her, both of us emitting a sad "aw," and run my hands through her dampened hair, my fingernails scraping her scalp as orgasm aftershocks ripple through her and her body hums, postcoital pliant.

King barks and we both tense.

I sigh and she laughs ruefully. Reluctant to settle back into the now, even though I bring glad tidings, I reach for my jacket in the front seat, pull out the check, unfold it, and show it to her. She gasps.

"Right?" I say. "Right?"

I explain, and she sits there, mouth open, eyes wide, looking like a little girl, confused, even a little irritated.

King starts barking repeatedly, further breaking the postcoital endorphin spell.

"We should go in," Beth says. "This . . . this is amazing. You don't think it'll bounce, do you?"

"Nope," I say, pulling up my pants. "I don't. Now. Where's my surprise? And where's my boy?"

We walk inside, and Evan bodychecks me with a Katie-like shout.

"Hey!" I say. "You're awake! Mommy said you were asleep!"

Beth gasps behind me, sounding like an orgasm aftershock but mostly just shock, as in, *did he look out the window and see us fucking?* The car is still fogged up, so maybe not. But maybe. King barks on, but when I close the door, he stops.

Evan is wiry, heavier, and smells slightly different, more sour than sweet. He wraps his arms around me and climbs my trunk, saying *Papa, Papa, Papa* over and over again. My knees buckle a little as I gather him into my arms. Pain shoots up from my lower back.

"Careful, baby boy," Beth says, her hand at my belt loops. "Papa's tired."

I tighten my hug, and Evan starts bawling, arms squeezing my neck painfully. He sucks in air and wails, a dam burst.

Beth nods. "I knew this would come," she says. "It's OK, Evan, Papa's home. It's OK."

We all head to the futon couch and sit entangled in a three-person jumble of arms, hair, tears, and hands. Evan remains on my lap for some time, head against my chest, crying, trying to speak, unable to do so, then crying some more. He finds the scar on my right palm and traces it with his index finger. His tears soak the front of my factory-second Chaps button-down. After about fifteen minutes, the longest he's cried since he was a baby, he draws a deep, trembling breath and lets loose one last sob.

"It's OK, big guy," I say. "How you doing?"

"Katie will be so su-prised," he says, sounding like he's been up all night at a hardcore show. "Wait till you see, she's so smart now, she knows everything."

He's falling into the rhythm of our recent phone conversations. All about Katie.

"How're *you* doing, though?" I ask.

He melts down for another five minutes, during which Beth strokes him and coos like when he was an infant. Finally, he calms.

"Play Papa's song," he says to Beth, tugging on her dress. "Mommy. Play Papa's song for Papa."

Before she can respond, he disentangles from us and hops up, wiping tears. Red-faced but grinning, he runs into the kitchen.

"That's the first time he's cried since you left," Beth whispers and sniffs.

"What's he talking about?" I ask.

"Come on," she says, unsteady smile playing across her face.

As we enter the kitchen, which *still* reeks of Clorox and mold, Evan is standing on a chair and sliding a CD into a new black Sony boom box.

"New boom box?"

"Yeah," Beth says. "That's not the surprise, though."

"Papa's song! Papa's song!" Evan jumps to the floor and stands poised like he's about to take on an opponent.

A synthetic beat fills the kitchen, followed by a reverb'd female vocal humming a familiar melody over synthesizer chords and a chugging guitar. The voice is scratchy and soulful.

> *Trying to explain all these things I'm*
> *feeling*
> *Deep down in my secret heart*
> *Trying to define all these dreams I*
> *dream*
> *All these spinning wheels, they're all*
> *going nowhere, nowhere fast*
> *I'm filling to the brim and bursting at the*
> *seams*
> *Let me stay awhile, now*
> *When words fail me*
> *When words fail me*
> *When words fail me.*

It's my song, written for Beth. "Words Fail Me." My melody, my words, dressed up in expensive-sounding arrangements, sped up a little, decidedly funkier in a modern pop R & B kind of way. A couple of chords are a little different, and some phrases are repeated. But it's clearly my tune. Beth's tune.

I'd demo'd "Words Fail Me" on a cassette four-track twelve years ago, hoping Stereoblind would record it for our Polygram debut *Psycho Delic*. Mark Opitz and Tristan had rejected it. My hissy, drum machine/acoustic guitar/vocal version, sung into a cheap microphone on East Seventh, was track one on a mixtape I'd given Beth over a decade ago.

And now Sasha is singing it. And it sounds like a hit. I sink into a chair, my heart pounding, hands clammy.

"OK," Beth says. "Here's what happened: Sasha loves '80s music and she was making a video for 'Kiss Me You Fool,' and she wanted it to look '80s, so she wanted a shot of someone loading a cassette into one of those huge ghetto blasters. We get to the set, near Chelsea Piers . . ."

"When did this happen . . . ?"

"Like three weeks ago? And the props guy, poor guy, had everything *but* a cassette. And I had that mixtape you gave me that included my song."

"You had it with you? *Loverman Mix 1?*"

"Yes. All love songs. I was listening to it on the way down to the city . . ."

"No. Where was it?"

"In a box of special stuff. I've got other stuff in there, too. But I had the tape in my pocketbook. I didn't want to leave it in the car . . ."

"Stop talking!" Evan says. "Here it comes!" An almost-metal-sounding guitar solo blazes into the song. Evan writhes and gyrates. Beth and I laugh and just watch him as the song plays on for a few more minutes. Sasha's usually irritating overuse of melisma is infrequent, thank God. Her vocal, raw and not very processed, adds depth and contour to my melody.

> *Please hear my call*
> *When I say nothing at all*

As the song fades, Evan executes a Bob Fosse-esque ending to his dance. We clap, and Beth starts talking.

"So during a break, Sasha actually played the tape. Mixtapes fascinate her, and when I told her my husband made it for me, she actually got weepy because no one's ever made her a mixtape and never will, as cassettes are on their way out. She cried. She's like that. Kind of a mess. And I say, 'This song, Grant wrote it for me,' and that was the coup de grace. She was bowled over. She played the song over and over, then had an assistant go someplace while we were on lunch break and make a digital copy, she liked it so much.

"I was going to call you and tell you, but I didn't want to seem manipulative, and it was so hard talking to you on the phone. And I didn't want to get your hopes up about anything. Should I have called you?"

"It's OK," I say. "I get it. I do."

"So yesterday I get a FedEx envelope from LA with this track and a note. Here it is. I was actually gonna call you today."

She gets a handwritten note from the kitchen table. Evan, meanwhile, is replaying the song. Beth and I retreat back to the living room.

> *Dear Beth,*
>
> *My producer Linda P loves this tune like I do, so we knocked out this version in her home studio. Linda wants it to be lead-off single on my next album, dropping next March. Hope you and your husband like it. He and I need to talk bees-knees, though, ASAP. Please have him call me.*
>
> *Peace,*
> *S*

"Bees knees?" I ask.

"Business," Beth says. "The gal is all business."

"Bees knees!" Evan says from the doorway and runs and jumps into my arms again.

chapter 21

bees knees

Around noon the next day, a bright, crisp May Saturday, I get Sasha on her cell.

"Beth!" Sasha says by way of hello. Her speaking voice is lower than her singing voice, throaty and worn, a smoker's purr.

I'm still not accustomed to people responding to caller ID and saying whatever name pops up instead of a traditional greeting. With the addition of my existing nerves, Sasha's mistaken salutation throws me off for a few mush-mouthed moments.

"Hello . . . ?" she says, confused, her voice a little distorted. "Bethy?"

"Hey Sasha, it's actually Grant, Grant Kelly. You said to call."

"Grant? Grant. Oh yeah! Grant! The husband! The Loverman!"

"Yeah, the husband. You, uh, said to call? About the song. 'Words Fail Me'?"

A long pause, during which I hear waves crashing in the background. In the Shulz House living room, Evan is watching *Powerpuff Girls* on Cartoon Network. Time Warner Cable finally made it to this far-flung hamlet while I was in Goldsboro and hooked up the Victorian and Shulz House, but Ricky and Jen refused the service. Beth sits at my perch in the kitchen, watching as I pace in front of the refrigerator. The weight of her gaze is a bit much, so I turn my eyes to the greening maples on the lower half of Mt. Marie. A murder of crows zips by.

"That song!" Sasha finally says in an exaggerated stage whisper. "I so love that song! 'Words Fail Me'!" She sings the chorus.

"Thank you," I say.

"You heard my demo?"

"Yeah, it sounds great," I say. She's just like Paul; the star fishing for compliments. "It's such a surprise, Sasha. I'm really glad you like it."

"I love it. And my producer Linda loves it. She's a freak for '80s stuff like me."

"I actually wrote it in 1990 . . ."

"Doesn't matter, Loverman. I'd like it to be the lead single off my next album."

"So I hear," I say, my pulse racing.

"Here's the thing, though. I get a co-write for the stuff I put in there."

The one or two word changes and the additional chord or two?

"And you publish through my record company, Universal."

A chill rises through the heat in my torso. I'm about to say yes, but something stops me.

"That cool with you?" she says. "Universal'll give you a nice advance, I'm sure. Probably twenty K. Maybe twenty-five."

I hum through a tightening jaw.

"You there, Loverman?"

"Oh yeah, I'm here. I hear you."

"You hear that other thing?"

"What other thing?"

"That's your ship coming in, Loverman."

"How . . . much writing credit you talking about?"

Beth flails in my peripheral vision, her hands motioning slow down, or cool down, or something.

"I was thinking fifty-fifty," Sasha's voice drops, chills. "On both words and music, Loverman."

I sink to the floor in front of the refrigerator. Beth sits at the edge of her chair, gazing at me expectantly, eyes huge like a Keane child. Time stops. Even the waves in the background of Sasha's phone signal cease.

Evan walks in and stops in his tracks, looking to me, his mom, then back at me.

"How about sixty-forty?" I say.

To my surprise, Sasha bounces back with a chirpy "OK!"

I should have said seventy-thirty. But at least I said something.

~

Trip sits at a picnic table grading papers in the shade of a huge, lone hemlock tree in his backyard. A few feet away, in the bright afternoon sun, Katie and Evan—clad in filthy overalls, straw cowboy hats, and too-big gloves—dig in a raised garden bed, each using trowels to mulch black soil with fertilizer and what looks like river sediment. Evan headed over by himself an hour or so ago while I finalized plans for "Words Fail Me" with Sasha's manager, Ari. More business talk with the folks at Universal Publishing on Monday, and contracts arriving via FedEx, but for now, I am done, done, done with my chess moves. The potential ramifications of what I've agreed to hover in a dream space, shimmery, without actual form, yet emanating a magnetic energy I hope to find a way to ignore. No such luck yet, but I'm thinking my long-delayed confrontation with Trip might do the trick. With an onerous sleep debt staking its claim, I head over on leaden feet to confront my former best friend.

Trip looks up as I approach. He smiles thinly, gesturing to me to have a seat. He's rested, hale, sun-kissed. But nervous.

"Gardening?" I say dumbly, pointing at the kids.

"Yeah, Jen's got me into it," he says, glad, like me, for a superficial topic to talk about. "She gave me a bunch of seedlings—tomatoes, summer squash, cukes, corn—and I'm gonna see if I've got the touch. Katie loves it. Seems like it's in her blood."

"Maybe it is . . ."

"Katie," he calls. "Say hello to Mr. Grant!"

Katie looks up and waves her trowel. "Hewwo Mistah Gwant!" she yells and smiles big. "How ah you?" I give the thumbs-up, which she returns. Evan looks at me, then nods at her, his eyes raised with a *can you believe it?*

Trip's face breaks into a huge smile, the first genuine smile I've seen from him in ages. It knocks years from him. "She's coming along great, especially since . . ."

"Yeah, I heard. Christa came to visit me, you know."

"Yeah, I know. She's back at her folks'. Called me this morning. She's really happy you're not at your mom's anymore."

I nod and drum my fingers on the table. A heaviness fills the space between us. The kids laugh amid buzzing insects and cawing crows.

"Look, Grant . . ." Trip taps the tabletop. "We gotta move on from this. Katie's doing so well, and as much as everything that happened was fucking awful, I wonder if she'd be like she is without Christa and me separating. She wouldn't. We'd all still be miserable. I wish I'd known to make that happen before all the shit went down, but we can't go back and change it."

"I'm so sorry, Trip, I was . . ."

"It was all fucked up, I know that. It's still fucked up, but . . . look at that."

He points to the kids, who are watching a massive bird soaring over the mountain. An eagle, circling over prey. My old friend, I know in an instant, as my blood pressure spikes and my fatigue vanishes.

"Eagaaaah!" Katie squeals. Evan laughs and flaps his arms for her, circling the raised bed.

"Eagahhh!" Katie says again, pointing, her body rigid with excitement.

Trip and I hoot and yell with the kids.

"That's more important than our drunken bullshit," Trip says, "which is in the past, and good riddance to it all. Really."

The eagle disappears in the maples, and the kids resume their mulching, which appears barely productive in a gardening sense yet fun.

"Is that silt they're mixing in?" I ask.

"Yep. Great fertilizer. May as well use what nature brought to my door, if you know what I mean."

I nod. And remember. "Katie ever have bad memories of . . . that night?" I ask.

"Nope," he says. "Not that I can tell. I do. But she doesn't. She sleeps like a rock next to me every night, which I gotta say, beats Ambien as a sleep aid. I bet she saw some even worse shit in China."

"Thanks, by the way, for saving my life."

"Don't mention it. You'd do the same for me. And we might've lost you guys but for Beth, you know."

I nod and cast a glance at Evan. "I can't believe my kid saw a guy drown."

"He's resilient," Trip says. "Us old folks forget that. And, you know, he's surrounded by love. That helps." His cool blue gaze meets mine. "I'm glad you came back, Grant. I won't lie and say I'm not still fucking pissed. I am. But I'm seeing the big picture for the first time in, I don't know, forever. Taking the long view. I'm clearheaded, sober, no more Ambien. And for fuck's sake, I started another draft of *Shadow World* while you were gone."

"That's great."

"Yeah, feels good. Feels like I know a bit more about apocalypse now, and I can use that info." He raises his eyebrows at me. "You know what *apocalypse* means, literally translated?"

"Uh . . . the end of the world, right?"

"Actually, translated from Greek, it means a revelation of knowledge, a lifting of the veil, after which, everything changes."

chapter 22

dear parents

*Casa de Christa, Oliver, Summer, and
Katie
5078 Franklin Avenue
Los Angeles, California 90027*

*The Kellys
45 Cross Street
Hudson, NY 12534*

June 28, 2015

Dearest Parents,

*Here it is. HERE IT IS. You asked for it
you got it. For your silver anniversary, a
real live letter, not email, text, Facebook/
Crackbook message or any lame-o-ness,
but my SAD (cursive what is THAT?)
handwriting on actual paper, stuffed
into the SASE you gave me bringing you
up-to-date on my West Coast Summer
Adventures with ol pal o' mine Katie. You
can also thank Katie herself, who bet her
little sister I'd never sit down and write
an actual old-school letter. Summer said
I would and so she wins five bucks from
Katie once I am done. Summer should
have bet 50 bucks, though cuz her big
sis can afford it (new ads on her channel:
Wendy's and Home Depot) but Summer
is little and not allowed on YouTube yet,*

*so how would she know? And Christa
says she's keeping most of Katie's money
in a trust anyway, but Katie can get $
when she asks nicely and doesn't act
crazy. She's a little better at that.*

*She's still super competitive, though.
She says her vlog trust will exceed the
college $ Padrino left me in his will. We
have a wager on it.*

*I am a fan of LA. We went to LACMA a
couple days ago to see the Rivera show,
and then yesterday we went to the Walk
of Fame with Katie's friend Sam to shoot
some vid of Katie for her KayTeez vlog,
and people recognized her from that
Us mag thing "Teen Tubers!" (VOMIT).
Katie waited till Sam was rolling and
yelled at some Scientologists doing
"audits" on the sidewalk, which was
funny and scary. She uploaded it last
night and got 1223 more subscribers!
Total subs: 8 MILLION. She did it to
annoy her stepdad who was raised Sci-
entologist. He's very cool, although not
around much cuz he's shooting that reality show about house flippers. We were
gonna go to the beach, but Katie still has
that water phobia thing, so we didn't.*

*Katie and I were talking about Mt. Marie
Days. She remembers 2 things: the
garden (every time she smells cucum-
bers she remembers us planting stuff
and seeing that eagle . . . don't know if*

*I remember that) and when we moved
to Hudson and she had that fit. She
remembers moving to Catskill after that
so her dad could teach at that school.
She has lots of memories of us making movies with her dad's phone—her
early vlog stuff. She likes LA but misses
Catskill (what???) and is going back to
her old Waldorf School so we'll see her
more, but she said she will come back
here to visit a lot, maybe go to college
out here. She and Summer are hilarious
together. Nonstop Comedy Gold. Summer is a Mini Me of her mom—they have
the same nose—and her crazy hair even
got her in a commercial for Target.*

*I almost forgot. I heard WFM in the
mall the other day. Some older girls
were singing it if you care, doing Sasha
moves and all. Katie pointed at me and
yelled, "His dad wrote that song and
his mom works for Sasha AND Sasha's
little sister, Skyler!" The girls got freaked
out, and Katie got some footage of it.
Hilarious.*

*Do you really think the new studio will
be done when I get back? I hope hope
hope so. I have more ideas for that
mural, esp. since seeing the Rivera stuff.
A mural over your mixing console! You're
welcome! And Mom—I hope your poetry
workshop is going good. When we went
to Book Soup I found that anthology
with your poem in it. Christa bought it*

*for Katie, and I'm bringing it home for
you to sign for her.*

*That's it. My hand hurts. What a day.
The day I wrote my first letter. I see the
appeal. I guess.*

*Thanks for sending me on this adven-
ture. Happy Anniversary!!!!!*

Evan

the end

songs

KISS MY RING

I was the pauper
Who became the king
You want what I got
Well you gotta sing
It's not very much
It's everything
So kiss my ring, kiss my ring.

I was the leper
Now I'm Mr. Clean
You wanna be here
Then go where I been
Make yourself a mess
When you make the scene
And kiss my ring, kiss my ring.

Everybody's got to stand in line
sometime.

I was the dreamer
Now I am the dream
If you want change
Then join my regime
Make yourself a mess
When you make the scene
And kiss my ring, kiss my ring.

Everybody's got to stand in line
sometime.

WORDS FAIL ME

All this conversation, I just keep on
talking
I'm not saying nothing at all
I'm circling around what I really want to
say
Looking for the right lines, fumbling for
the phrases
But everything's so tired and cold
Every word upon my lips just gets in the
way.

CHORUS:
Let me stay a while now
When words fail me, please hear my call
When words fail me, when I say nothing
at all

Trying to explain all the things I'm
feeling
Deep down in secret heart
Trying to define all these dreams I
dream
All these spinning wheels, they're all
going nowhere
Nowhere fast
I'm filling to the brim and bursting at the
seams.

CHORUS

WHAT THE FUNK IS UP?

I'm lookin' at the sky I say, what the funk
is up?
I'm lookin' in your eye I say, what the
funk is up?
It's a psychedelic situation, an
immaculate
creation, making the entire nation say
What the funk is up?

I wake up in my bed I say, what the funk
is up?
I'm getting out the lead I say, what the
funk is up?
It's a polyphonic exploration, an
automatic
invocation, making the entire nation say
What the funk is up? What the funk is
up?

CHORUS:
Everybody thinks they know where we're
goin'
But no one wants to know where we
been
You and me we see what they're showin'
We know what's coming 'round the bend
. . . again

I'm lookin' at the clouds I say, what the
funk is up?
I'm dancin' out loud I say, what the funk
is up?

It's a tragicomic realization, a quadro-
phonic exultation, making the entire
nation say
What the funk is up? What the funk is
up?

CHORUS

A STRANGER TO YOU

So this is what it takes
To make your will break
And open you up like a rose
So this brings that soul kiss
Dripping like dew
Ripping through your favorite clothes.

When you do not recognize me without
my mask
When an act of kindness is too much to
ask
When I'm a stranger to you, I love what
we do.

So this quickens your heart
'Til it breaks apart
And all the good stuff spills out
So this makes you see red
Shakes up our bed
This taste of wonder and doubt.

When you see the traces of another man
in me
The road not taken isn't such a sad
mystery
And when I'm a stranger to you, I love
what we do.

So this makes your blood flow
Deep down below
Like when we met years ago
You say sweetness and grace
A familiar face
But part of you says that's not so.

Only when the mirror breaks does it
show what's true
When more than one reflection looks
back at you
And when I'm a stranger to you, I love
what we do.

PERFECTLY BROKEN

When I bring you back to life in my dark
fantasies
I'm sitting there beside you and I'm
shouting begging please
And this song ceases to exist
My power is just far too great for you to
resist.

And we're perfectly broken
Nothing is too much to bear
Perfectly broken
Nothing to repair.

Saturated, soaked with sound
And running in the red
Pumped all full of chemicals
So we sleep like the dead.
The kiss it left a scar that will remain
I close my eyes and I can see what's left
of the stain.

And we're perfectly broken
Nothing is too much to bear
Perfectly broken
Nothing to repair.

acknowledgements:

Thank you first and foremost to my wife, Holly, and son, Jack; without your love and encouragement this book would not exist. Thanks to my brother, Britt, my mother, and my extended family for support; to Lou Aronica and all at The Story Plant for believing in my work; to my agent, Susan Golomb, for faith, and for taking it to the bridge, and to Scott Cohen for going to the mat; to Ellenora Cage, for introducing me to Lou; to Rosanne Cash, whose late '90s statement, "You really should sharpen your prose pencil" was a crucial spark; to Perdita Finn, for unshakable belief; to the Glaring Omissions—Minda, Suzanne, Miriam, Howard, Violet, Scott, Maureen—for constructive criticism. . . your fingerprints are all over this book; to my editors for putting me on deadline; to Nora Tamada, for the copyedits and inspiring margin notes; to Mark Lerner for the stellar cover and the studio time; to enthusiastic early readers Laura Sandlin, John Draper, Martin Keith, Laurie Gwen Shapiro, Tara Lee, Euphrosyne Bloom, Jennifer Haase, Abbe Aronson, and Jacqueline Burt; to writer peers whose work emboldened me: Greg Olear, Sean Beaudoin, Janet Steen, Martha Frankel, Teresa Giordano, Nina Shengold, Shawn Amos, Nelly Reifler, Tony Fletcher, Bev Donofrio, and Jana Martin; to Mimi Cross, who listened and co-dreamed; to Jackie Kellechan at the Golden Notebook for giving me a venue; to Sarah Lazin for asking what I was working on, thereby setting this ball in motion; to James Morgan and Jay Sherman-Godfrey, for helming the music, and to Lukas for making it swing; to dearly departed friends Todd and Luis, for showing me bravery; to my beloved '80s pen pal Matthew Best; and to my grandmother Gammie and Big Brother Raymond, who loved getting my letters.

Thanks also to all who give me enthusiastic comments online and share my work.

about the author

Robert Burke Warren is a musician and writer whose work has appeared in *Paste, Salon, The Bitter Southerner, The Good Men Project, The Rumpus, The Woodstock Times, Texas Music, Brooklyn Parent, Chronogram, The Weeklings,* and the Da Capo anthology, *The Show I'll Never Forget.* He lives in the Catskill Mountains with his family. This is his first novel.